“北京第二外国语学院精品教材建设”项目资助

A Guide to Foreign Literary Canons

外国文学经典导读

◎龙 云 编著

南京大学出版社

图书在版编目(CIP)数据

外国文学经典导读 : A Guide to Foreign Literary Canons / 龙云编著. — 南京 :南京大学出版社，2021.9

ISBN 978-7-305-24670-8

Ⅰ. ①外… Ⅱ. ①龙… Ⅲ. ①文学-外国文学-高等学校-教材-英文 Ⅳ. ①D75

中国版本图书馆 CIP 数据核字(2021)第号

出版发行 南京大学出版社
社　　址 南京市汉口路 22 号　　邮　编 210093
出 版 人 金鑫荣

书　　名 外国文学经典导读
A Guide to Foreign Literary Canons
编　　著 龙　云
责任编辑 裴维维　　编辑热线 025-83592123

照　　排 南京南琳图文制作有限公司
印　　刷 南京百花彩色印刷广告制作有限责任公司
开　　本 787×1092 1/16 印张 13 字数 390 千
版　　次 2021 年 9 月第 1 版 2021 年 9 月第 1 次印刷
ISBN 978-7-305-24670-8
定　　价 42.00 元

网址：http://www.njupco.com
官方微博：http://weibo.com/njupco
官方微信号：njupress
销售咨询热线：(025) 83594756

前 言

全球化时代，随着课程改革的国际化趋势的发展，我国对高等教育质量和人才培养模式提出了更高的要求，外国文学教学模式也面临着改革和创新的巨大要求和挑战。随着文学导读和文学赏析等课程的开设，近些年来国内高校开始为英语专业本科生和研究生开设“外国文学经典导读”等相关课程，以拓宽学生的文学和文化视野。

一、使用对象

本书是为提高高校英语专业学生阅读和赏析文学经典作品的能力而编写的教材，适合高校英语专业核心课程或高校大学生通识课程的教学使用，也适合对外国文学作品感兴趣的自学者使用。

二、编写原则和特点

本书坚持“提升理解、赏析、思辨能力”的原则，所选的文章都是能够彰显作家创作特色和主题风格的代表性作品。问题设置上力争能够指导学生对重点的把握，同时注重激发学生深入思考，具有启发性和思辨性相结合的特点。

三、教材构成

本书包含十二个单元，每个单元包括作家介绍、主题介绍、术语解释、作品选段和问题理解五个部分。通过本书的学习，学生可以掌握作家的生平、作品主题、创作特点和思想内涵，进而对多样题材的外国文学经典的创作特色、思想内涵和时代影响形成大致的了解。

教师和学习者可根据教学进度和兴趣特点对本教材的内容安排进行适当调整和有选择性地使用。在本教材的编写过程中，参考了国内外出版的相关书籍，对这些作者表示深深的感谢。由于编者水平有限，书中错误、缺点和不足之处在所难免，敬请大家不吝批评指正。

龙云

2021 年 5 月于北京

Contents

Unit 1

Louisa May Alcott: *Little Women*

Louisa May Alcott (1832—1888), the second of four daughters, was born in Germantown, Pennsylvania, and raised in Boston and Concord, Massachusetts. Her father was a noted New England Transcendentalist, philosopher and educator. Her mother was the practical parent, the one who often took menial jobs to feed the family. Louisa May Alcott was raised in poverty. The family moved around a lot. They often depended on the kindness of friends and relatives to survive. Alcott and her sisters were put to work as soon as they were of age to help support the family. Yet she was brought up with the likes of Ralph Waldo Emerson, Henry David Thoreau and Nathaniel Hawthorne as neighbors, teachers, role models and close family friends. Although severely impoverished, Alcott's childhood was apparently unforgettable. Taught by her father, Alcott was deeply influenced by his transcendentalist thought and experimental educational philosophies. Ralph Waldo Emerson's personal library of classics and philosophy was available for use to the young Alcott, and Henry David Thoreau taught her botany.

Louisa May Alcott's father Bronson Alcott founded several schools, but all of them failed, forcing his wife and her daughters to undertake the financial support of the family. Abba Bronson believed in her husband and often picked up the slack. She protected her daughters from the hard realities of life when they all lived at Fruitlands, a Transcendental commune that was a miserable failure. The family was allowed to eat only what the land provided: no meat, milk or eggs. They could wear only linen, as the cotton industry exploited the slaves in the South. Louisa and her sisters were encouraged to spend their time at the commune playing, picnicking and roaming the fields. Louisa later wrote a gentle satire about this time in her life, called *Transcendental Wild Oats*. At one point, when her husband was unable to produce an income, Abba went to work in Boston as one of the first social workers and earned at thirty dollars a month. She also was in charge of an employment agency for women in domestic service and once ran a boarding house. She did these things at a time when genteel women did not work. Later, Alcott often remarked that her entire career was inspired by her desire to compensate for her family's early discomfort.

Alcott taught school, took in sewing, and worked briefly as a domestic servant. At the age of sixteen she began writing, convinced that she could eventually earn enough money to alleviate the family's poverty. In 1851, her first poem was published in the magazine under the pseudonym Flora Fairfield, bringing Alcott little money but a great deal of confidence. It was during the ensuing years that Alcott published a number of sensational serial stories, which were both popular and lucrative. For Louisa May Alcott, writing was an early passion, her career as an author began with poverty and short stories that appeared in popular magazines. In her sketch "Transcendental Oats," Louisa May Alcott described in an amusing way the experience of a year at Fruitlands, where an attempt was made to establish an ideal community. Miss Alcott was obliged to be a wage-earner to help out the family income, and so taught school, served as a governess and at times worked as a seamstress. Weary of this, she wrote stories of a sensational nature, which were remunerative financially, but unsatisfactory to her as a literary pursuit, and she abandoned this style of writing. In a Washington hospital she served as a nurse for a time, but the work was so hard that she failed in health, and when she recovered, she had to find new fields of work; then she traveled as attendant to an invalid, and with her visited Europe.

Louisa May Alcott's works were attracted by many children generation by generation. Since her first creation was published when she was 16-year-old, she has born abundant fruit in the field of writing. Her first and biggest success was based on her experience with her sisters and was written in response to a publisher who asked her to write a story for girls. It took her two and a half months to write and was an immediate success. Henry James called Alcott the "novelist of children." Her other children novels include: *An Old-Fashioned Girl*, *Little Men* (based on a school her widowed sister ran), *Eight Cousins*, *Rose in Bloom*, *Under the Lilacs*, *Jack and Jill*, *Jo's Boys* and *A Garland for Girls*. Her books portray nineteenth century domestic middle-class life realistically, since so much of her work is based on her own family life, which was however sometimes unconventional.

Theme

Little Women is a coming-of-age story of four sisters in Civil War New England. Together they face hardships and poverty all the while trying to reach their castles in the air. More than that however, *Little Women* is a morality tale. Each chapter not only contains the lives and adventures of the four sisters, but lessons on how to be a good person, and how to achieve happiness in life. These values are centered upon God, family, and love. Though money, people, and childhood dreams come and go, Marmee's wisdom about happiness never seems to falter. The dreams of the writer, artist, and pianist in the family all fall behind the happiness they find in their respective households.

Term

Fiction: Fiction usually refers to literature consisting of invented narrative, especially the novel and short story. Today fiction almost becomes the synonym of novel. Broadly speaking, the term novel is applied to a prose work of some length "tale or piece of news." In a narrow sense, a novel is a realistic fiction, complete in itself and contains the essential elements of story, character, and setting. Traditional fiction centers on the characterization of characters and describes social life and the conflicts exiting in human life.

Excerpt

Chapter I Playing Pilgrims

"Christmas won't be Christmas without any presents," grumbled Jo, lying on the rug.

"It's so dreadful to be poor!" sighed Meg, looking down at her old dress.

"I don't think it's fair for some girls to have plenty of pretty things, and other girls nothing at all," added little Amy, with an injured sniff.

"We've got father and mother and each other," said Beth, contentedly, from her corner.

The four young faces on which the firelight shone brightened at the cheerful words, but darkened again as Jo said sadly:

"We haven't got father, and shall not have him for a long time." She didn't say "perhaps never", but each silently added it, thinking of father far away, where the fighting was.

Nobody spoke for a minute; then Meg said in an altered tone:

"You know the reason mother proposed not having any presents this Christmas was because it is going to be a hard winter for everyone; and she thinks we ought not to spend money for pleasure when our men are suffering so in the army. We can't do much, but we can make our little sacrifices, and ought to do it gladly. But I am afraid I don't"; and Meg shook her head, and she thought regretfully of all the pretty things she wanted.

"But I don't think the little we should spend would do any good. We've each got a dollar, and the army wouldn't be much helped by our giving that. I agree not to expect anything from mother or you, but I do want to buy Undine and Sintram for myself; I've wanted it so long," said Jo, who was a bookworm.

"I planned to spend mine on new music," said Beth, with a little sigh, which no one heard but the hearth-brush and kettle-holder.

"I shall get a nice box of Faber's drawing pencils; I really need them," said Amy, decidedly.

"Mother didn't say anything about our money, and she won't wish us to give up everything. Let's each buy what we want, and have a little fun; I'm sure we work hard enough to earn it," cried Jo, examining the heels of her shoes in a gentlemanly manner.

"I know I do—teaching those tiresome children nearly all day when I am longing to enjoy myself at home," began Meg, in the complaining tone again.

"You don't have half such a hard time as I do," said Jo. "How would you like to be shut up for hours with a nervous, fussy old lady, who keeps you trotting, is never satisfied, and worries you till you're ready to fly out of the window or cry?"

"It's naughty to fret; but I do think washing dishes and keeping things tidy is the worst work in the world. It makes me cross; and my hands get so stiff, I can't practice well at all"; and Beth looked at her rough hands with a sigh that anyone could hear that time.

"I don't believe any of you suffer as I do." cried Amy; "for you don't have to go to school with impertinent girls, who plague you if you don't know your lessons, and laugh at your dresses, and label your father if he isn't rich, and insult you when your nose isn't nice."

"If you mean libel, I'd say so, and not talk about labels, as if papa was a pickle-bottle," advised Jo, laughing.

"I know what I mean, and you needn't be satirical about it. It's proper to use good words, and improve your vocabulary," returned Amy, with dignity.

"Don't peck at one another, children. Don't you wish we had the money papa lost when we were little, Jo? Dear me! how happy and good we'd be, if we had no worries!" said Meg, who could remember better times.

"You said, the other day, you thought we were a deal happier than the King children, for they were fighting and fretting all the time, in spite of their money."

"So I did, Beth. Well, I think we are; for, though we do have to work, we make fun for ourselves, and are a pretty jolly set, as Jo would say."

"Jo does use such slang words!" observed Amy, with a reproving look at the long figure stretched on the rug. Jo immediately sat up, put her hands in her pockets, and began to whistle.

"Don't, Jo; it's so boyish!"

"That's why I do it."

"I detest rude, unlady-like girls!"

"I hate affected, niminy-piminy chits!"

"Birds in their little nests agree," sang Beth, the peacemaker, with such a funny face that both sharp voices softened to a laugh, and the "pecking" ended for that time.

"Really, girls, you are both to be blamed," said Meg, beginning to lecture in her elder-sisterly fashion. "You are old enough to leave off boyish tricks, and to behave better Josephine. It didn't matter so much when you were a little girl; but now you are so tall, and turn up your hair, you should remember that you are a young lady."

"I'm not! And if turning up my hair makes me one, I'll wear it in two tails till I'm twenty." cried Jo, pulling off her net, and shaking down her chestnut mane. "I hate to think I've got to grow up, and he Miss March and wear long gowns, and look as prim as a China-aster! It's bad enough to be a girl, anyway, when I like boys' games and work and manners! I can't get over my disappointment in not being a boy; and it's worse than ever now, for I'm dying to go and fight with papa, and I can only stay at home and knit, like a poky old woman!" And Jo shook the blue army sock till the needles rattled like castanets, and her ball bounded across the room.

"Poor Jo! It's too had, but it can't he helped; so you must try to be contented with making your name boyish, and playing brother to us girls," said Beth, stroking the rough head at her knee with a hand that all the dish-washing and dusting in the world could not make ungentle in it touch.

"As for you, Amy," continued Meg, "you are altogether too particular and prim. Your airs are funny now; but you'll grow up an affected little goose, if you don't take care. I like your nice manners and refined ways of speaking when you don't try to be elegant; but your absurd words are as bad as Jo's slang."

"If Jo is a tomboy and Amy a goose, what am I, please?" asked Beth, ready to share the lecture.

"You're a dear, and nothing else," answered Meg, warmly; and no one contradicted her, for the "Mouse" was the pet of the family.

As young readers like to know "how people look," we will take this moment to give them a little sketch of the four sisters, who sat knitting away in the twilight, while the December snow fell quietly without, and the fire crackled cheerfully within. It was a comfortable old room, though the carpet was faded and the furniture very plain; for a good picture or two hung on the walls, books filled the recesses, chrysanthemums and Christmas roses bloomed in the windows, and a pleasant atmosphere of home-peace pervaded it.

Margaret, the eldest of the four, was sixteen, and very pretty, being plump and fair, with large eyes, plenty of soft, brown hair, a sweet mouth, and white hands, of which she was rather vain. Fifteen-year-old Jo was very tall, thin, and brown, and reminded one of a colt; for she never seemed to know what to do with her long limbs, which were very much in her way. She had a decided mouth, a comical nose, and sharp, grey eyes, which appeared to see everything, and were by turns fierce, funny, or thoughtful. Her long, thick hair was her one beauty; but it was usually bundled into a net, to be out of her way. Round shoulders had Jo, big hands and feet, a fly-away look to her clothes, and the uncomfortable appearance of a girl who was rapidly shooting up into a woman, and didn't like it. Elizabeth, or Beth, as everyone called her-was a rosy, smooth-haired, bright-eyed girl of thirteen, with a shy manner, a timid voice, and a peaceful expression, which was seldom disturbed. Her father called her "Little Miss Tranquility," and the name suited her excellently; for she seemed to live in a happy world of her own, only venturing out to meet the few whom she trusted and loved. Amy, though the youngest, was a most important person —in her own opinion at least. A regular snow-maiden, with blue eyes, and yellow hair, curling on her shoulders, pale and slender, and always carrying herself like a young lady mindful of her manners. What the characters of the four sisters were we will leave to be found out.

The clock struck six; and, having swept up the hearth, Beth put a pair of slippers down to warm. Somehow the sight of the old shoes had a good effect upon the girls; for Mother was coming, and everyone brightened to welcome her. Meg stopped lecturing, and lighted the lamp, Amy got out of the easy-chair without being asked, and Jo forgot how tired she was as she sat up to hold the slippers nearer to the blaze.

"They are quite worn out; Marmee must have a new pair."

"I thought I'd get her some with my dollar," said Beth.

"No, I shall!" cried Amy.

"I'm the oldest," began Meg, but Jo cut in with a decided.

"I'm the man of the family now papa is away, and I shall provide the slippers, for he told me to take special care of Mother while he was gone."

"I'll tell you what we'll do," said Beth, "let's each get her something for Christmas, and not get anything for ourselves."

"That's like you, dear! What will we get?" exclaimed Jo. Everyone thought soberly for a minute; then Meg announced as if the idea was suggested by the sight of her own pretty hands, "I shall give her a nice pair of gloves."

"Army shoes, best to be had," cried Jo.

"Some handkerchiefs, all hemmed," said Beth.

"I'll get a little bottle of cologne; she likes it, and it won't cost much, so I'll have some left to buy my pencils," added Amy.

"How will we give the things?" asked Meg.

"Put them on the table, and bring her in and see her open the bundles. Don't you remember how we used to do on our birthdays?" answered Jo.

"I used to be so frightened when it was my turn to sit in the big chair with the crown on, and see you all come marching round to give the presents, with a kiss. I liked the things and the kisses, but it was dreadful to have you sit looking at me while I opened the bundles," said Beth, who was toasting her face and the bread for tea, at the same time.

"Let Marmee think we are getting things for ourselves, and then surprise her. We must go shopping tomorrow afternoon, Meg; there is so much to do about the play for Christmas night," said Jo, marching up and down, with her hands behind her back and her nose in the air.

"I don't mean to act any more after this time; I'm getting too old for such things," observed Meg, who was as much a child as ever about "dressing-up" frolics.

"You won't stop, I know, as long as you can trail round in a white gown with your hair down, and wear gold-paper jewelry. You are the best actress we've got, and there'll be an end of everything if you quit the boards," said Jo. "We ought to rehearse tonight. Come here, Amy, and do the fainting scene, for you are as stiff as a poker in that."

"I can't help it; I never saw anyone faint, and I don't choose to make myself all black and blue, tumbling flat as you do. If I can go down easily, I'll drop: if I can't, I shall fall into a chair and be graceful; I don't care if Hugo does come at me with a pistol," returned Amy, who was not gifted with dramatic power but was chosen because she was small enough to be borne out shrieking by the villain of the piece.

"Do it this way: clasp your hands so, and stagger across the room, crying frantically, 'Roderigo! save me! save me!' and away went Jo, with a melodramatic scream which was truly thrilling." Amy followed, but she poked her hands out stiffly before her, and jerked herself along as if she went by machinery; and her "Ow!" was more suggestive of pins being run into her than of fear and anguish. Jo gave a despairing groan, and Meg laughed outright, while Beth let her bread burn as she watched the fun with interest.

"It's no use! Do the best you can when the time comes, and if the audience laugh, don't blame me. Come on, Meg."

Then things went smoothly, for Don Pedro defied the world in a speech of two pages without a single break; Hagar, the witch, chanted an awful incantation over her kettleful of simmering toads, with weird effect; Roderigo rent his chains asunder manfully, and Hugo died in agonies of remorse and arsenic, with a wild "Ha! ha!"

"It's the best we've had yet," said Meg, as the dead villain sat up and rubbed his elbows.

"I don't see how you can write and act such splendid things, Jo. You're a regular Shakespeare!" exclaimed Beth, who firmly believed that her sisters were gifted with wonderful genius in all things.

"Not quite," replied Jo modestly. "I do think *The Witch's Curse, an Operatic Tragedy*, is rather a nice thing; but I'd like to try Macbeth, if we only had a trap-door for Banquo. I always wanted to do the killing part. Is that a dagger I see before me?" muttered Jo, rolling her eyes and clutching at the air, as she had seen a famous tragedian do.

"No, it's the toasting fork, with Mother's shoe on it instead of the bread. Beth's stage-struck!" cried Meg, and the rehearsal ended in a general burst of laughter.

"Glad to find you so merry, my girls," said a cheery voice at the door, and actors and audience turned to welcome a tall, motherly lady, with a "can-I-help-you" look about her which was truly delightful. She was not elegantly dressed but a noble-looking woman, and tire girls thought the grey cloak and unfashionable bonnet covered the most splendid mother in the world.

"Well, dearies, how have you got on today? There was so much to do, getting the boxes ready to go tomorrow, that I didn't come home to dinner. Has anyone called, Beth? How is your cold, Meg? Jo, you look tired to death. Come and kiss me, baby."

While making these maternal inquiries, Mrs. March got her wet things off, her warm slippers on, and sitting down in the easy-chair, drew Amy to her lap, preparing to enjoy the happiest hour of her busy day. The girls flew about, trying to make things comfortable, each in her own way. Meg arranged the tea-table; Jo brought wood and set chairs, dropping, overturning, and clattering everything she touched; Beth trotted to and fro between parlor and kitchen, quiet and busy; while Amy gave directions to everyone, as she sat with her hands folded.

As they gathered about the table, Mrs. March said, with a particularly happy face, "I've got a treat for you after supper."

A quick, bright smile went round like a streak of sunshine. Beth clapped her hands, regardless of the biscuit she held, and Jo tossed up her napkin, crying, "A letter! a letter! Three cheers for Father!"

"Yes, a nice long letter. He is well, and thinks he shall get through the cold season better than we feared. He sends all sorts of loving wishes for Christmas, and an especial message to you girls," said Mrs. March, patting her pocket as if she had got a treasure there.

"Hurry and get done! Don't stop to quirk your little finger, and simper over your plate, Amy," cried Jo, choking in her tea, and dropping her bread, butter side down, on the carpet in her haste to get at the treat. Beth ate no more, but crept away, to sit in her shadowy corner and brood over the delight to come, till the others were ready.

"I think it was so splendid of father to go as chaplain when he was too old to be drafted, and not strong enough for a soldier," said Meg, warmly.

"Don't I wish I could go as a drummer, a *vivan*—what's its name? or a nurse, so I could be near him and help him," exclaimed Jo, with a groan.

"It must be very disagreeable to sleep in a tent, and eat all sorts of bad-tasting things, and drink out of a tin mug," sighed Amy.

"When will he come home, Marmee?" asked Beth, with a little quiver in her voice.

"Not for many months, dear, unless he is sick. He will stay and do his work faithfully as long as he can, and we won't ask for him back a minute sooner than he can be spared. Now come and hear the letter."

They all drew to the fire, mother in the big chair, with Beth at her feet, Meg and Amy perched on either arm of the chair, and Jo leaning on the back, where no one would see any sign of emotion if the letter should happen to be touching. Very few letters were written in those hard times that were not touching, especially those which fathers sent home. In this one little was said of the hardships endured, the dangers faced, or the home-sickness conquered; it was a cheerful, hopeful letter, full of lively descriptions of camp life, marches, and military news; and only at the end did the writer's heart overflow with fatherly love and longing for the little girls at home.

"Give them all my dear love and a kiss. Tell them I think of them by day, pray for them by night, and find my best comfort in their affection at all times. A year seems very long to wait before I see them, but remind them that while we wait we may all work, so that these hard days need not be wasted. I know they will remember all I said to them, that they will be loving children to you, will do their duty faithfully, fight their bosom enemies bravely and conquer themselves so beautifully, that when I come back to them I may be fonder and prouder than ever of my little women."

Everybody sniffed when they came to that part; Jo wasn't ashamed of the great tear that dropped off the end of her nose, and Amy never minded the rumpling of her curls as she hid her face on her mother's shoulder and sobbed out, "I am a selfish girl! but I'll truly try to be better, so he may not be disappointed in me by and by."

"We all will!" cried Meg. "I think too much of my looks, and hate to work, but won't any more, if I can help it."

"I'll try and be what he loves to call me, 'a little woman,' and not be rough and wild; but do my duty here instead of wanting to be somewhere else," said Jo, thinking that keeping her temper at home was a much harder task than facing a rebel or two down South.

Beth said nothing, but wiped away her tears with the blue army sock, and began to knit with all her might, losing no time in doing the duty that lay nearest her, while she resolved in her quiet little soul to be all that father hoped to find her when the year brought round the happy coming home.

Mrs. March broke the silence that followed Jo's words, by saying in her cheery voice, "Do you remember how you used to play Pilgrim's Progress when you were little things? Nothing delighted you more than to have me tie my piece-bags on your backs for burdens, give you hats and sticks and rolls of paper, and let you travel through the house from the cellar, which was the City of Destruction, up, up, to the housetop, where you had all the lovely things you could collect to make a Celestial City."

"What fun it was, especially going by the lions, fighting Apollyon, and passing through the Valley where the hobgoblins were!" said Jo.

"I liked the place where the bundles fell off and tumbled downstairs," said Meg.

"My favourite part was when we came out on the flat roof where our flowers and arbors and pretty things were, and all stood and sang for joy up there in the sunshine," said Beth, smiling, as if that pleasant moment had come back to her.

"I don't remember much about it, except that I was afraid of the cellar and the dark entry, and always liked the cake and milk we had up at the top. If I wasn't too old for such things, I'd rather like to play it over again," said Amy, she began to talk of renouncing childish things at the mature age of twelve.

"We never are too old for this, my dear, because it is a play we are playing all the time in one way or another. Our burdens are here, our road is before us, and the longing for goodness and happiness is the guide that leads us through many troubles and mistakes to the peace which is a true Celestial City. Now, my little pilgrims, suppose you begin again, not in play, but in earnest, and see how far on you can get before Father comes home."

"Really, Mother? Where are our bundles?" asked Amy, who was a very literal young lady.

"Each of you told what your burden was just now, except Beth; I rather think she hasn't got any," said her mother.

"Yes, I have; mine is dishes and clusters, and envying girls with nice pianos, and being afraid of people."

Beth's bundle was such a funny one that everybody wanted to laugh; but nobody did, for it would have hurt her feelings very much.

"Let us do it," said Meg, thoughtfully. "It is only another name for trying to be good, and the story may help us; for though we do want to be good, it's hard work, and we forget, and don't do our best."

"We were in the Slough of Despond tonight, and Mother came and pulled us out as Help did in the book. We ought to have our roll of directions like Christian. What shall we do about that?" asked Jo, delighted with the fancy which lent a little romance to the very dull task of doing her duty.

"Look under your pillows on Christmas morning, and you will find your guide-book" replied Mrs. March.

They talked over the new plan while old Hannah cleared the table; then out came the four little work-baskets, and the needles flew as the girls made sheets for Aunt March. It was uninteresting sewing, but tonight no one grumbled. They adopted Jo's plan of dividing the long seams into four parts, and calling the quarters Europe, Asia, Africa, and America, and in that way got on capitally, especially when they talked about the different countries, as they stitched their way through them.

At nine they stopped work, and sang, as usual, before they went to bed.

No one but Beth could get much music out of the old piano; but she had a way of softly touching the yellow keys, and making a pleasant accompaniment to the simple songs they sang. Meg had a voice like a flute, and she and her mother led the little choir. Amy chirped like a cricket, and Jo wandered through the airs at her own sweet will, always coming out at the wrong place with a croak or a quaver that spoilt the most pensive tune. They had always done this from the time they could lisp:

Crinkle, crinkle, 'ittle' tar,

and it had become a household custom, for the mother was a born singer. The first sound in the morning was her voice, as she went about the house singing like a lark; and the last sound at night was the same cheery sound, for the girls never grew too old for that familiar lullaby.

Chapter Ⅸ Meg Goes to *Vanity Fair*

"I do think it was the most fortunate thing in the world that those children should have the measles just now," said Meg, one April day, as she stood packing the "go abroady" trunk in her room, surrounded by her sisters.

"And so nice of Annie Moffat not to forget her promise. A whole fortnight of fun will be regularly splendid," replied Jo, looking like a windmill as she folded skirts with her long arms.

"And such lovely weather, I'm so glad of that," added Beth, tidily sorting neck and hair ribbons in her best box, lent for the great occasion.

"I wish I was going to have a fine time and wear all these nice things," said Amy with her mouth full of pins, as she artistically replenished her sister's cushion.

"I wish you were all going, but as you can't, I shall keep my adventures to tell you when I come back. I'm sure it's the least I can do when you have been so kind, lending me things and helping me get ready," said Meg, glancing round the room at the very simple outfit, which seemed nearly perfect in their eyes.

"What did Mother give you out of the treasure box?" asked Amy, who had not been present at the opening of a certain cedar chest in which Mrs. March kept a few relics of past splendor, as gifts for her girls when the proper time came.

"A pair of silk stockings, that pretty carved fan, and a lovely blue sash. I wanted the violet silk, but there isn't time to make it over, so I must be contented with my old tarlatan."

"It will look nice over my new muslin skirt, and the sash will set it off beautifully. I wish I hadn't smashed my coral bracelet, for you might have had it," said Jo, who loved to give and lend, but whose possessions were usually too dilapidated to be of much use.

"There is a lovely old-fashioned pearl set in the treasure chest, but Mother said real flowers were the prettiest ornament for a young girl, and Laurie promised to send me all I want," replied Meg. "Now, let me see, there's my new gray walking suit, just curl up the feather in my hat, Beth, then my poplin for Sunday and the small party, it looks heavy for spring, doesn't it? The violet silk would be so nice. Oh, dear!"

"Never mind, you've got the tarlatan for the big party, and you always look like an angel in white," said Amy, brooding over the little store of finery in which her soul delighted.

"It isn't low-necked, and it doesn't sweep enough, but it will have to do. My blue housedress looks so well, turned and freshly trimmed, that I feel as if I'd got a new one. My silk sacque isn't a bit the fashion, and my bonnet doesn't look like Sallie's. I didn't like to say anything, but I was sadly disappointed in my umbrella. I told Mother black with a white handle, but she forgot and bought a green one with a yellowish handle. It's strong and neat, so I ought not to complain, but I know I shall feel ashamed of it beside Annie's silk one with a gold top," sighed Meg, surveying the little umbrella with great disfavor.

"Change it," advised Jo.

"I won't be so silly, or hurt Marmee's feelings, when she took so much pains to get my things. It's a nonsensical notion of mine, and I'm not going to give up to it. My silk stockings and two pairs of new gloves are my comfort. You are a dear to lend me yours, Jo. I feel so rich and sort of elegant, with two new pairs, and the old ones cleaned up for common." And Meg took a refreshing peep at her glove box.

"Annie Moffat has blue and pink bows on her nightcaps. Would you put some on mine?" she asked, as Beth brought up a pile of snowy muslins, fresh from Hannah's hands.

"No, I wouldn't, for the smart caps won't match the plain gowns without any trimming on them. Poor folks shouldn't rig," said Jo decidedly.

"I wonder if I shall ever be happy enough to have real lace on my clothes and bows on my caps?" said Meg impatiently.

"You said the other day that you'd be perfectly happy if you could only go to Annie Moffat's," observed Beth in her quiet way.

"So I did! Well, I am happy, and I won't fret, but it does seem as if the more one gets the more one wants, doesn't it? There now, the trays are ready, and everything in but my ball dress, which I shall leave for Mother to pack," said Meg, cheering up, as she glanced from the half-filled trunk to the many times pressed and mended white tarlatan, which she called her "ball dress" with an important air.

The next day was fine, and Meg departed in style for a fortnight of novelty and pleasure. Mrs. March had consented to the visit rather reluctantly, fearing that Margaret would come back more discontented than she went. But she begged so hard, and Sallie had promised to take good care of her, and a little pleasure seemed so delightful after a winter of irksome work that the mother yielded, and the daughter went to take her first taste of fashionable life.

The Moffats were very fashionable, and simple Meg was rather daunted, at first, by the splendor of the house and the elegance of its occupants. But they were kindly people, in spite of the frivolous life they led, and soon put their guest at her ease. Perhaps Meg felt, without understanding why, that they were not particularly cultivated or intelligent people, and that all their gilding could not quite conceal the ordinary material of which they were made. It certainly was agreeable to fare sumptuously, drive in a fine carriage, wear her best frock every day, and do nothing but enjoy herself. It suited her exactly, and soon she began to imitate the manners and conversation of those about her, to put on little airs and graces, use French phrases, crimp her hair, take in her dresses, and talk about the fashions as well as she could. The more she saw of Annie Moffat's pretty things, the more she envied her and sighed to be rich. Home now looked bare and dismal as she thought of it, work grew harder than ever, and she felt that she was a very destitute and much-injured girl, in spite of the new gloves and silk stockings.

She had not much time for repining, however, for the three young girls were busily employed in "having a good time." They shopped, walked, rode, and called all day, went to theaters and operas or frolicked at home in the evening, for Annie had many friends and knew how to entertain them. Her older sisters were very fine young ladies, and one was engaged, which was extremely interesting and romantic, Meg thought. Mr. Moffat was a fat, jolly old gentleman, who knew her father, and Mrs. Moffat, a fat, jolly old lady, who took as great a fancy to Meg as her daughter had done. Everyone petted her, and "Daisey," as they called her, was in a fair way to have her head turned.

When the evening for the small party came, she found that the poplin wouldn't do at all, for the other girls were putting on thin dresses and making themselves very fine indeed. So out came the tarlatan, looking older, limper, and shabbier than ever beside Sallie's crisp new one. Meg saw the girls glance at it and then at one another, and her cheeks began to burn, for with all her gentleness she was very proud. No one said a word about it, but Sallie offered to dress her hair, and Annie to tie her sash, and Belle, the engaged sister, praised her white arms. But in their kindness Meg saw only pity for her poverty, and her heart felt very heavy as she stood by herself, while the others laughed, chattered, and flew about like gauzy butterflies. The hard, bitter feeling was getting pretty bad, when the maid brought in a box of flowers. Before she could speak, Annie had the cover off, and all were exclaiming at the lovely roses, heath, and fern within.

"It's for Belle, of course, George always sends her some, but these are altogether ravishing," cried Annie, with a great sniff.

"They are for Miss March, the man said. And here's a note," put in the maid, holding it to Meg.

"What fun! Who are they from? Didn't know you had a lover," cried the girls, fluttering about Meg in a high state of curiosity and surprise.

"The note is from Mother, and the flowers from Laurie," said Meg simply, yet much gratified that he had not forgotten her.

"Oh, indeed!" said Annie with a funny look, as Meg slipped the note into her pocket as a sort of talisman against envy, vanity, and false pride, for the few loving words had done her good, and the flowers cheered her up by their beauty.

Feeling almost happy again, she laid by a few ferns and roses for herself, and quickly made up the rest in dainty bouquets for the breasts, hair, or skirts of her friends, offering them so prettily that Clara, the elder sister, told her she was "the sweetest little thing she ever saw," and they looked quite charmed with her small attention. Somehow the kind act finished her despondency, and when all the rest went to show themselves to Mrs. Moffat, she saw a happy, bright-eyed face in the mirror, as she laid her ferns against her rippling hair and fastened the roses in the dress that didn't strike her as so very shabby now.

She enjoyed herself very much that evening, for she danced to her heart's content. Everyone was very kind, and she had three compliments. Annie made her sing, and some one said she had a remarkably fine voice. Major Lincoln asked who "the fresh little girl with the beautiful eyes" was, and Mr. Moffat insisted on dancing with her because she "didn't dawdle, but had some spring in her," as he gracefully expressed it. So altogether she had a very nice time, till she overheard a bit of conversation, which disturbed her extremely. She was sitting just inside the conservatory, waiting for her partner to bring her an ice, when she heard a voice ask on the other side of the flowery wall ...

"How old is he?" "Sixteen or seventeen, I should say," replied another voice.

"It would be a grand thing for one of those girls, wouldn't it? Sallie says they are very intimate now, and the old man quite dotes on them."

"Mrs. M. has made her plans, I dare say, and will play her cards well, early as it is. The girl evidently doesn't think of it yet," said Mrs. Moffat.

"She told that fib about her momma, as if she did know, and colored up when the flowers came quite prettily. Poor thing! She'd be so nice if she was only got up in style. Do you think she'd be offended if we offered to lend her a dress for Thursday?" asked another voice.

"She's proud, but I don't believe she'd mind, for that dowdy tarlatan is all she has got. She may tear it tonight, and that will be a good excuse for offering a decent one."

Here Meg's partner appeared, to find her looking much flushed and rather agitated. She was proud, and her pride was useful just then, for it helped her hide her mortification, anger, and disgust at what she had just heard. For, innocent and unsuspicious as she was, she could not help understanding the gossip of her friends. She tried to forget it, but could not, and kept repeating to herself, "Mrs. M. has made her plans," "that fib about her mamma," and "dowdy tarlatan," till she was ready to cry and rush home to tell her troubles and ask for advice. As that was impossible, she did her best to seem gay, and being rather excited, she succeeded so well that no one dreamed what an effort she was making. She was very glad when it was all over and she was quiet in her bed, where she could think and wonder and fume till her head ached and her hot cheeks were cooled by a few natural tears. Those foolish, yet well meant words, had opened a new world to Meg, and much disturbed the peace of the old one in which till now she had lived as happily as a child. Her innocent friendship with Laurie was spoiled by the silly speeches she had overheard. Her faith in her mother was a little shaken by the worldly plans attributed to her by Mrs. Moffat, who judged others by herself, and the sensible resolution to be contented with the simple wardrobe which suited a poor man's daughter was weakened by the unnecessary pity of girls who thought a shabby dress one of the greatest calamities under heaven.

Poor Meg had a restless night, and got up heavy-eyed, unhappy, half resentful toward her friends, and half ashamed of herself for not speaking out frankly and setting everything right. Everybody dawdled that morning, and it was noon before the girls found energy enough even to take up their worsted work. Something in the manner of her friends struck Meg at once. They treated her with more respect, she thought, took quite a tender interest in what she said, and looked at her with eyes that plainly betrayed curiosity. All this surprised and flattered her, though she did not understand it till Miss Belle looked up from her writing, and said, with a sentimental air ...

"Daisy, dear, I've sent an invitation to your friend, Mr. Laurence, for Thursday. We should like to know him, and it's only a proper compliment to you."

Meg colored, but a mischievous fancy to tease the girls made her reply demurely, "You are very kind, but I'm afraid he won't come."

"Why not, Cherie?" asked Miss Belle.

"He's too old."

"My child, what do you mean? What is his age, I beg to know!" cried Miss Clara.

"Nearly seventy, I believe," answered Meg, counting stitches to hide the merriment in her eyes.

"You sly creature! Of course we meant the young man," exclaimed Miss Belle, laughing.

"There isn't any, Laurie is only a little boy." And Meg laughed also at the queer look which the sisters exchanged as she thus described her supposed lover.

"About you age," Nan said.

"Nearer my sister Jo's, I am seventeen in August," returned Meg, tossing her head.

"It's very nice of him to send you flowers, isn't it?" said Annie, looking wise about nothing.

"Yes, he often does, to all of us, for their house is full, and we are so fond of them. My mother and old Mr. Laurence are friends, you know, so it is quite natural that we children should play together." And Meg hoped they would say no more.

"It's evident Daisy isn't out yet," said Miss Clara to Belle with a nod.

"Quite a pastoral state of innocence all round," returned Miss Belle with a shrug.

"I'm going out to get some little matters for my girls. Can I do anything for you, young ladies?" asked Mrs. Moffat, lumbering in like an elephant in silk and lace.

"No, thank you, ma'am," replied Sallie. "I've got my new pink silk for Thursday and don't want a thing."

"Nor I ..." began Meg, but stopped because it occurred to her that she did want several things and could not have them.

"What shall you wear?" asked Sallie.

"My old white one again, if I can mend it fit to be seen, it got sadly torn last night," said Meg, trying to speak quite easily, but feeling very uncomfortable.

"Why don't you send home for another?" said Sallie, who was not an observing young lady.

"I haven't got any other." It cost Meg an effort to say that, but Sallie did not see it and exclaimed in amiable surprise, "Only that? How funny ..." She did not finish her speech, for Belle shook her head at her and broke in, saying kindly ...

"Not at all. Where is the use of having a lot of dresses when she isn't out yet? There's no need of sending home, Daisy, even if you had a dozen, for I've got a sweet blue silk laid away, which I've outgrown, and you shall wear it to please me, won't you, dear?"

"You are very kind, but I don't mind my old dress if you don't, it does well enough for a little girl like me," said Meg.

"Now do let me please myself by dressing you up in style. I admire to do it, and you'd be a regular little beauty with a touch here and there. I shan't let anyone see you till you are done, and then we'll burst upon them like Cinderella and her godmother going to the ball," said Belle in her persuasive tone.

Meg couldn't refuse the offer so kindly made, for a desire to see if she would be "a little beauty" after touching up caused her to accept and forget all her former uncomfortable feelings toward the Moffats.

On the Thursday evening, Belle shut herself up with her maid, and between them they turned Meg into a fine lady. They crimped and curled her hair, they polished her neck and arms with some fragrant powder, touched her lips with coralline salve to make them redder, and Hortense would have added "a soupcon of rouge," if Meg had not rebelled. They laced her into a sky-blue dress, which was so tight she could hardly breathe and so low in the neck that modest Meg blushed at herself in the mirror. A set of silver filagree was added, bracelets, necklace, brooch, and even earrings, for Hortense tied them on with a bit of pink silk which did not show. A cluster of tea-rose buds at the bosom and a ruche, reconciled Meg to the display of her pretty, white shoulders, and a pair of high-heeled silk boots satisfied the last wish of her heart. A lace handkerchief, a plumy fan, and a bouquet in a shoulder holder finished her off, and Miss Belle surveyed her with the satisfaction of a little girl with a newly dressed doll.

"Mademoiselle is chatmante, tres jolie, is she not?" cried Hortense, clasping her hands in an affected rapture.

"Come and show yourself," said Miss Belle, leading the way to the room where the others were waiting.

As Meg went rustling after, with her long skirts trailing, her earrings tinkling, her curls waving, and her heart beating, she felt as if her fun had really begun at last, for the mirror had plainly told her that she was "a little beauty". Her friends repeated the pleasing phrase enthusiastically, and for several minutes she stood, like a jackdaw in the fable, enjoying her borrowed plumes, while the rest chattered like a party of magpies.

"While I dress, do you drill her, Nan, in the management of her skirt and those French heels, or she will trip herself up. Take your silver butterfly, and catch up that long curl on the left side of her head, Clara, and don't any of you disturb the charming work of my hands," said Belle, as she hurried away, looking well pleased with her success.

"You don't look a bit like yourself, but you are very nice. I'm nowhere beside you, for Belle has heaps of taste, and you're quite French, I assure you. Let your flowers hang, don't be so careful of them, and be sure you don't trip," returned Sallie, trying not to care that Meg was prettier than herself.

Keeping that warning carefully in mind, Margaret got safely downstairs and sailed into the drawing rooms where the Moffats and a few early guests were assembled. She very soon discovered that there is a charm about fine clothes which attracts a certain class of people and secures their respect. Several young ladies, who had taken no notice of her before, were very affectionate all of a sudden. Several young gentlemen, who had only stared at her at the other party, now not only stared, but asked to be introduced, and said all manner of foolish but agreeable things to her, and several old ladies, who sat on the sofas, and criticized the rest of the party, inquired who she was with an air of interest. She heard Mrs. Moffat reply to one of them ...

"Daisy March—father a colonel in the army—one of our first families, but reverses of fortune, you know; intimate friends of the Laurences; sweet creature, I assure you; my Ned is quite wild about her."

"Dear me!" said the old lady, putting up her glass for another observation of Meg, who tried to look as if she had not heard and been rather shocked at Mrs. Moffat's fibs.

The "queer feeling" did not pass away, but she imagined herself acting the new part of fine lady and so got on pretty well, though the tight dress gave her a side-ache, the train kept getting under her feet, and she was in constant fear lest her earrings should fly off and get lost or broken. She was flirting her fan and laughing at the feeble jokes of a young gentleman who tried to be witty, when she suddenly stopped laughing and looked confused, for just opposite, she saw Laurie. He was staring at her with undisguised surprise, and disapproval also, she thought, for though he bowed and smiled, yet something in his honest eyes made her blush and wish she had her old dress on. To complete her confusion, she saw Belle nudge Annie, and both glance from her to Laurie, who, she was happy to see, looked unusually boyish and shy.

"Silly creatures, to put such thoughts into my head. I won't care for it, or let it change me a bit," thought Meg, and rustled across the room to shake hands with her friend.

"I'm glad you came, I was afraid you wouldn't." she said, with her most grown-up air.

"Jo wanted me to come, and tell her how you looked, so I did," answered Laurie, without turning his eyes upon her, though he half smiled at her maternal tone.

"What shall you tell her?" asked Meg, full of curiosity to know his opinion of her, yet feeling ill at ease with him for the first time.

"I shall say I didn't know you, for you look so grown-up and unlike yourself, I'm quite afraid of you," he said, fumbling at his glove button.

"How absurd of you! The girls dressed me up for fun, and I rather like it. Wouldn't Jo stare if she saw me?" said Meg, bent on making him say whether he thought her improved or not.

"Yes, I think she would," returned Laurie gravely. "Don't you like me so?" asked Meg.

"No, I don't," was the blunt reply.

"Why not?" in an anxious tone.

He glanced at her frizzled head, bare shoulders, and fantastically trimmed dress with an expression that abashed her more than his answer, which had not particle of his usual politeness in it.

"I don't like fuss and feathers."

That was altogether too much from a lad younger than herself, and Meg walked away, saying petulantly, "You are the rudest boy I ever saw." Feeling very much ruffled, she went and stood at a quiet window to cool her cheeks, for the tight dress gave her an uncomfortably brilliant color. As she stood there, Major Lincoln passed by, and a minute after she heard him saying to his mother ...

"They are making a fool of that little girl. I wanted you to see her, but they have spoiled her entirely. She's nothing but a doll tonight."

"Oh, dear!" sighed Meg. "I wish I'd been sensible and worn my own things, then I should not have disgusted other people, or felt so uncomfortable and ashamed of myself."

She leaned her forehead on the cool pane, and stood half hidden by the curtains, never minding that her favorite waltz had begun, till some one touched her, and turning, she saw Laurie, looking penitent, as he said, with his very best bow and his hand out ...

"Please forgive my rudeness, and come and dance with me."

"I'm afraid it will be to disagreeable to you," said Meg, trying to look offended and failing entirely.

"Not a bit of it, I'm dying to do it. Come, I'll be good. I don't like your gown, but I do think you are just splendid." And he waved his hands, as if words failed to express his admiration.

Meg smiled and relented, and whispered as they stood waiting to catch the time, "Take care my skirt doesn't trip you up. It's the plague of my life and I was a goose to wear it."

"Pin it round your neck, and then it will be useful," said Laurie, looking down at the little blue boots, which he evidently approved of.

Away they went fleetly and gracefully, for having practiced at home, they were well matched, and the blithe young couple were a pleasant sight to see, as they twirled merrily round and round, feeling more friendly than ever after their small tiff.

"Laurie, I want you to do me a favor, will you?" said Meg, as he stood fanning her when her breath gave out, which it did very soon though she would not own why.

"Won't I!" said Laurie, with alacrity.

"Please don't tell them at home about my dress tonight. They won't understand the joke, and it will worry Mother."

"Then why did you do it?" said Laurie's eyes, so plainly that Meg hastily added ...

"I shall tell them myself all about it, and 'fess' to Mother how silly I've been. But I'd rather do it myself. So you'll not tell, will you?"

"I give you my word I won't, only what shall I say when they ask me?"

"Just say I looked pretty well and was having a good time."

"I'll say the first with all my heart, but how about the other? You don't look as if you were having a good time. Are you?" And Laurie looked at her with an expression which made her answer in a whisper ...

"No, not just now. Don't think I'm horrid. I only wanted a little fun, but this sort doesn't pay, I find, and I'm getting tired of it."

"Here comes Ned Moffat. What does he want?" said Laurie, knitting his black brows as if he did not regard his young host in the light of a pleasant addition to the party.

"He put his name down for three dances, and I suppose he's coming for them. What a bore!" said Meg, assuming a languid air which amused Laurie immensely.

He did not speak to her again till suppertime, when he saw her drinking champagne with Ned and his friend Fisher, who were behaving "like a pair of fools," as Laurie said to himself, for he felt a brotherly sort of right to watch over the Marches and fight their battles whenever a defender was needed.

"You'll have a splitting headache tomorrow, if you drink much of that. I wouldn't, Meg, your mother doesn't like it, you know," he whispered, leaning over her chair, as Ned turned to refill her glass and Fisher stooped to pick up her fan.

"I'm not Meg tonight, I'm 'a doll' who does all sorts of crazy things. Tomorrow I shall put away my 'fuss and feathers' and be desperately good again," she answered with an affected little laugh.

"Wish tomorrow was here, then," muttered Laurie, walking off, ill-pleased at the change he saw in her.

Meg danced and flirted, chattered and giggled, as the other girls did. After supper she undertook the German, and blundered through it, nearly upsetting her partner with her long skirt, and romping in a way that scandalized Laurie, who looked on and meditated a lecture. But he got no chance to deliver it, for Meg kept away from him till he came to say good night.

"Remember!" she said, trying to smile, for the splitting headache had already begun.

"Silence a la mort," replied Laurie, with a melodramatic flourish, as he went away.

This little bit of byplay excited Annie's curiosity, but Meg was too tired for gossip and went to bed, feeling as if she had been to a masquerade and hadn't enjoyed herself as much as she expected. She was sick all the next day, and on Saturday went home, quite used up with her fortnight's fun and feeling that she had "sat in the lap of luxury" long enough.

"It does seem pleasant to be quiet, and not have company manners on all the time. Home is a nice place, though it isn't splendid," said Meg, looking about her with a restful expression, as she sat with her mother and Jo on the Sunday evening.

"I'm glad to hear you say so, dear, for I was afraid home would seem dull and poor to you after your fine quarters," replied her mother, who had given her many anxious looks that day. For motherly eyes are quick to see any change in children's faces.

Meg had told her adventures gayly and said over and over what a charming time she had had, but something still seemed to weigh upon her spirits, and when the younger girls were gone to bed, she sat thoughtfully staring at the fire, saying little and looking worried. As the clock struck nine and Jo proposed bed, Meg suddenly left her chair and, taking Beth's stool, leaned her elbows on her mother's knee, saying bravely ...

"Marmee, I want to'fess.'"

"I thought so. What is it, dear?"

"Shall I go away?" asked Jo discreetly.

"Of course not. Don't I always tell you everything? I was ashamed to speak of it before the younger children, but I want you to know all the dreadful things I did at the Moffats'."

"We are prepared," said Mrs. March, smiling but looking a little anxious.

"I told you they dressed me up, but I didn't tell you that they powdered and squeezed and frizzled, and made me look like a fashion plate. Laurie thought I wasn't proper. I know he did, though he didn't say so, and one man called me 'a doll'. I knew it was silly, but they flattered me and said I was a beauty, and quantities of nonsense, so I let them make a fool of me."

"Is that all?" asked Jo, as Mrs. March looked silently at the downcast face of her pretty daughter, and could not find it in her heart to blame her little follies.

"No, I drank champagne and romped and tried to flirt, and was altogether abominable," said Meg self-reproachfully.

"There is something more, I think." And Mrs. March smoothed the soft cheek, which suddenly grew rosy as Meg answered slowly ...

"Yes. It's very silly, but I want to tell it, because I hate to have people say and think such things about us and Laurie."

Then she told the various bits of gossip she had heard at the

Moffats', and as she spoke, Jo saw her mother fold her lips tightly, as if ill pleased that such ideas should be put into Meg's innocent mind.

"Well, if that isn't the greatest rubbish I ever heard," cried Jo indignantly. "Why didn't you pop out and tell them so on the spot?"

"I couldn't, it was so embarrassing for me. I couldn't help hearing at first, and then I was so angry and ashamed, I didn't remember that I ought to go away."

"Just wait till I see Annie Moffat, and I'll show you how to settle such ridiculous stuff. The idea of having 'plans' and being kind to Laurie because he's rich and may marry us by-and-by! Won't he shout when I tell him what those silly things say about us poor children?" And Jo laughed, as if on second thoughts the thing struck her as a good joke.

"If you tell Laurie, I'll never forgive you! She mustn't, must she, Mother?" said Meg, looking distressed.

"No, never repeat that foolish gossip, and forget it as soon as you can," said Mrs. March gravely. "I was very unwise to let you go among people of whom I know so little, kind, I dare say, but worldly, ill-bred, and full of these vulgar ideas about young people. I am more sorry than I can express for the mischief this visit may have done you, Meg."

"Don't be sorry, I won't let it hurt me. I'll forget all the bad and remember only the good, for I did enjoy a great deal, and thank you very much for letting me go. I'll not be sentimental or dissatisfied, Mother. I know I'm a silly little girl, and I'll stay with you till I'm fit to take care of myself. But it is nice to be praised and admired, and I can't help saying I like it," said Meg, looking half ashamed of the confession.

"That is perfectly natural, and quite harmless, if the liking does not become a passion and lead one to do foolish or unmaidenly things. Learn to know and value the praise which is worth having, and to excite the admiration of excellent people by being modest as well as pretty, Meg."

Margaret sat thinking a moment, while Jo stood with her hands behind her, looking both interested and a little perplexed, for it was a new thing to see Meg blushing and talking about admiration, lovers, and things of that sort. And Jo felt as if during that fortnight her sister had grown up amazingly, and was drifting away from her into a world where she could not follow.

"Mother, do you have 'plans,' as Mrs. Moffat said?" asked Meg bashfully.

"Yes, my dear, I have a great many, all mothers do, but mine differ somewhat from Mrs. Moffat's, I suspect. I will tell you some of them, for the time has come when a word may set this romantic little head and heart of yours right, on a very serious subject. You are young, Meg, but not too young to understand me, and mothers' lips are the fittest to speak of such things to girls like you. Jo, your turn will come in time, perhaps, so listen to my 'plans' and help me carry them out, if they are good."

Jo went and sat on one arm of the chair, looking as if she thought they were about to join in some very solemn affair. Holding a hand of each, and watching the two young faces wistfully, Mrs. March said, in her serious yet cheery way ...

"I want my daughters to be beautiful, accomplished, and good. To be admired, loved, and respected. To have a happy youth, to be well and wisely married, and to lead useful, pleasant lives, with as little care and sorrow to try them as God sees fit to send. To be loved and chosen by a good man is the best and sweetest thing which can happen to a woman, and I sincerely hope my girls may know this beautiful experience. It is natural to think of it, Meg, right to hope and wait for it, and wise to prepare for it, so that when the happy time comes, you may feel ready for the duties and worthy of the joy. My dear girls, I am ambitious for you, but not to have you make a dash in the world, marry rich men merely because they are rich, or have splendid houses, which are not homes because love is wanting. Money is a needful and precious thing, and when well used, a noble thing, but I never want you to think it is the first or only prize to strive for. I'd rather see you poor men's wives, if you were happy, beloved, contented, than queens on thrones, without self-respect and peace."

"Poor girls don't stand any chance, Belle says, unless they put themselves forward," sighed Meg.

"Then we'll be old maids," said Jo stoutly.

"right, Jo. Better be happy old maids than unhappy wives, or unmaidenly girls, running about to find husbands," said Mrs. March decidedly. "Don't be troubled, Meg, poverty seldom daunts a sincere lover. Some of the best and most honored women I know were poor girls, but so love-worthy that they were not allowed to be old maids. Leave these things to time. Make this home happy, so that you may be fit for homes of your own, if they are offered you, and contented here if they are not. One thing remember, my girls. Mother is always ready to be your confidante, Father to be your friend, and both of hope and trust that our daughters, whether married or single, will be the pride and comfort of out lives."

"We will, Marmee, we will!" cried both, with all their hearts, as she bade them good night.

(选自 Louisa May Alcott. *Little Women*. New York: W. W. Norton & Company, Inc., 2004. pp. 11 - 19, 71 - 84.)

Questions

1. How do you interpret the title of the novel *Little Women*?
2. Why wasn't the girls' father at home during that Christmas?
3. Why Meg feels that the Moffats are not particular cultivated or intelligent?
4. How do you understand "vanity fair" in the title of Chapter 9?
5. Why does Meg regret her behavior at the party?

Unit 2

Kate Chopin: "The Story of an Hour"

Kate Chopin (1851—1904) was born in St. Louis, Missouri, the daughter of an immigrant Irishman, Thomas O'Flaherty and a French-American mother, Eliza Faris. She was one of five children, but both her sisters died in infancy and her brothers died in their twenties. When she was five years old, Kate was sent to a Catholic boarding school. Just months later, her father died in a train accident, and she was sent back to live with her mother and her grand-mother, all widowed. After two years in their care, she returned to that Catholic school and finished at the top of her class. She grew up from early childhood with intelligent and independent women both at home and at school with the nuns. Her childhood lacked male role models and she rarely witnessed to the tradition of female submission and male domination. That is to say, this lack would also prevent her from experiencing what was basically a fundamental social concept of her time—the tradition of submission of women to men in all social spheres, but especially that of marriage. Kate Chopin's upbringing in a household of women and her education by nuns in a school for girls, may not have prepared her to completely accept the societal limitations of such a role. While it is true that she would have been instructed in the basic duties of being both a wife and a mother, and also taught subordination of the self to a "higher" masculine authority, her primary role models, both at home and at school, were women. Therefore, Kate would have been quite accustomed to seeing women in positions of autonomy and authority. It is often speculated that the inconsistency between training and experience in her life, contributed to the later development of her strong female characters, many of whom are stifled by their marital relationships. The themes of female freedom and sexual awareness were undoubtedly the result of the atmosphere she was raised.

Kate Chopin began writing seriously at the age of 39, when she would have already experienced many life situations. She found her central focus rapidly, and wrote stories whose colorful characters and lush settings often masked the seriousness of their themes. Not greatly involved in the politics of her time, she was nonetheless influenced by such classic masters as Maupassant who would have awakened her, to ideas such as personal liberty and freedom. Kate Chopin enjoyed the immediate success. She was often asked to attend conferences and give speeches and was widely celebrated for the majority of her short but prolific career. When Kate Chopin had just been nationally praised for her collection of stories *Bayou Folk* (1894), she wrote "The Story of an Hour" (1894), a tale about a woman who felt enslaved in her marriage. The story was turned down by magazine editors for its challenged conventional social behavior. However, feminist critics championed this story intensively.

It is *The Awakening*, published in 1899 that makes Kate Chopin finally come into her own as a novelist. By degrees discovering her sense of self as a person and an artist, the protagonist, Edna Pontellier, slowly emerges from her semi-conscious state as wife and mother and "awakens" into full-blooming vibrancy and womanhood at the end of the novel. A barrage of critical abuse followed the novel's publication and, unfortunately for her later admirers, extinguished her period of creativity. Chopin died of a brain hemorrhage in 1904 after a strenuous day at the St. Louis World's Fair, where she had been a regular visitor. Until *The Awakening* was rediscovered in the 1970s as an early masterpiece of American realism and a superb rendering of female experience that she was regarded as a great female writer.

Theme

This story is about a woman who felt enslaved in her marriage and when she was told that her husband suddenly died, she thought that she would be free from then on. But her husband came home unexpectedly, and she died from shock and disappointment, rather than joy as the doctor's diagnosis. "The Story of an Hour" reflects women's low social positions and their eagerness for freedom and independence.

Term

Irony: A subtly humorous perception of inconsistency, in which an apparently straightforward statement or event is undermined by its context so as to give it a very different significance. At its simplest, in verbal irony, it involves a discrepancy between what is said and what is really meant. The more sustained structural irony in literature involves the use of a naive or deluded hero or unreliable narrator, whose view of the world differs widely from the true circumstance recognized by the author and readers; literary irony thus flatters its readers' intelligence at the expense of a character (or fictional narrator). A similar sense of detached superiority is achieved by dramatic irony, in which the audience knows more about a character's situation than the character does, foreseeing an outcome contrary to the character's expectations, and thus ascribing a sharply different sense to some of the character's own statements.

Text

The Story of an Hour

Knowing that Mrs. Mallard was afflicted with a heart trouble, great care was taken to break to her as gently as possible the news of her husband's death.

It was her sister Josephine who told her, in broken sentences; veiled hints that revealed in half concealing. Her husband's friend Richards was there, too, near her. It was he who had been in the newspaper office when intelligence of the railroad disaster was received, with Brently Mallard's name leading the list of "killed." He had only taken the time to assure himself of its truth by a second telegram, and had hastened to forestall any less careful, less tender friend in bearing the sad message.

She did not hear the story as many women have heard the same, with a paralyzed inability to accept its significance. She wept at once, with sudden, wild abandonment, in her sister's arms. When the storm of grief had spent itself, she went away to her room alone. She would have no one follow her.

There stood, facing the open window, a comfortable, roomy armchair. Into this she sank, pressed down by a physical exhaustion that haunted her body and seemed to reach into her soul.

She could see in the open square before her house the tops of trees that were all aquiver with the new spring life. The delicious breath of rain was in the air. In the street below a peddler was crying his wares. The notes of a distant song which some one was singing reached her faintly, and countless sparrows were twittering in the eaves.

There were patches of blue sky showing here and there through the clouds that had met and piled one above the other in the west facing her window.

She sat with her head thrown back upon the cushion of the chair, quite motionless, except when a sob came up into her throat and shook her, as a child who has cried itself to sleep continues to sob in its dreams.

She was young, with a fair, calm face, whose lines bespoke repression and even a certain strength. But now there was a dull stare in her eyes, whose gaze was fixed away off yonder on one of those patches of blue sky. It was not a glance of reflection, but rather indicated a suspension of intelligent thought.

There was something coming to her and she was waiting for it, fearfully. What was it? She did not know; it was too subtle and elusive to name. But she felt it, creeping out of the sky, reaching toward her through the sounds, the scents, the color that filled the air.

Now her bosom rose and fell tumultuously. She was beginning to recognize this thing that was approaching to possess her, and she was striving to beat it back with her will—as powerless as her two white slender hands would have been.

When she abandoned herself, a little whispered word escaped her slightly parted lips. She said it over and over under her breath: "Free, free, free!" The vacant stare and the look of terror that had followed it went from her eyes. They stayed keen and bright. Her pulses beat fast, and the coursing blood warmed and relaxed every inch of her body.

She did not stop to ask if it were or were not a monstrous joy that held her. A clear and exalted perception enabled her to dismiss the suggestion as trivial.

She knew that she would weep again when she saw the kind, tender hands folded in death; the face that had never looked save with love upon her, fixed and gray and dead. But she saw beyond that bitter moment a long procession of years to come that would belong to her absolutely. And she opened and spread her arms out to them in welcome.

There would be no one to live for during those coming years; she would live for herself. There would be no powerful will bending hers in that blind persistence with which men and women believe they have a right to impose a private will upon a fellow-creature. A kind intention or a cruel intention made the act seem no less a crime as she looked upon it in that brief moment of illumination.

And yet she had loved him—sometimes. Often she had not. What did it matter! What could love, the unsolved mystery, count for in face of this possession of self-assertion which she suddenly recognized as the strongest impulse of her being!

"Free! Body and soul free!" she kept whispering.

Josephine was kneeling before the closed door with her lips to the keyhole, imploring for admission. "Louise, open the door! I beg, open the door—you will make yourself ill. What are you doing Louise? For heaven's sake open the door."

"Go away. I am not making myself ill." No; she was drinking in a very elixir of life through that open window.

Her fancy was running riot along those days ahead of her. Spring days, and summer days, and all sorts of days that would be her own. She breathed a quick prayer that life might be long. It was only yesterday she had thought with a shudder that life might be long.

She arose at length and opened the door to her sister's importunities. There was a feverish triumph in her eyes, and she carried herself unwittingly like a goddess of Victory. She clasped her sister's waist, and together they descended the stairs. Richards stood waiting for them at the bottom.

Some one was opening the front door with a latchkey. It was Brently Mallard who entered, a little travel-stained, composedly carrying his grip-sack and umbrella. He had been far from the scene of accident, and did not even know there had been one. He stood amazed at Josephine's piercing cry; at Richards' quick motion to screen him from the view of his wife.

But Richards was too late.

When the doctors came they said she had died of heart disease—of joy that kills.

(选自 Kate Chopin. "The Story of an Hour," *The Awakening and Selected Stories*. Sandra M. Gilbert ed. New York: The Penguin Group, 1969. pp. 213－215.)

Questions

1. How would you describe the character of Mrs. Mallad?
2. Is the plot plausible? How would you interpret the ending of the story?
3. Why did Mrs. Mallad rejoice at her husband's death?
4. Please give some examples of irony in the story.
5. What are the causes leading to Mrs. Mallad's death?

Unit 3

Johann Wolfgang von Goethe: *The Sorrows of Young Werther*

Johann Wolfgang von Goethe (1749—1832) was born in Frankfurt am Main, the first child of a lawyer Johann Caspar Goethe, and Katherine Elisabeth Textor. Goethe had a comfortable childhood and he was greatly influenced by his mother who encouraged his literary aspirations. After troubles at school, he received an exceptionally wide education at home. At the age of 16, Goethe began to study law at Leipzig University (1765—1768), and he also studied drawing with Adam Oeser. An unhappy love affair inspired Goethe's first play *The Lover's Caprice* (1767). In literature, Goethe gained early fame with *The Sorrows of Young Werther* (1774), but his most famous work is the poetic drama *Faust*—his most enduring work, which is one of the peaks of world literature. The first part was published in 1808, the second part shortly after Goethe's death. Most of Goethe's works have been translated into English, notably by T. Carlyle.

In Weimar his great love was Charlotte von Stein, an older married woman, but the relationship remained platonic. After Goethe's emotional dependence on Charlotte ended, he lived happily and unmarried with Christiane Vulpius, who became Goethe's mistress in 1789. In spite of public pressure, it was not until 1806 when they married.

The Sorrows of Young Werther is somewhat autobiographical. In 1772, when Goethe was an obscure young legal apprentice living in Wetzlar (in which, presumably, Werther is set), he developed an impossible passion for Charlotte Buff, who was engaged to his friend, Kestner. Goethe himself, in his later years, spoke of the effect of his book, comparing it to a small spark that exploded a mine full of gunpowder. He wrote in his autobiography *My Life: Poetry and Truth*: "The explosion Werther caused was so far-reaching because the young people of that era had already undermined themselves; and the shock was so great because everyone could now burst forth with his own exaggerated demands, unsatisfied passions, and imaginary sufferings." The book remains Goethe's most popular work—more popular, even than *Faust*. The book stands as a near-perfectly crafted narrative, carefully observed and expertly executed with many paradoxical details included. Not only is the work a time capsule of sorts, allowing us a glimpse into an age of unrivaled passion and morbidity, but it also transcends its time as a meditation on the extremities of youthful sorrows.

In 1792 Goethe accompanied Duke Charles Augustus as official historian in the allied campaign against revolutionary France. He appreciated the principles of the French Revolution but resented the methods employed. A reformer in his own small state, Goethe wished to see social change accomplished from above.

The opinions of Goethe are recorded not only in his own writings but also in conversations recorded by his secretary J. P. Eckermann and in extensive correspondence with the composer Zelter and with Schiller, Byron, Carlyle, Manzoni, and others. It can never overestimate Goethe's great influences on the subsequent history of German literature.

Theme

In *The Sorrows of Young Werther*, through Werther's conflict with society, Goethe protests for strangling talented and aspiring young people at that time in Germany, which awakens self-consciousness of young generations. The tragedy of Werther represents the young German bourgeoisie who demanded to get rid of the feudal shackles, but the incompetence of the German bourgeoisie does not allow them to resist feudal oppression, which leads to Werther's suicide. The novel embodies the main features of the Sturm und Drang movement, including supporting anti-feudalism and anti-traditional thought of hierarchy, getting closing to nature, praising geniuses and heroes to awaken national consciousness, pursuing individual freedom, promoting the liberation of personality and the expression of individual emotions, combining the personal experience with the imagination, taking violence to resist, lamenting the rotten social status.

Term

(Storm & Stress)

Storm and Stress: Sturm und Drang refers to the German literary movement of the late 18th century that exalted nature, feeling, and human individualism and sought to overthrow the Enlightenment cult of Rationalism. The movement took its name from the 1776 play "Sturm und Drang," a work by one of its proponents, dramatist and novelist Friedrich von Klinger. During this movement, individual subjectivity and, in particular, the extreme emotions were given free expression in reaction to the perceived constraints of rationalism imposed by the Enlightenment. In such a historical background, the spirit of the times expressed in *The Sorrows of Young Werther* is the ideal of the social reality under the unreasonable reform of the emerging bourgeoisie, that is, "personality liberation," "emotional freedom," "return to nature" and so on.

Excerpt

Preface

I have carefully collected whatever I have been able to learn of the story of poor Werther, and here present it to you, knowing that you will thank me for it. To his spirit and character you cannot refuse your admiration and love: to his fate you will not deny your tears.

And thou, good soul, who sufferest the same distress as he endured once, draw comfort from his sorrows; and let this little book be thy friend, if, owing to fortune or through thine own fault, thou canst not find a dearer companion.

MAY 4.

How happy I am that I am gone! My dear friend, what a thing is the heart of man! To leave you, from whom I have been inseparable, whom I love so dearly, and yet to feel happy! I know you will forgive me. Have not other attachments been specially appointed by fate to torment a head like mine? Poor Leonora! and yet I was not to blame. Was it my fault, that, whilst the peculiar charms of her sister afforded me an agreeable entertainment, a passion for me was engendered in her feeble heart? And yet am I wholly blameless? Did I not encourage her emotions? Did I not feel charmed at those truly genuine expressions of nature, which, though but little mirthful in reality, so often amused us? Did I not—but oh! what is man, that he dares so to accuse himself? My dear friend I promise you I will improve; I will no longer, as has ever been my habit, continue to ruminate on every petty vexation which fortune may dispense; I will enjoy the present, and the past shall be for me the past. No doubt you are right, my best of friends, there would be far less suffering amongst mankind, if men—and God knows why they are so fashioned—did not employ their imaginations so assiduously in recalling the memory of past sorrow, instead of bearing their present lot with equanimity. Be kind enough to inform my mother that I shall attend to her business to the best of my ability, and shall give her the earliest information about it. I have seen my aunt, and find that she is very far from being the disagreeable person our friends allege her to be. She is a lively, cheerful woman, with the best of hearts. I explained to her my mother's wrongs with regard to that part of her portion which has been withheld from her. She told me the motives and reasons of her own conduct, and the terms on which she is willing to give up the whole, and to do more than we have asked. In short, I cannot write further upon this subject at present; only assure my mother that all will go on well. And I have again observed, my dear friend, in this trifling affair, that misunderstandings and neglect occasion more mischief in the world than even malice and wickedness. At all events, the two latter are of less frequent occurrence.

In other respects I am very well off here. Solitude in this terrestrial paradise is a genial balm to my mind, and the young spring cheers with its bounteous promises my oftentimes misgiving heart. Every tree, every bush, is full of flowers; and one might wish himself transformed into a butterfly, to float about in this ocean of perfume, and find his whole existence in it.

The town itself is disagreeable; but then, all around, you find an inexpressible beauty of nature. This induced the late Count M to lay out a garden on one of the sloping hills which here intersect each other with the most charming variety, and form the most lovely valleys. The garden is simple; and it is easy to perceive, even upon your first entrance, that the plan was not designed by a scientific gardener, but by a man who wished to give himself up here to the enjoyment of his own sensitive heart. Many a tear have I already shed to the memory of its departed master in a summer-house which is now reduced to ruins, but was his favorite resort, and now is mine. I shall soon be master of the place. The gardener has become attached to me within the last few days, and he will lose nothing thereby.

MAY 10.

A wonderful serenity has taken possession of my entire soul, like these sweet mornings of spring which I enjoy with my whole heart. I am alone, and feel the charm of existence in this spot, which was created for the bliss of souls like mine. I am so happy, my dear friend, so absorbed in the exquisite sense of mere tranquil existence, that I neglect my talents. I should be incapable of drawing a single stroke at the present moment; and yet I feel that I never was a greater artist than now. When, while the lovely valley teems with vapor around me, and the meridian sun strikes the upper surface of the impenetrable foliage of my trees, and but a few stray gleams steal into the inner sanctuary, I throw myself down among the tall grass by the trickling stream; and, as I lie close to the earth, a thousand unknown plants are noticed by me: when I hear the buzz of the little world among the stalks, and grow familiar with the countless indescribable forms of the insects and flies, then I feel the presence of the Almighty, who formed us in his own image, and the breath of that universal love which bears and sustains us, as it floats around us in an eternity of bliss; and then, my friend, when darkness overspreads my eyes, and heaven and earth seem to dwell in my soul and absorb its power, like the form of a beloved mistress, then I often think with longing, Oh, would I could describe these conceptions, could impress upon paper all that is living so full and warm within me, that it might be the mirror of my soul, as my soul is the mirror of the infinite God! Oh my friend—but it is too much for my strength—I sink under the weight of the splendor of these visions!

MAY 12.

I know not whether some deceitful spirits haunt this spot, or whether it be the warm, celestial fancy in my own heart which makes everything around me seem like paradise. In front of the house is a fountain,—a fountain to which I am bound by a charm like Melusina and her sisters. Descending a gentle slope, you come to an arch, where, some twenty steps lower down, water of the clearest crystal gushes from the marble rock. The narrow wall which encloses it above, the tall trees which encircle the spot, and the coolness of the place itself, —everything imparts a pleasant but sublime impression. Not a day passes on which I do not spend an hour there. The young maidens come from the town to fetch water, —innocent and necessary employment, and formerly the occupation of the daughters of kings. As I take my rest there, the idea of the old patriarchal life is awakened around me. I see them, our old ancestors, how they formed their friendships and contracted alliances at the fountain-side; and I feel how fountains and streams were guarded by beneficent spirits. He who is a stranger to these sensations has never really enjoyed cool repose at the side of a fountain after the fatigue of a weary summer day.

MAY 13.

You ask if you shall send me books. My dear friend, I beseech you, for the love of God, relieve me from such a yoke! I need no more to be guided, agitated, heated. My heart ferments sufficiently of itself. I want strains to lull me, and I find them to perfection in my Homer. Often do I strive to allay the burning fever of my blood; and you have never witnessed anything so unsteady, so uncertain, as my heart. But need I confess this to you, my dear friend, who have so often endured the anguish of witnessing my sudden transitions from sorrow to immoderate joy, and from sweet melancholy to violent passions? I treat my poor heart like a sick child, and gratify its every fancy. Do not mention this again: there are people who would censure me for it.

MAY 15.

The common people of the place know me already, and love me, particularly the children. When at first I associated with them, and inquired in a friendly tone about their various trifles, some fancied that I wished to ridicule them, and turned from me in exceeding ill-humor. I did not allow that circumstance to grieve me: I only felt most keenly what I have often before observed. Persons who can claim a certain rank keep themselves coldly aloof from the common people, as though they feared to lose their importance by the contact; whilst wanton idlers, and such as are prone to bad joking, affect to descend to their level, only to make the poor people feel their impertinence all the more keenly.

I know very well that we are not all equal, nor can be so; but it is my opinion that he who avoids the common people, in order not to lose their respect, is as much to blame as a coward who hides himself from his enemy because he fears defeat.

The other day I went to the fountain, and found a young servant-girl, who had set her pitcher on the lowest step, and looked around to see if one of her companions was approaching to place it on her head. I ran down, and looked at her. "Shall I help you, pretty lass?" said I. She blushed deeply. "Oh, sir!" she exclaimed. "No ceremony!" I replied. She adjusted her head-gear, and I helped her. She thanked me, and ascended the steps.

MAY 17.

I have made all sorts of acquaintances, but have as yet found no society. I know not what attraction I possess for the people, so many of them like me, and attach themselves to me; and then I feel sorry when the road we pursue together goes only a short distance. If you inquire what the people are like here, I must answer, "The same as everywhere." The human race is but a monotonous affair. Most of them labor the greater part of their time for mere subsistence; and the scanty portion of freedom which remains to them so troubles them that they use every exertion to get rid of it. Oh, the destiny of man!

But they are a right good sort of people. If I occasionally forget myself, and take part in the innocent pleasures which are not yet forbidden to the peasantry, and enjoy myself, for instance, with genuine freedom and sincerity, round a well-covered table, or arrange an excursion or a dance opportunely, and so forth, all this produces a good effect upon my disposition; only I must forget that there lie dormant within me so many other qualities which moulder uselessly, and which I am obliged to keep carefully concealed. Ah! this thought affects my spirits fearfully. And yet to be misunderstood is the fate of the like of us.

Alas, that the friend of my youth is gone! Alas, that I ever knew her! I might say to myself, "You are a dreamer to seek what is not to be found here below." But she has been mine. I have possessed that heart, that noble soul, in whose presence I seemed to be more than I really was, because I was all that I could be. Good heavens! Did then a single power of my soul remain unexercised? In her presence could I not display, to its full extent, that mysterious feeling with which my heart embraces nature? Was not our intercourse a perpetual web of the finest emotions, of the keenest wit, the varieties of which, even in their very eccentricity, bore the stamp of genius? Alas! the few years by which she was my senior brought her to the grave before me. Never can I forget her firm mind or her heavenly patience.

A few days ago I met a certain young V—, a frank, open fellow, with a most pleasing countenance. He has just left the university, does not deem himself overwise, but believes he knows more than other people. He has worked hard, as I can perceive from many circumstances, and, in short, possesses a large stock of information. When he heard that I am drawing a good deal, and that I know Greek (two wonderful things for this part of the country), he came to see me, and displayed his whole store of learning, from Batteaux to Wood, from

De Piles to Winkelmann: he assured me he had read through the first part of Sultzer's theory, and also possessed a manuscript of Heyne's work on the study of the antique. I allowed it all to pass.

I have become acquainted, also, with a very worthy person, the district judge, a frank and open-hearted man. I am told it is a most delightful thing to see him in the midst of his children, of whom he has nine. His eldest daughter especially is highly spoken of. He has invited me to go and see him, and I intend to do so on the first opportunity. He lives at one of the royal hunting-lodges, which can be reached from here in an hour and a half by walking, and which he obtained leave to inhabit after the loss of his wife, as it is so painful to him to reside in town and at the court.

There have also come in my way a few other originals of a questionable sort, who are in all respects undesirable, and most intolerable in their demonstration of friendship. Good-bye. This letter will please you: it is quite historical.

JUNE 16.

"Why do I not write to you?" You lay claim to learning, and ask such a question. You should have guessed that I am well—that is to say—in a word, I have made an acquaintance who has won my heart: I have—I know not.

To give you a regular account of the manner in which I have become acquainted with the most amiable of women would be a difficult task. I am a happy and contented mortal, but a poor historian.

An angel! Nonsense! Everybody so describes his mistress; and yet I find it impossible to tell you how perfect she is, or why she is so perfect: suffice it to say she has captivated all my senses. So much simplicity with so much understanding—so mild, and yet so resolute—a mind so placid, and a life so active.

But all this is ugly balderdash, which expresses not a single character nor feature. Some other time—but no, not some other time, now, this very instant, will I tell you all about it. Now or never. Well, between ourselves, since I commenced my letter, I have been three times on the point of throwing down my pen, of ordering my horse, and riding out. And yet I vowed this morning that I would not ride to-day, and yet every moment I am rushing to the window to see how high the sun is.

I could not restrain myself—go to her I must. I have just returned, Wilhelm; and whilst I am taking supper I will write to you. What a delight it was for my soul to see her in the midst of her dear, beautiful children, —eight brothers and sisters!

But, if I proceed thus, you will be no wiser at the end of my letter than you were at the beginning. Attend, then, and I will compel myself to give you the details.

I mentioned to you the other day that I had become acquainted with S—, the district judge, and that he had invited me to go and visit him in his retirement, or rather in his little kingdom. But I neglected going, and perhaps should never have gone, if chance had not discovered to me the treasure which lay concealed in that retired spot. Some of our young people had proposed giving a ball in the country, at which I consented to be present. I offered my hand for the evening to a pretty and agreeable, but rather commonplace, sort of girl from the immediate neighborhood; and it was agreed that I should engage a carriage, and call upon Charlotte, with my partner and her aunt, to convey them to the ball. My companion informed me, as we drove along through the park to the hunting-lodge, that I should make the acquaintance of a very charming young lady. "Take care," added the aunt, "that you do not lose your heart." "Why?" said I. "Because she is already engaged to a very worthy man," she replied, "who is gone to settle his affairs upon the death of his father, and will succeed to a very considerable inheritance." This information possessed no interest for me. When we arrived at the gate, the sun was setting behind the tops of the mountains. The atmosphere was heavy; and the ladies expressed their fears of an approaching storm, as masses of low black clouds were gathering in the horizon. I relieved their anxieties by pretending to be weather-wise, although I myself had some apprehensions lest our pleasure should be interrupted.

I alighted; and a maid came to the door, and requested us to wait a moment for her mistress. I walked across the court to a well-built house, and, ascending the flight of steps in front, opened the door, and saw before me the most charming spectacle I had ever witnessed. Six children, from eleven to two years old, were running about the hall, and surrounding a lady of middle height, with a lovely figure, dressed in a robe of simple white, trimmed with pink ribbons. She was holding a rye loaf in her hand, and was cutting slices for the little ones all around, in proportion to their age and appetite. She performed her task in a graceful and affectionate manner; each claimant awaiting his turn with outstretched hands, and boisterously shouting his thanks. Some of them ran away at once, to enjoy their evening meal; whilst others, of a gentler disposition, retired to the courtyard to see the strangers, and to survey the carriage in which their Charlotte was to drive away. "Pray forgive me for giving you the trouble to come for me, and for keeping the ladies waiting: but dressing, and arranging some household duties before I leave, had made me forget my children's supper; and they do not like to take it from any one but me." I uttered some indifferent compliment: but my whole soul was absorbed by her air, her voice, her manner; and I had scarcely recovered myself when she ran into her room to fetch her gloves and fan. The young ones threw inquiring glances at me from a distance; whilst I approached the youngest, a most delicious little creature. He drew back; and Charlotte, entering at the very moment, said, "Louis, shake hands with your cousin." The little fellow obeyed willingly; and I could not resist giving him a hearty kiss, notwithstanding his rather dirty face. "Cousin," said I to Charlotte, as I handed her down, "do you think I deserve the happiness of being related to you?" She replied, with a ready smile, "Oh! I have such a number of cousins, that I should be sorry if you were the most undeserving of them." In taking leave, she desired her next sister, Sophy, a girl about eleven years old, to take great care of the children, and to say good-bye to papa for her when he came home from his ride. She enjoined to the little ones to obey their sister Sophy as they would herself, upon which some promised that they would; but a little fair-haired girl, about six years old, looked discontented, and said, "But Sophy is not you, Charlotte; and we like you best." The two eldest boys had clambered up the carriage; and, at my request, she permitted them to accompany us a little way through the forest, upon their promising to sit very still, and hold fast.

We were hardly seated, and the ladies had scarcely exchanged compliments, making the usual remarks upon each other's dress, and upon the company they expected to meet, when Charlotte stopped the carriage, and made her brothers get down. They insisted upon kissing her hands once more; which the eldest did with all the tenderness of a youth of fifteen, but the other in a lighter and more careless manner. She desired them again to give her love to the children, and we drove off.

The aunt inquired of Charlotte whether she had finished the book she had last sent her. "No," said Charlotte; "I did not like it: you can have it again. And the one before was not much better." I was surprised, upon asking the title, to hear that it was ____. (We feel obliged to suppress the passage in the letter, to prevent any one from feeling aggrieved; although no author need pay much attention to the opinion of a mere girl, or that of an unsteady young man.)

I found penetration and character in everything she said: every expression seemed to brighten her features with new charms,—with new rays of genius, —which unfolded by degrees, as she felt herself understood.

"When I was younger," she observed, "I loved nothing so much as romances. Nothing could equal my delight when, on some holiday, I could settle down quietly in a corner, and enter with my whole heart and soul into the joys or sorrows of some fictitious Leonora. I do not deny that they even possess some charms for me yet. But I read so seldom, that I prefer books suited exactly to my taste. And I like those authors best whose scenes describe my own situation in life, —and the friends who are about me, whose stories touch me with interest, from resembling my own homely existence, —which, without being absolutely paradise, is, on the whole, a source of indescribable happiness."

I endeavored to conceal the emotion which these words occasioned, but it was of slight avail; for, when she had expressed so truly her opinion of "The Vicar of Wakefield," and of other works, the names of which I omit (Though the names are omitted, yet the authors mentioned deserve Charlotte's approbation, and will feel it in their hearts when they read this passage. It concerns no other person.), I could no longer contain myself, but gave full utterance to what I thought of it: and it was not until Charlotte had addressed herself to the two other ladies, that I remembered their presence, and observed them sitting mute with astonishment. The aunt looked at me several times with an air of raillery, which, however, I did not at all mind.

We talked of the pleasures of dancing. "If it is a fault to love it," said Charlotte, "I am ready to confess that I prize it above all other amusements. If anything disturbs me, I go to the piano, play an air to which I have danced, and all goes right again directly."

You, who know me, can fancy how steadfastly I gazed upon her rich dark eyes during these remarks, how my very soul gloated over her warm lips and fresh, glowing cheeks, how I became quite lost in the delightful meaning of her words, so much so, that I scarcely heard the actual expressions. In short, I alighted from the carriage like a person in a dream, and was so lost to the dim world around me, that I scarcely heard the music which resounded from the illuminated ballroom.

The two Messrs. Andran and a certain N. N. (I cannot trouble myself with the names), who were the aunt's and Charlotte's partners, received us at the carriage-door, and took possession of their ladies, whilst I followed with mine.

We commenced with a minuet. I led out one lady after another, and precisely those who were the most disagreeable could not bring themselves to leave off. Charlotte and her partner began an English country dance, and you must imagine my delight when it was their turn to dance the figure with us. You should see Charlotte dance. She dances with her whole heart and soul: her figure is all harmony, elegance, and grace, as if she were conscious of nothing else, and had no other thought or feeling; and, doubtless, for the moment, every other sensation is extinct.

She was engaged for the second country dance, but promised me the third, and assured me, with the most agreeable freedom, that she was very fond of waltzing. "It is the custom here," she said, "for the previous partners to waltz together; but my partner is an indifferent waltzer, and will feel delighted if I save him the trouble. Your partner is not allowed to waltz, and, indeed, is equally incapable: but I observed during the country dance that you waltz well; so, if you will waltz with me, I beg you would propose it to my partner, and I will propose it to yours." We agreed, and it was arranged that our partners should mutually entertain each other.

We set off, and, at first, delighted ourselves with the usual graceful motions of the arms. With what grace, with what ease, she moved! When the waltz commenced, and the dancers whirled around each other in the giddy maze, there was some confusion, owing to the incapacity of some of the dancers. We judiciously remained still, allowing the others to weary themselves; and, when the awkward dancers had withdrawn, we joined in, and kept it up famously together with one other couple, — Andran and his partner. Never did I dance more lightly. I felt myself more than mortal, holding this loveliest of creatures in my arms, flying, with her as rapidly as the wind, till I lost sight of every other object; and O Wilhelm, I vowed at that moment, that a maiden whom I loved, or for whom I felt the slightest attachment, never, never should waltz with any one else but with me, if I went to perdition for it! —you will understand this.

We took a few turns in the room to recover our breath. Charlotte sat down, and felt refreshed by partaking of some oranges which I had had secured,—the only ones that had been left; but at every slice which, from politeness, she offered to her neighbors, I felt as though a dagger went through my heart.

We were the second couple in the third country dance. As we were going down (and Heaven knows with what ecstasy I gazed at her arms and eyes, beaming with the sweetest feeling of pure and genuine enjoyment), we passed a lady whom I had noticed for her charming expression of countenance; although she was no longer young. She looked at Charlotte with a smile, then, holding up her finger in a threatening attitude, repeated twice in a very significant tone of voice the name of "Albert."

"Who is Albert," said I to Charlotte, "if it is not impertinent to ask?" She was about to answer, when we were obliged to separate, in order to execute a figure in the dance; and, as we crossed over again in front of each other, I perceived she looked somewhat pensive. "Why need I conceal it from you?" she said, as she gave me her hand for the promenade. "Albert is a worthy man, to whom I am engaged." Now, there was nothing new to me in this (for the girls had told me of it on the way); but it was so far new that I had not thought of it in connection with her whom, in so short a time, I had learned to prize so highly. Enough, I became confused, got out in the figure, and occasioned general confusion; so that it required all Charlotte's presence of mind to set me right by pulling and pushing me into my proper place.

The dance was not yet finished when the lightning which had for some time been seen in the horizon, and which I had asserted to proceed entirely from heat, grew more violent; and the thunder was heard above the music. When any distress or terror surprises us in the midst of our amusements, it naturally makes a deeper impression than at other times, either because the contrast makes us more keenly susceptible, or rather perhaps because our senses are then more open to impressions, and the shock is consequently stronger. To this cause I must ascribe the fright and shrieks of the ladies. One sagaciously sat down in a corner with her back to the window, and held her fingers to her ears; a second knelt down before her, and hid her face in her lap; a third threw herself between them, and embraced her sister with a thousand tears; some insisted on going home; others, unconscious of their actions, wanted sufficient presence of mind to repress the impertinence of their young partners, who sought to direct to themselves those sighs which the lips of our agitated beauties intended for heaven. Some of the gentlemen had gone down-stairs to smoke a quiet cigar, and the rest of the company gladly embraced a happy suggestion of the hostess to retire into another room which was provided with shutters and curtains. We had hardly got there, when Charlotte placed the chairs in a circle; and, when the company had sat down in compliance with her request, she forthwith proposed a round game.

I noticed some of the company prepare their mouths and draw themselves up at the prospect of some agreeable forfeit. "Let us play at counting," said Charlotte. "Now, pay attention: I shall go round the circle from right to left; and each person is to count, one after the other, the number that comes to him, and must count fast; whoever stops or mistakes is to have a box on the ear, and so on, till we have counted a thousand." It was delightful to see the fun. She went round the circle with upraised arm. "One," said the first; "two," the second; "three," the third; and so on, till Charlotte went faster and faster. One made a mistake, instantly a box on the ear; and, amid the laughter that ensued, came another box; and so on, faster and faster. I myself came in for two. I fancied they were harder than the rest, and felt quite delighted. A general laughter and confusion put an end to the game long before we had counted as far as a thousand. The party broke up into little separate knots: the storm had ceased, and I followed Charlotte into the ballroom. On the way she said, "The game banished their fears of the storm." I could make no reply. "myself," she continued, "was as much frightened as any of them; but by affecting courage, to keep up the spirits of the others, I forgot my apprehensions." We went to the window. It was still thundering at a distance: a soft rain was pouring down over the country, and filled the air around us with delicious odours. Charlotte leaned forward on her arm; her eyes wandered over the scene; she raised them to the sky, and then turned them upon me; they were moistened with tears; she placed her hand on mine and said, "Klopstock!" at once I remembered the magnificent ode which was in her thoughts: I felt oppressed with the weight of my sensations, and sank under them. It was more than I could bear. I bent over her hand, kissed it in a stream of delicious tears, and again looked up to her eyes. Divine Klopstock! why didst thou not see thy apotheosis in those eyes? And thy name so often profaned, would that I never heard it repeated!

(选自 Johann Wolfgang von Goethe. *The Sorrows of Young Werther*. New York: Signet Classics, 1962. pp. 6 - 28)

Questions

1. What kind of a young man was Werther?
2. What kind of mood was he in when he first arrived at the small town?
3. What kind of attractive woman was Charlotte in Werther's eyes?
4. What do you think of Werther's love for Charlotte?
5. What are the causes for Werther's tragedy?

Unit 4

Walt Whitman: "There Was a Child Went Forth"

Walt Whitman was born on the West Hills of Long Island, New York. His mother, Louisa Van Velsor, whom he adored, was barely literate. She never read Whitman's poetry, but gave him unconditional love. His father of English lineage, was a carpenter and builder of houses, and a stern disciplinarian. He was too burdened with the struggle to support his ever-growing family of nine children, four of whom were handicapped.

Young Walt, the second of nine, was withdrawn from public school at the age of eleven to help support the family. At the age of twelve he started to learn the printer's trade, and fell in love with the written and printed word. He was mainly self-taught by reading voraciously. In 1836, at the age of 17, he began his career as an innovative teacher in the one-room school houses of Long Island. He permitted his students to call him by his first name, and devised learning games for them in arithmetic and spelling. He continued to teach school until 1841, when he turned to journalism as a full-time career. He soon became editor for a number of Brooklyn and New York papers. Whitman went to New Orleans in 1848, where he was editor for a brief time of *New Orleans Crescent*. It was in New Orleans that he experienced at first hand the viciousness of slavery in the slave markets of that city.

On his return to Brooklyn in the fall of 1848, he founded a "free soil" newspaper *Brooklyn Freeman*. Between 1848 and 1855 he developed the style of poetry that so astonished Ralph Waldo Emerson. When *Leaves of Grass* reached him as a gift in July, 1855, the Dean of American Letters thanked him for "the wonderful gift" and said that he rubbed his eyes a little "to see if the sunbeam was no illusion." This book was notable for its frank delight in and praise of the senses. This cluster of poems was a breakthrough: it broke the regular style. All of it is written in unconventional verse and rhythm. At the same time, the heart of Whitman's poems was a radically new, sympathetic view of women and African Americans and their significance to his vision of an egalitarian society. He envisioned the poet as a hero, savior and a prophet, one who led the community by his expressions of the truth. Whitman's poetry praised nature and the individual human's role in it. However, Whitman did not diminish the role of the mind or the spirit; rather, he elevated the human mind, deeming both worthy of poetic praise.

Whitman adopted "free verse", that is, poetry without a fixed beat or regular rhyme scheme. A looser and more open-ended syntactical structure is frequently favored. Lines and sentences of different lengths are left lying side by side just as things are, undisturbed and separate. There are few compound sentences to draw objects and experiences into a system of hierarchy. Whitman was the first American to use free verse extensively. By using "free verse," Whitman turned the poem into an open field, an area of vital possibility where the reader can allow his own imagination to play. However, there is a strong sense of being rhythmical in the poems. The reader can feel the rhythm of Whitman's thought and cadences of his feeling. Parallelism and phonetic recurrence at the beginning of the lines also contribute to the musicality of his poems.

One of the great innovators in American literature, in both the content and form of his poetry, Whitman was the first American poet to write free verse, which he did with great skill and success. His experiments with free-verse rhythms and realistic imagery inspired many twentieth-century poets.

Theme

This poem describes the growth of a child who learned about the world around him and improved himself accordingly. It roughly corresponds to Whitman's own growth and development from youth to old age, expressing the poet's identification of his consciousness with all objects and forms, and the list of things which he himself identifies with is large and comprehensive. The continual process of becoming is at the heart of the poem. In short, the poem describes the development and improvement of a child's cognition.

Terms

Poetry: It's the language that is sung, chanted, spoken, or written according to some pattern of recurrence that emphasizes the relationships between words on the basis of sound as well as sense. This pattern is always a rhythm or meter, which may be supplemented by rhyme or alliteration or both. The demands of verbal patterning usually make poetry a more condensed medium than prose or everyday speech, often involving variations in syntax, the use of special words and phrases peculiar to poets, and a more frequent and more elaborate use of figures of speech, principally metaphor and simile. Poetry is generally employed in those utterances and writings that call for heightened intensity of emotion, dignity of expression, or subtlety of meditation.

Free Verse: Free verse is poetry that has an irregular rhythm and line length, and that attempts to avoid any predetermined verse structure; instead, it uses the cadences of natural speech. While it alternates stressed and unstressed syllables as stricter verse forms do, free verse does so in a looser way. Whitman's poetry is an example of free verse at its most impressive.

Text

There Was a Child Went Forth

THERE was a child went forth every day;
And the first object he look'd upon, that object he became;
And that object became part of him for the day, or a certain part of the day, or for many years, or stretching cycles of years.

The early lilacs became part of this child,
And grass, and white and red morning-glories, and white and red clover, and the song of the phoebe-bird,
And the Third-month lambs, and the sow's pink-faint litter, and the mare's foal, and the cow's calf,
And the noisy brood of the barn-yard, or by the mire of the pond-side,
And the fish suspending themselves so curiously below there—and the beautiful curious liquid,
And the water-plants with their graceful flat heads—all became part of him.

The field-sprouts of Fourth-month and Fifth-month became part of him;
Winter-grain sprouts, and those of the light-yellow corn, and the esculent roots of the garden,
And the apple-trees cover'd with blossoms, and the fruit afterward,

and wood-berries, and the commonest weeds by the road;

And the old drunkard staggering home from the out-house of the tavern, whence he had lately risen,

And the school-mistress that pass'd on her way to the school,

And the friendly boys that pass'd—and the quarrelsome boys,

And the tidy and fresh-cheek'd girls—and the barefoot negro boy and girl,

And all the changes of city and country, wherever he went.

His own parents, he that had father'd him, and she that had conceived him in her womb, and birth'd him,

They gave this child more of themselves than that;

They gave him afterward every day—they became part of him.

The mother at home, quietly placing the dishes on the supper-table;

The mother with mild words—clean her cap and gown, a wholesome odor falling off her person and clothes as she walks by;

The father, strong, self-sufficient, manly, mean, anger'd, unjust;

The blow, the quick loud word, the tight bargain, the crafty lure,

The family usages, the language, the company, the furniture—the yearning and swelling heart,

Affection that will not be gainsay'd—the sense of what is real—the thought if, after all, it should prove unreal,

The doubts of day-time and the doubts of night-time—the curious whether and how,

Whether that which appears so is so, or is it all flashes and specks?

Men and women crowding fast in the streets—if they are not flashes and specks, what are they?

The streets themselves, and the facades of houses, and goods in the windows,

Vehicles, teams, the heavy-plank'd wharves—the huge crossing at the ferries,

The village on the highland, seen from afar at sunset—the river between,

Shadows, aureola and mist, the light falling on roofs and gables of white or brown, three miles off,

The schooner near by sleepily dropping down the tide—the little boat slack-tow'd astern,

The hurrying tumbling waves, quick-broken crests, slapping,

The strata of color'd clouds, the long bar of maroon-tint, away solitary by itself—the spread of purity it lies motionless in,

The horizon's edge, the flying sea-crow, the fragrance of salt marsh and shore mud;

These became part of that child who went forth every day, and who now goes, and will always go forth every day.

(选自 Walt Whitman. *Complete Poetry and Collected Prose*. New York: Literary Classics of the United States, Inc., 1982. pp. 213 – 215.)

Questions

1. The poem describes the influences in the child's process of becoming. Which influence do you think is the most lasting? Why?
2. How do the child's parents become "part of him"?
3. Which do you think has greater influence on the life of a person, heredity or environment?
4. In what sense is the child's journey endless, and his quest ceaseless?
5. What is the implication of this poem?

Unit 5

Ralph Waldo Emerson: *Nature*

Ralph Waldo Emerson was born in Boston in 1803. He graduated from Harvard, taught school for a short time, and then became pastor of the Second Church of Boston in 1829. He resigned his position two years later and began in literary life. He was a prominent essayist, philosopher, and poet. He was the chief spokesman of the spiritual movement—New England Transcendentalism.

Emerson was responsible for bringing Transcendentalism to New England, and he was recognized throughout his life as the leader of the movement. Transcendentalism is the view that the basic truths of the universe lie beyond the knowledge one obtains from his senses, a knowledge that a Transcendentalist regards as the mere appearance of things. In other words, basic truths lie beyond what your eyes and ears tell you, because you can only see and hear the appearance of things, not the truth. Physical appearance is deceptive. What one can see is not always true. Basic truths can be reached only through instinct and intuition and are a matter of private experience.

Emerson was one of the most influential of American thinkers. After visiting Europe, Emerson settled in Concord and soon drew about him a remarkable circle of writers including his closest friend Henry David Thoreau. They gathered at one another's homes of an afternoon and talked about literature, philosophy and moral matters. Eventually the group named itself the Transcendental Club. Emerson believed above all in individualism, independence of mind, and self-reliance. For Emerson, individualism was idealistic. He would have people trust in "divine providence," live in harmony with nature and with what he called Oversoul, the universal spirit that is the source of all unity and growth.

Emerson's essays exerted important influences upon so many American writers, including Thoreau, Whitman, Dickinson, and Frost. Yet his great influence extended beyond the literary community to the American people at large. His optimism, his belief in the vast possibilities of mind and spirit, and his doctrine of self-reliance well suited a democratic, progressive nation. His teaching and words led to the intellectual emancipation from old conventions. *Nature* was published anonymously in 1836, containing an introduction and eight brief chapters which discuss the love of nature, the uses of nature, the idealist philosophy in relation to nature, evidences of spirit in the material universe, and the potential expansion of human souls and works that will result from a general return to direct, immediate contact with the natural environment. *Essays* was published in 1841. Emerson's lasting reputation began with the publication of this. Many of his famous essays are included in this, which convey the best of his philosophical discussions and transcendental pursuits, such as *The American Scholar*, *Self-Reliance*, *The Over-Soul*, *Essays*: *Second Series*. As an essayist, Emerson was a master of style. He encouraged American scholars to break free of European influences and create a new American culture.

Emerson's health started to fail after the partial burning of his house in 1872. He made his last tour abroad in 1872—1873, and then withdrew more and more from public life. Emerson died on April 27, 1882 in Concord.

Theme

Nature: It is one of Emerson's best-known and most influential essays. *Nature* is a lyrical expression of the harmony Emerson felt between himself and nature. The main idea of the essay is that nature inspires spiritual understanding in human being. Emerson expresses the following transcendentalist ideas in the essay: (1) Nature is a great teacher; (2) Nature is noble; (3) Nature is a source of comfort; (4) Human beings are a part of nature; (5) The individual's perception of nature depends on his or her state of mind; (6) By contemplation nature, the individual can transcend to a higher spiritual plane.

Term

Essay: "Essay" derives from the French essai, meaning "experiment," "attempt." Essay is understood to be a fairly short prose composition, in style often familiarly conversational and in subject either self-revelatory or illustrative of social manners and types. Generally speaking, essay should be a kind of chat-like prose that expounds an opinion, a judgment or an experience in a free style, but careful and precise in language and subtle and profound in meaning.

Excerpt

Chapter Ⅳ Language

Language is a third use which nature subserves to man. Nature is the vehicle of thought, and in a simple, double and threefold degree.

1. Words are signs of natural facts.
2. Particular natural facts are symbols of particular spiritual facts.
3. Nature is the symbol of spirit.

1) Words are signs of natural facts. The use of natural history is to give us aid in supernatural history: the use of the outer creation, to give us language for the beings and changes of the inward creation. Every word which is used to express a moral or intellectual fact, if traced to its root, is turned to be borrowed from some material or intellectual appearance. *Right* means *straight*; *wrong* means *twisted*. *Spirit* primarily means *wind*; *transgression*, the crossing of a *line*; *supercilious*, the *raising of the eyebrow*. We say the *heart* to express emotion, the *head* to denote thought; and *thought* and *emotion* are words borrowed from sensible things, and now appropriated to spiritual nature. Most of the process by which this transformation is made, is hidden from us in the remote time when language was framed; but the same tendency may be daily observed in children. Children and savages use only nouns or names of things, which they convert into verbs, and apply to analogous mental acts.

2) But this origin of all words that convey a spiritual import, —so conspicuous a fact in the history of language, —is our least debt to nature. It is not words only that are emblematic; it is things which are emblematic. Every natural fact is a symbol of some spiritual fact. Every appearance in nature corresponds to some state of the mind, and that state of the mind can only be described by presenting that natural appearance as its picture. An enraged man is a lion, a cunning man is a fox, a firm man is a rock, a learned man is a torch. A lamb is innocence; a snake is subtle spite; flowers express to us the delicate affections. Light and darkness are our familiar expression for knowledge and ignorance; and heat for love. Visible distance behind and before us, is respectively our image of memory and hope.

Who looks upon a river in a meditative hour, and is not reminded of the flux of all things? Throw a stone into the stream, and the circles that propagate themselves are the beautiful type of all influence. Man is conscious of a universal soul within or behind his individual life, wherein, as in a firmament, the natures of Justice, Truth, Love, Freedom, arise and shine. This universal soul, he calls Reason: it is not mine, or thine, or his, but we are its; we are its property and men. And the blue sky in which the private earth is buried, the sky with its eternal calm, and full of everlasting orbs, is the type of Reason. That which, intellectually considered, we call Reason, considered in relation to nature, we call Spirit. Spirit is the Creator. Spirit hath life in itself. And man in all ages and countries, embodies it in his language, as the FATHER.

It is easily seen that there is nothing lucky or capricious in these analogies, but that they are constant, and pervade nature. These are not the dreams of a few poets, here and there, but man is an analogist, and studies relations in all objects. He is placed in the centre of beings, and a ray of relation passes from every other being to him. And neither can man be understood without these objects, nor these objects without man. All the facts in natural history taken by themselves, have no value, but are barren, like a single sex. But marry it to human history, and it is full of life. Whole Floras, all Linnaeus' and Buffon's volumes, are dry catalogues of facts; but the most trivial of these facts, the habit of a plant, the organs, or work, or noise of an insect, applied to the illustration of a fact in intellectual philosophy, or, in any way associated to human nature, affects us in the most lively and agreeable manner. The seed of a plant, —to what affecting analogies in the nature of man, is that little fruit made use of, in all discourse, up to the voice of Paul, who calls the human corpse a seed, —"It is sown a natural body; it is raised a spiritual body." The motion of the earth round its axis, and round the sun, makes the day, and the year. These are certain amounts of brute light and heat. But is there no intent of an analogy between man's life and the seasons? And do the seasons gain no grandeur or pathos from that analogy? The instincts of the ant are very unimportant, considered as the ant's; but the moment a ray of relation is seen to extend from it to man, and the little drudge is seen to be a monitor, a little body with a mighty heart, then all its habits, even that said to be recently observed, that it never sleeps, become sublime.

Because of this radical correspondence between visible things and human thoughts, savages, who have only what is necessary, converse in figures. As we go back in history, language becomes more picturesque, until its infancy, when it is all poetry; or all spiritual facts are represented by natural symbols. The same symbols are found to make the original elements of all languages. It has moreover been observed, that the idioms of all languages approach each other in passages of the greatest eloquence and power. And as this is the first language, so is it the last. This immediate dependence of language upon nature, this conversion of an outward phenomenon into a type of somewhat in human life, never loses its power to affect us. It is this which gives that piquancy to the conversation of a strong-natured farmer or back-woodsman, which all men relish.

A man's power to connect his thought with its proper symbol, and so to utter it, depends on the simplicity of his character, that is, upon his love of truth, and his desire to communicate it without loss. The corruption of man is followed by the corruption of language. When simplicity of character and the sovereignty of ideas is broken up by the prevalence of secondary desires, the desire of riches, of pleasure, of power, and of praise, —and duplicity and falsehood take place of simplicity and truth, the power over nature as an interpreter of the will, is in a degree lost; new imagery ceases to be created, and old words are perverted to stand for things which are not; a paper currency is employed, when there is no bullion in the vaults. In due time, the fraud is manifest, and words lose all power to stimulate the understanding or the affections. Hundreds of writers may be found in every long-civilized nation, who for a short time believe, and make others believe, that they see and utter truths, who do not of themselves clothe one thought in its natural garment, but who feed unconsciously on the language created by the primary writers of the country, those, namely, who hold primarily on nature.

But wise men pierce this rotten diction and fasten words again to visible things; so that picturesque language is at once a commanding certificate that he who employs it, is a man in alliance with truth and God. The moment our discourse rises above the ground line of familiar facts, and is inflamed with passion or exalted by thought, it clothes itself in images. A man conversing in earnest, if he watch his intellectual processes, will find that a material image, more or less luminous, arises in his mind, contemporaneous with every thought, which furnishes the vestment of the thought. Hence, good writing and brilliant discourse are perpetual allegories. This imagery is spontaneous. It is the blending of experience with the present action of the mind. It is proper creation. It is the working of the Original Cause through the instruments he has already made.

These facts may suggest the advantage which the country-life possesses for a powerful mind, over the artificial and curtailed life of cities. We know more from nature than we can at will communicate. Its light flows into the mind evermore, and we forget its presence. The poet, the orator, bred in the woods, whose senses have been nourished by their fair and appeasing changes, year after year, without design and without heed, —shall not lose their lesson altogether, in the roar of cities or the broil of politics. Long hereafter, amidst agitation and terror in national councils, —in the hour of revolution, —these solemn images shall reappear in their morning lustre, as fit symbols and words of the thoughts which the passing events shall awaken. At the call of a noble sentiment, again the woods wave, the pines murmur, the river rolls and shines, and the cattle low upon the mountains, as he saw and heard them in his infancy. And with these forms, the spells of persuasion, the keys of power are put into his hands.

3) We are thus assisted by natural objects in the expression of particular meanings. But how great a language to convey such pepper-corn informations! Did it need such noble races of creatures, this profusion of forms, this host of orbs in heaven, to furnish man with the dictionary and grammar of his municipal speech? Whilst we use this grand cipher to expedite the affairs of our pot and kettle, we feel that we have not yet put it to its use, neither are able. We are like travellers using the cinders of a volcano to roast their eggs. Whilst we see that it always stands ready to clothe what we would say, we cannot avoid the question, whether the characters are not significant of themselves. Have mountains, and waves, and skies, no significance but what we consciously give them, when we employ them as emblems of our thoughts? The world is emblematic. Parts of speech are metaphors, because the whole of nature is a metaphor of the human mind. The laws of moral nature answer to those of matter as face to face in a glass. "The visible world and the relation of its parts, is the dial plate of the invisible." The axioms of physics translate the laws of ethics. Thus, "the whole is greater than its part;" "reaction is equal to action;" "the smallest weight may be made to lift the greatest, the difference of weight being compensated by time;" and many the like propositions, which have an ethical as well as physical sense. These propositions have a much more extensive and universal sense when applied to human life, than when confined to technical use.

In like manner, the memorable words of history, and the proverbs of nations, consist usually of a natural fact, selected as a picture or parable of a moral truth. Thus; A rolling stone gathers no moss; A bird in the hand is worth two in the bush; A cripple in the right way, will beat a racer in the wrong; Make hay while the sun shines; T is hard to carry a full cup even; Vinegar is the son of wine; The last ounce broke the camel's back; Long-lived trees make roots first; —and the like. In their primary sense these are trivial facts, but we repeat them for the value of their analogical import. What is true of proverbs, is true of all fables, parables, and allegories.

This relation between the mind and matter is not fancied by some poet, but stands in the will of God, and so is free to be known by all men. It appears to men, or it does not appear. When in fortunate hours we ponder this miracle, the wise man doubts, if, at all other times, he is not blind and deaf;

> "Can these things be,
> And overcome us like a summer's cloud,
> Without our special wonder?"

for the universe becomes transparent, and the light of higher laws than its own, shines through it. It is the standing problem which has exercised the wonder and the study of every fine genius since the world began; from the era of the Egyptians and the Brahmins, to that of Pythagoras, of Plato, of Bacon, of Leibnitz, of Swedenborg. There sits the Sphinx at the road-side, and from age to age, as each prophet comes by, he tries his fortune at reading her riddle. There seems to be a necessity in spirit to manifest itself in material forms; and day and night, river and storm, beast and bird, acid and alkali, preexist in necessary Ideas in the mind of God, and are what they are by virtue of preceding affections, in the world of spirit. A Fact is the end or last issue of spirit. The visible creation is the terminus or the circumference of the invisible world. "Material objects," said a French philosopher, "are necessarily kinds of *scoriae* of the substantial thoughts of the Creator, which must always preserve an exact relation to their first origin; in other words, visible nature must have a spiritual and moral side."

The doctrine is abstruse, and though the images of "garment," "scoriae," "mirror,"etc., may stimulate the fancy, we must summon the aid of subtler and more vital expositors to make it plain. "Every scripture is to be interpreted by the same spirit which gave it forth," —is the fundamental law of criticism. A life in harmony with nature, the love of truth and of virtue, will purge the eyes to understand her text. By degrees we may come to know the primitive sense of the permanent objects of nature, so that the world shall be to us an open book, and every form significant of its hidden life and final cause.

A new interest surprises us, whilst, under the view now suggested, we contemplate the fearful extent and multitude of objects; since "every object rightly seen, unlocks a new faculty of the soul." That which was unconscious truth, becomes, when interpreted and defined in an object, a part of the domain of knowledge, —a new weapon in the magazine of power.

（选自 Ralph Waldo Emerson. "Nature," *The Norton Anthology: American Literature*. Julia Reidhead ed. New York: W. W. Norton & Company, Inc., 2008. pp. 500 - 504.）

Questions

1. What is nature? What are the functions of nature?
2. Give an example how nature impresses you.
3. What is language? How is language related to nature according to Emerson?
4. Have you experienced "a meditative hour" when you are reminded the flux of all things?
5. Why is country life advantageous for a power mind?

Unit 6

George Bernard Shaw: *Pygmalion*

George Bernard Shaw (1856—1950), Irish dramatist, literary critic, a socialist spokesman, and a leading figure in the 20th century theater. Shaw was a freethinker, a supporter of women's rights and an advocate of equality of income. In 1925 he was awarded the Nobel Prize for Literature. Shaw accepted the honor but refused the money. Shaw is considered as the second greatest English playwright, behind only Shakespeare.

Shaw was born in 1856 in a lower-middle class family of Scottish-Protestant ancestry. His father was a failed corn-merchant, with a drinking problem. His mother was a professional singer and a voice teacher claiming to have a unique and original approach to singing. At the age of 15, he started to work as a junior clerk. When Shaw was 16 years old, his mother left her husband and son and moved to London. Shaw lived with his father, completing his schooling, and working as a clerk for an estate office which he hated just as much as school. In 1876, Shaw left his father and moved to London, living with his mother's families. There he pursued a career in journalism and writing. The first medium he tried as a creative writer was prose, completing five novels. He read eagerly, in public libraries and in the British Museum reading room. And he became involved in politics. In order to catch the attention of the crowd, he developed an energetic and aggressive speaking style that is evident in all of his writing. Shaw did not return to Ireland for nearly thirty years. Shaw began his literary career by writing music and theatre criticism, and novels, including the semi-autobiographical *Immaturity* without much success. Shaw founded a socialist political organization dedicated to transforming Britain into a socialist state, not by revolution but by systematic progressive legislation. Shaw lectured for the organization, and wrote pamphlets on the progressive arts.

In 1895 Shaw became a drama critic for the *Saturday Review*. These articles were later collected in *Our Theatres in The Nineties* (1932). Shaw also wrote music, art and drama criticism for *Dramatic Review* (1885—86), *Our Corner* (1885—86), *The Pall Mall Gazette* (1885—88), *The World* (1886—94), and *The Star* (1888—90). His music criticism has been collected in *Shaw's Music* (1981). In 1898 Shaw married the wealthy girl.

In 1904, Harley Barker, an actor, director and playwright twenty years younger than Shaw, took over the management of the Court Theatre and set it up as an experimental theatre specializing in new and progressive drama. Over the next three seasons, Barker produced ten plays by Shaw who was actually the director of his own plays, and Shaw began writing new plays. Over the next ten years, all but one of Shaw's plays was produced. Shaw, who had become financially independent on marrying, now became quite wealthy. Throughout the decade, he remained active in committees dedicated to ending dramatic censorship, and to establishing a National Theatre. In 1914, the outbreak of war changed Shaw's life. For Shaw, the war represented the bankruptcy of the capitalist system, the last desperate gasps of the 19th-century empires, and a tragic waste of young lives, all under the guise of patriotism. He expressed his opinions in a series of newspaper articles under the title *Common Sense About the War*. These articles proved to be a disaster for Shaw's public stature: he was treated as an outcast in his London, and there was even talk of his being tried for treason. His dramatic output halted and he succeeded in writing only one major play during the war years, Heartbreak House, into which he projected his bitterness and despair about British politics and society. After the war, Shaw found his dramatic voice again and rebuilt his reputation, first with a series of five plays about "creative evolution." In 1925 he was awarded the Nobel Prize for Literature. Several theatre companies in the United States began producing his plays, old and new, on a regular basis. In the late 1920s, a Shaw festival was established in England.

Shaw's early plays including *Widower's Houses*, which criticized slum landlords were not well received. His "unpleasant plays," ideological attacks on the evils of capitalism and explorations of moral and social problems, were followed with more entertaining but equally principled productions. *Major Barbara* depicted an officer of the Salvation Army, who learned from her father, a manufacturer of armaments, that money and power could be better weapons against evil than love. *Pygmalion* was originally written for the actress Mrs. Patrick Campbell, and became later the basis for two films and a musical. With *Saint Joan* he was again accepted by the post-war public. His plays dealt with issues such as poverty and women's rights and implied that socialism could help solve the problems created by capitalism—a view that many Europeans considered heresy during the First World War.

In his later life, Shaw lived the rest of his life as an international celebrity, traveled the world, and continually was involved in local and international politics. He visited the Soviet Union at the invitation of Stalin; and he came briefly to the United States at the invitation of William Randolph Hearst for a lecture at the Metropolitan Opera House in New York, and for lunch at Hearst's castle. And he continued to write thousands of letters and over a dozen more plays. In 1950, Shaw fell off a ladder and died a few days later of complications from the injury, at the age 94.

Theme

Professor Higgins transforms a common flower girl into a graceful lady, which is quite like that the sculptor Pygmalion in the Ovidian legend carves a beautiful statue out of shapeless ivory. Higgins effects this amazing transformation by teaching Eliza to speak correctly and beautifully. This cultural crash-course is simply a scientific experiment for Higgins who focuses upon his task of passing of Eliza as a duchess with absolute concentration and objectivity. He is amazed to find that he cannot control all the variables of his experiment since nobody can control the human heart. Higgins realizes that he should not have ignored the humanity of his subject. Professor Higgins stands for the principle of rationality and the intellect while Eliza represents natural warmth and affection of the heart.

Term

Drama: It's a composition in verse or prose designed for performance in the theater, in which actors take the roles of the characters, perform the indicated action, and utter the written dialogue. The common alternative name for a dramatic composition is play.

Excerpt

Act Ⅲ

It is Mrs. Higgins's at-home day. Nobody has yet arrived. Her drawing-room, in a flat on Chelsea embankment, has three windows looking on the river; and the ceiling is not so lofty as it would be in an older house of the same pretension. The windows are open, giving access to a balcony with flowers in pots. If you stand with your face to the windows, you have the fireplace on your left and the door in the right-hand wall close to the corner nearest the windows.

Mrs. Higgins was brought up on Morris and Burne Jones; and her room, which is very unlike her son's room in Wimpole Street, is not crowded with furniture and little tables and nicknacks. In the middle of the room there is a big ottoman; and this, with the carpet, the Morris wall-papers, and the Morris chintz window curtains and brocade covers of the ottoman and its cushions, supply all the ornament, and are much too handsome to be hidden by odds and ends of useless things. A few good oil-paintings from the exhibitions in the Grosvenor Gallery thirty years ago (the Burne Jones, not the Whistler side of them) are on the walls. The only landscape is a Cecil Lawson on the scale of a Rubens. There is a portrait of Mrs. Higgins as she was when she defied fashion in her youth in one of the beautiful Rossettian costumes which, when caricatured by people who did not understand, led to the absurdities of popular estheticism in the eighteen-seventies.

In the corner diagonally opposite the door Mrs. Higgins, now over sixty and long past taking the trouble to dress out of the fashion, sits writing at an elegantly simple writing-table with a bell button within reach of her hand. There is a Chippendale chair further back in the room between her and the window nearest her side. At the other side of the room, further forward, is an Elizabethan chair roughly carved in the taste of Inigo Jones. On the same side a piano in a decorated case. The corner between the fireplace and the window is occupied by a divan cushioned in Morris chintz.

It is between four and five in the afternoon.

The door is opened violently; and Higgins enters with his hat on.

MRS. HIGGINS [*dismayed*] Henry [*scolding him*]! What are you doing here to-day? It is my at home day: you promised not to come. [*As he bends to kiss her, she takes his hat off, and presents it to him*].

HIGGINS. Oh bother! [*He throws the hat down on the table*].

MRS. HIGGINS. Go home at once.

HIGGINS [*kissing her*] I know, mother. I came on purpose.

MRS. HIGGINS. But you mustn't. I'm serious, Henry. You offend all my friends: they stop coming whenever they meet you.

HIGGINS. Nonsense! I know I have no small talk; but people don't mind. [He sits on the settee].

MRS. HIGGINS. Oh! don't they? Small talk indeed! What about your large talk? Really, dear, you mustn't stay.

HIGGINS. I must. I've a job for you. A phonetic job.

MRS. HIGGINS. No use, dear. I'm sorry; but I can't get round your vowels; and though I like to get pretty postcards in your patent shorthand, I always have to read the copies in ordinary writing you so thoughtfully send me.

HIGGINS. Well, this isn't a phonetic job.

MRS. HIGGINS. You said it was.

HIGGINS. Not your part of it. I've picked up a girl.

MRS. HIGGINS. Does that mean that some girl has picked you up?

HIGGINS. Not at all. I don't mean a love affair.

MRS. HIGGINS. What a pity!

HIGGINS. Why?

MRS. HIGGINS. Well, you never fall in love with anyone under forty-five. When will you discover that there are some rather nice-looking young women about?

HIGGINS. Oh, I can't be bothered with young women. My idea of a loveable woman is something as like you as possible. I shall never get into the way of seriously liking young women: some habits lie too deep to be changed. [*Rising abruptly and walking about, jingling his money and his keys in his trouser pockets*] Besides, they're all idiots.

MRS. HIGGINS. Do you know what you would do if you really loved me, Henry?

HIGGINS. Oh bother! What? Marry, I suppose?

MRS. HIGGINS. No. Stop fidgeting and take your hands out of your pockets. [*With a gesture of despair, he obeys and sits down again*]. That's a good boy. Now tell me about the girl.

HIGGINS. She's coming to see you.

MRS. HIGGINS. I don't remember asking her.

HIGGINS. You didn't. I asked her. If you'd known her you wouldn't have asked her.

MRS. HIGGINS. Indeed! Why?

HIGGINS. Well, it's like this. She's a common flower girl. I picked her off the kerbstone.

MRS. HIGGINS. And invited her to my at-home!

HIGGINS [*rising and coming to her to coax her*] Oh, that'll be all right. I've taught her to speak properly; and she has strict orders as to her behavior. She's to keep to two subjects: the weather and everybody's health—Fine day and How do you do, you know—and not to let herself go on things in general. That will be safe.

MRS. HIGGINS. Safe! To talk about our health! about our insides! perhaps about our outsides! How could you be so silly, Henry?

HIGGINS [impatiently] Well, she must talk about something. [*He controls himself and sits down again*]. Oh, she'll be all right: don't you fuss. Pickering is in it with me. I've a sort of bet on that I'll pass her off as a duchess in six months. I started on her some months ago; and she's getting on like a house on fire. I shall win my bet. She has a quick ear; and she's been easier to teach than my middle-class pupils because she's had to learn a complete new language. She talks English almost as you talk French.

MRS. HIGGINS. That's satisfactory, at all events.

HIGGINS. Well, it is and it isn't.

MRS. HIGGINS. What does that mean?

HIGGINS. You see, I've got her pronunciation all right; but you have to consider not only how a girl pronounces, but what she pronounces; and that's where—

They are interrupted by the parlor-maid, announcing guests.

THE PARLOR-MAID. Mrs. and Miss Eynsford Hill. [*She withdraws*].

HIGGINS. Oh Lord! [*He rises; snatches his hat from the table; and makes for the door; but before he reaches it his mother introduces him*].

Mrs. and Miss Eynsford Hill are the mother and daughter who sheltered from the rain in Covent Garden. The mother is well bred, quiet, and has the habitual anxiety of straitened means. The daughter has acquired a gay air of being very much at home in society: the bravado of genteel poverty.

MRS. EYNSFORD HILL [*to Mrs. Higgins*] How do you do? [*They shake hands*].

MISS EYNSFORD HILL. How d'you do? [*She shakes*].

MRS. HIGGINS [*introducing*] My son Henry.

MRS. EYNSFORD HILL. Your celebrated son! I have so longed to meet you, Professor Higgins.

HIGGINS [*glumly, making no movement in her direction*] Delighted. [*He backs against the piano and bows brusquely*].

Miss EYNSFORD HILL [*going to him with confident familiarity*] How do you do?

HIGGINS [*staring at her*] I've seen you before somewhere. I haven't the ghost of a notion where; but I've heard your voice. [*Drearily*] It doesn't matter. You'd better sit down.

MRS. HIGGINS. I'm sorry to say that my celebrated son has no manners. You mustn't mind him.

MISS EYNSFORD HILL [*gaily*] I don't. [*She sits in the Elizabethan chair*].

MRS. EYNSFORD HILL [*a little bewildered*] Not at all. [*She sits on the ottoman between her daughter and Mrs. Higgins, who has turned her chair away from the writing-table*].

HIGGINS. Oh, have I been rude? I didn't mean to be.

He goes to the central window, through which, with his back to the company, he contemplates the river and the flowers in Battersea Park on the opposite bank as if they were a frozen dessert.

The parlor-maid returns, ushering in Pickering.

THE PARLOR-MAID. Colonel Pickering [*She withdraws*].

PICKERING. How do you do, Mrs. Higgins?

MRS. HIGGINS. So glad you've come. Do you know Mrs. Eynsford Hill—Miss Eynsford Hill? [*Exchange of bows. The Colonel brings the Chippendale chair a little forward between Mrs. Hill and Mrs. Higgins, and sits down*].

PICKERING. Has Henry told you what we've come for?

HIGGINS [*over his shoulder*] We were interrupted: damn it!

MRS. HIGGINS. Oh Henry, Henry, really!

MRS. EYNSFORD HILL [*half rising*] Are we in the way?

MRS. HIGGINS [*rising and making her sit down again*] No, no. You couldn't have come more fortunately: we want you to meet a friend of ours.

HIGGINS [*turning hopefully*] Yes, by George! We want two or three people. You'll do as well as anybody else.

The parlor-maid returns, ushering Freddy.

THE PARLOR-MAID. Mr. Eynsford Hill.

HIGGINS [*almost audibly, past endurance*] God of Heaven! another of them.

FREDDY [*shaking hands with Mrs. Higgins*] Ahdedo?

MRS. HIGGINS. Very good of you to come. [*Introducing*] Colonel Pickering.

FREDDY [*bowing*] Ahdedo?

MRS. HIGGINS. I don't think you know my son, Professor Higgins.

FREDDY [*going to Higgins*] Ahdedo?

HIGGINS [*looking at him much as if he were a pickpocket*] I'll take my oath I've met you before somewhere. Where was it?

FREDDY. I don't think so.

HIGGINS [*resignedly*] It don't matter, anyhow. Sit down. He shakes Freddy's hand, and almost slings him on the ottoman with his face to the windows; then comes round to the other side of it.

HIGGINS. Well, here we are, anyhow! [*He sits down on the ottoman next Mrs. Eynsford Hill, on her left.*] And now, what the devil are we going to talk about until Eliza comes?

MRS. HIGGINS. Henry: you are the life and soul of the Royal Society's soirees; but really you're rather trying on more commonplace occasions.

HIGGINS. Am I? Very sorry. [*Beaming suddenly*] I suppose I am, you know. [*Uproariously*] Ha, ha!

MISS EYNSFORD HILL [*who considers Higgins quite eligible matrimonially*] I sympathize. I haven't any small talk. If people would only be frank and say what they really think!

HIGGINS [*relapsing into gloom*] Lord forbid!

MRS. EYNSFORD HILL [*taking up her daughter's cue*] But why?

HIGGINS. What they think they ought to think is bad enough, Lord knows; but what they really think would break up the whole show. Do you suppose it would be really agreeable if I were to come out now with what I really think?

MISS EYNSFORD HILL [*gaily*] Is it so very cynical?

HIGGINS. Cynical! Who the dickens said it was cynical? I mean it wouldn't be decent.

MRS. EYNSFORD HILL [*seriously*] Oh! I'm sure you don't mean that, Mr. Higgins.

HIGGINS. You see, we're all savages, more or less. We're supposed to be civilized and cultured—to know all about poetry and philosophy and art and science, and so on; but how many of us know even the meanings of these names? [*To Miss Hill*] What do you know of poetry? [*To Mrs. Hill*] What do you know of science? [*Indicating Freddy*] What does he know of art or science or anything else? What the devil do you imagine I know of philosophy?

MRS. HIGGINS [*warningly*] Or of manners, Henry?

THE PARLOR-MAID [*opening the door*] Miss Doolittle. [*She withdraws*].

HIGGINS [*rising hastily and running to Mrs. Higgins*] Here she is, mother. [*He stands on tiptoe and makes signs over his mother's head to Eliza to indicate to her which lady is her hostess*].

Eliza, who is exquisitely dressed, produces an impression of such remarkable distinction and beauty as she enters that they all rise, quite flustered. Guided by Higgins's signals, she comes to Mrs. Higgins with studied grace.

LIZA [*speaking with pedantic correctness of pronunciation and great beauty of tone*] How do you do, Mrs. Higgins? [*She gasps slightly in making sure of the H in Higgins, but is quite successful*]. Mr. Higgins told me I might come.

MRS. HIGGINS [*cordially*] Quite right: I'm very glad indeed to see you.

PICKERING. How do you do, Miss Doolittle?

LIZA [*shaking hands with him*] Colonel Pickering, is it not?

MRS. EYNSFORD HILL. I feel sure we have met before, Miss Doolittle. I remember your eyes.

LIZA. How do you do? [*She sits down on the ottoman gracefully in the place just left vacant by Higgins*].

MRS. EYNSFORD HILL [*introducing*] My daughter Clara.

LIZA. How do you do?

CLARA [*impulsively*] How do you do? [*She sits down on the ottoman beside Eliza, devouring her with her eyes*].

FREDDY [*coming to their side of the ottoman*] I've certainly had the pleasure.

MRS. EYNSFORD HILL [*introducing*] My son Freddy.

LIZA. How do you do?

Freddy bows and sits down in the Elizabethan chair, infatuated.

HIGGINS [*suddenly*] By George, yes: it all comes back to me! [*They stare at him*]. Covent Garden! [*Lamentably*] What a damned thing!

MRS. HIGGINS. Henry, please! [*He is about to sit on the edge of the table*]. Don't sit on my writing-table: you'll break it.

HIGGINS [*sulkily*] Sorry.

He goes to the divan, stumbling into the fender and over the fire-irons on his way; extricating himself with muttered imprecations; and finishing his disastrous journey by throwing himself so impatiently on the divan that he almost breaks it. Mrs. Higgins looks at him, but controls herself and says nothing.

A long and painful pause ensues.

MRS. HIGGINS [*at last, conversationally*] Will it rain, do you think?

LIZA. The shallow depression in the west of these islands is likely to move slowly in an easterly direction. There are no indications of any great change in the barometrical situation.

FREDDY. Ha! ha! how awfully funny!

LIZA. What is wrong with that, young man? I bet I got it right.

FREDDY. Killing!

MRS. EYNSFORD HILL. I'm sure I hope it won't turn cold. There's so much influenza about. It runs right through our whole family regularly every spring.

LIZA [*darkly*] My aunt died of influenza: so they said.

MRS. EYNSFORD HILL [*clicks her tongue sympathetically*]!!!

LIZA [*in the same tragic tone*] But it's my belief they done the old woman in.

MRS. HIGGINS [*puzzled*] Done her in?

LIZA. Y-e-e-e-es, Lord love you! Why should she die of influenza? She come through diphtheria right enough the year before. I saw her with my own eyes. Fairly blue with it, she was. They all thought she was dead; but my father he kept ladling gin down her throat til she came to so sudden that she bit the bowl off the spoon.

MRS. EYNSFORD HILL [*startled*] Dear me!

LIZA [*piling up the indictment*] What call would a woman with that strength in her have to die of influenza? What become of her new straw hat that should have come to me? Somebody pinched it; and what I say is, them as pinched it done her in.

MRS. EYNSFORD HILL. What does doing her in mean?

HIGGINS [*hastily*] Oh, that's the new small talk. To do a person in means to kill them.

MRS. EYNSFORD HILL [*to Eliza, horrified*] You surely don't believe that your aunt was killed?

LIZA. Do I not! Them she lived with would have killed her for a hat-pin, let alone a hat.

MRS. EYNSFORD HILL. But it can't have been right for your father to pour spirits down her throat like that. It might have killed her.

LIZA. Not her. Gin was mother's milk to her. Besides, he'd poured so much down his own throat that he knew the good of it.

MRS. EYNSFORD HILL. Do you mean that he drank?

LIZA. Drank! My word! Something chronic.

MRS. EYNSFORD HILL. How dreadful for you!

LIZA. Not a bit. It never did him no harm what I could see. But then he did not keep it up regular. [*Cheerfully*] On the burst, as you might say, from time to time. And always more agreeable when he had a drop in. When he was out of work, my mother used to give him four pence and tell him to go out and not come back until he'd drunk himself cheerful and loving-like. There's lots of women has to make their husbands drunk to make them fit to live with. [*Now quite at her ease*] You see, it's like this. If a man has a bit of a conscience, it always takes him when he's sober; and then it makes him low-spirited. A drop of booze just takes that off and makes him happy. [*To Freddy, who is in convulsions of suppressed laughter*] Here! What are you sniggering at?

FREDDY. The new small talk. You do it so awfully well.

LIZA. If I was doing it proper, what was you laughing at? [To Higgins] Have I said anything I oughtn't?

MRS. HIGGINS [*interposing*] Not at all, Miss Doolittle.

LIZA. Well, that's a mercy, anyhow. [*Expansively*] What I always say is—

HIGGINS [*rising and looking at his watch*] Ahem!

LIZA [*looking round at him; taking the hint; and rising*] Well: I must go. [*They all rise. Freddy goes to the door*]. So pleased to have met you. Good-bye. [*She shakes hands with Mrs. Higgins*].

MRS. HIGGINS. Good-bye.

LIZA. Good-bye, Colonel Pickering.

PICKERING. Good-bye, Miss Doolittle. [*They shake hands*].

LIZA [*nodding to the others*] Good-bye, all.

FREDDY [*opening the door for her*] Are you walking across the Park, Miss Doolittle? If so—

LIZA. Walk! Not bloody likely. [*Sensation*]. I am going in a taxi. [*She goes out*].

Pickering gasps and sits down. Freddy goes out on the balcony to catch another glimpse of Eliza.

MRS. EYNSFORD HILL [*suffering from shock*] Well, I really can't get used to the new ways.

CLARA [*throwing herself discontentedly into the Elizabethan chair*]. Oh, it's all right, mamma, quite right. People will think we never go anywhere or see anybody if you are so old-fashioned.

MRS. EYNSFORD HILL. I daresay I am very old-fashioned; but I do hope you won't begin using that expression, Clara. I have got accustomed to hear you talking about men as rotters, and calling everything filthy and beastly; though I do think it horrible and unladylike. But this last is really too much. Don't you think so, Colonel Pickering?

PICKERING. Don't ask me. I've been away in India for several years; and manners have changed so much that I sometimes don't know whether I'm at a respectable dinner-table or in a ship's forecastle.

CLARA. It's all a matter of habit. There's no right or wrong in it. Nobody means anything by it. And it's so quaint, and gives such a smart emphasis to things that are not in themselves very witty. I find the new small talk delightful and quite innocent.

MRS. EYNSFORD HILL [*rising*] Well, after that, I think it's time for us to go.

Pickering and Higgins rise.

CLARA [*rising*] Oh yes: we have three at homes to go to still. Good-bye, Mrs. Higgins. Good-bye, Colonel Pickering. Good-bye, Professor Higgins.

HIGGINS [*coming grimly at her from the divan, and accompanying her to the door*] Good-bye. Be sure you try on that small talk at the three at-homes. Don't be nervous about it. Pitch it in strong.

CLARA [*all smiles*] I will. Good-bye. Such nonsense, all this early Victorian prudery!

HIGGINS [*tempting her*] Such damned nonsense!

CLARA. Such bloody nonsense!

MRS. EYNSFORD HILL [*convulsively*] Clara!

CLARA. Ha! ha! [*She goes out radiant, conscious of being thoroughly up to date, and is heard descending the stairs in a stream of silvery laughter*].

FREDDY [*to the heavens at large*] Well, I ask you [He gives it up, and comes to Mrs. Higgins]. Good-bye.

MRS. HIGGINS [*shaking hands*] Good-bye. Would you like to meet Miss Doolittle again?

FREDDY [*eagerly*] Yes, I should, most awfully.

MRS. HIGGINS. Well, you know my days.

FREDDY. Yes. Thanks awfully. Good-bye. [He goes out].

MRS. EYNSFORD HILL. Good-bye, Mr. Higgins.

HIGGINS. Good-bye. Good-bye.

MRS. EYNSFORD HILL [to Pickering] It's no use. I shall never be able to bring myself to use that word.

PICKERING. Don't. It's not compulsory, you know. You'll get on quite well without it.

MRS. EYNSFORD HILL. Only, Clara is so down on me if I am not positively reeking with the latest slang. Good-bye.

PICKERING. Good-bye [*They shake hands*].

MRS. EYNSFORD HILL [*to Mrs. Higgins*] You mustn't mind

Clara. [Pickering, catching from her lowered tone that this is not meant for him to hear, discreetly joins Higgins at the window]. We're so poor! and she gets so few parties, poor child! She doesn't quite know. [Mrs. Higgins, seeing that her eyes are moist, takes her hand sympathetically and goes with her to the door]. But the boy is nice. Don't you think so?

MRS. HIGGINS. Oh, quite nice. I shall always be delighted to see him.

MRS. EYNSFORD HILL. Thank you, dear. Good-bye. [*She goes out*].

HIGGINS [*eagerly*] Well? Is Eliza presentable [*he swoops on his mother and drags her to the ottoman, where she sits down in Eliza's place with her son on her left*]?

Pickering returns to his chair on her right.

MRS. HIGGINS. You silly boy, of course she's not presentable. She's a triumph of your art and of her dressmaker's; but if you suppose for a moment that she doesn't give herself away in every sentence she utters, you must be perfectly cracked about her.

PICKERING. But don't you think something might be done? I mean something to eliminate the sanguinary element from her conversation.

MRS. HIGGINS. Not as long as she is in Henry's hands.

HIGGINS [*aggrieved*] Do you mean that my language is improper?

MRS. HIGGINS. No, dearest: it would be quite proper—say on a canal barge; but it would not be proper for her at a garden party.

HIGGINS [deeply injured] Well I must say—

PICKERING [*interrupting him*] Come, Higgins: you must learn to know yourself. I haven't heard such language as yours since we used to review the volunteers in Hyde Park twenty years ago.

HIGGINS [*sulkily*] Oh, well, if you say so, I suppose I don't always talk like a bishop.

MRS. HIGGINS [*quieting Henry with a touch*] Colonel Pickering: will you tell me what is the exact state of things in Wimpole Street?

PICKERING [*cheerfully: as if this completely changed the subject*] Well, I have come to live there with Henry. We work together at my Indian Dialects; and we think it more convenient—

MRS. HIGGINS. Quite so. I know all about that: it's an excellent arrangement. But where does this girl live?

HIGGINS. With us, of course. Where would she live?

MRS. HIGGINS. But on what terms? Is she a servant? If not, what is she?

PICKERING [*slowly*] I think I know what you mean, Mrs. Higgins.

HIGGINS. Well, dash me if I do! I've had to work at the girl every day for months to get her to her present pitch. Besides, she's useful. She knows where my things are, and remembers my appointments and so forth.

MRS. HIGGINS. How does your housekeeper get on with her?

HIGGINS. Mrs. Pearce? Oh, she's jolly glad to get so much taken off her hands; for before Eliza came, she had to have to find things and remind me of my appointments. But she's got some silly bee in her bonnet about Eliza. She keeps saying "You don't think, sir": doesn't she, Pick?

PICKERING. Yes: that's the formula. "You don't think, sir." That's the end of every conversation about Eliza.

HIGGINS. As if I ever stop thinking about the girl and her confounded vowels and consonants. I'm worn out, thinking about her, and watching her lips and her teeth and her tongue, not to mention her soul, which is the quaintest of the lot.

MRS. HIGGINS. You certainly are a pretty pair of babies, playing with your live doll.

HIGGINS. Playing! The hardest job I ever tackled: make no mistake about that, mother. But you have no idea how frightfully interesting it is to take a human being and change her into a quite different human being by creating a new speech for her. It's filling up the deepest gulf that separates class from class and soul from soul.

PICKERING [*drawing his chair closer to Mrs. Higgins and bending over to her eagerly*] Yes: it's enormously interesting. I assure you, Mrs. Higgins, we take Eliza very seriously. Every week—every day almost—there is some new change. [*Closer again*] We keep records of every stage—dozens of gramophone disks and photographs—

HIGGINS [*assailing her at the other ear*] Yes, by George: it's the most absorbing experiment I ever tackled. She regularly fills our lives up; doesn't she, Pick?

PICKERING. We're always talking Eliza.

HIGGINS. Teaching Eliza.

PICKERING. Dressing Eliza.

MRS. HIGGINS. What!

HIGGINS. Inventing new Elizas.

HIGGINS (*speaking together*). You know, she has the most extraordinary quickness of ear:

PICKERING. I assure you, my dear Mrs. Higgins, that girl

HIGGINS. just like a parrot. I've tried her with every

PICKERING. is a genius. She can play the piano quite beautifully

HIGGINS. possible sort of sound that a human being can make—

PICKERING. We have taken her to classical concerts and to music

HIGGINS. Continental dialects, African dialects, Hottentot

PICKERING. halls; and it's all the same to her: she plays everything

HIGGINS. clicks, things it took me years to get hold of; and

PICKERING. she hears right off when she comes home, whether it's

HIGGINS. she picks them up like a shot, right away, as if she had

PICKERING. Beethoven and Brahms or Lehar and Lionel Morickton;

HIGGINS. been at it all her life.

PICKERING. though six months ago, she'd never as much as touched a piano.

MRS. HIGGINS [*putting her fingers in her ears, as they are by this time shouting one another down with an intolerable noise*] Sh—sh—sh—sh! [*They stop*].

PICKERING. I beg your pardon. [*He draws his chair back apologetically*].

HIGGINS. Sorry. When Pickering starts shouting nobody can get a word in edgeways.

MRS. HIGGINS. Be quiet, Henry. Colonel Pickering: don't you realize that when Eliza walked into Wimpole Street, something walked in with her?

PICKERING. Her father did. But Henry soon got rid of him.

MRS. HIGGINS. It would have been more to the point if her mother had. But as her mother didn't something else did.

PICKERING. But what?

MRS. HIGGINS [*unconsciously dating herself by the word*] A problem.

PICKERING. Oh, I see. The problem of how to pass her off as a lady.

HIGGINS. I'll solve that problem. I've half solved it already.

MRS. HIGGINS. No, you two infinitely stupid male creatures: the problem of what is to be done with her afterwards.

HIGGINS. I don't see anything in that. She can go her own way, with all the advantages I have given her.

MRS. HIGGINS. The advantages of that poor woman who was here just now! The manners and habits that disqualify a fine lady from earning her own living without giving her a fine lady's income! Is that what you mean?

PICKERING [*indulgently, being rather bored*] Oh, that will be all right, Mrs. Higgins. [He rises to go].

HIGGINS [*rising also*] We'll find her some light employment.

PICKERING. She's happy enough. Don't you worry about her. Good- bye. [He shakes hands as if he were consoling a frightened child, and makes for the door].

HIGGINS. Anyhow, there's no good bothering now. The thing's done. Good-bye, mother. [*He kisses her, and follows Pickering*].

PICKERING [*turning for a final consolation*] There are plenty of openings. We'll do what's right. Good-bye.

HIGGINS [*to Pickering as they go out together*] Let's take her to the Shakespeare exhibition at Earls Court.

PICKERING. Yes: let's. Her remarks will be delicious.

HIGGINS. She'll mimic all the people for us when we get home.

PICKERING. Ripping. [*Both are heard laughing as they go downstairs*].

MRS. HIGGINS [rises with an impatient bounce, and returns to her work at the writing-table. She sweeps a litter of disarranged papers out of her way; snatches a sheet of paper from her stationery case; and tries resolutely to write. At the third line she gives it up; flings down her pen; grips the table angrily and exclaims] Oh, men! men!! men!!!

(选自 George Bernard shaw. "Pygmalion," George Bernard Shaw's Plays. Sandie Byne ed. New York & London: w. w. Norton & Company, Inc., 2002. pp. 317 - 329.)

Questions

1. Describe the personality of Professor Higgins.
2. What do we learn from this play as language learners?
3. What is the underlying social satire of the play?
4. This play seems to tell us that "Manners are the happy way of doing things." What do you think of it?
5. It has been said that *Pygmalion* is not a play about turning a flower girl into a duchess, but one about turning a woman into a human being with her own mind and independence. Do you agree?

Unit 7

Khaled Hosseini: *The Kite Runner*

Khaled Hosseini (1965—) was born in Kabul, Afghanistan, the eldest of five children. He is an Afghan-born American novelist and physician. His father, Nasser worked as a diplomat for the Ministry of Foreign Affairs in Kabul while his mother worked as a Persian language teacher at a girl's high school. Regarding his ethnicity, Hosseini stated, "I'm not pure anything ... There's a Pashtun part of me, a Tajik part of me." His mother's family is believed to be from the Mohammadzai tribe of Pashtuns. Hosseini describes his upbringing as privileged. He spent eight years of his childhood in the middle-class Wazir Akbar Khan neighborhood in Kabul. Hosseini does not recall his sister, Raya, ever suffering discrimination for being a female. Kabul itself was "a growing, thriving, cosmopolitan city" where he regularly flew kites with a number of cousins. In 1970, Hosseini and his family moved to Iran where his father worked for the Embassy of Afghanistan in Tehran. In 1973, Hosseini's family returned to Kabul, and Hosseini's youngest brother was born in July of that year. In 1976, when Hosseini was 11 years old, his father secured a job in Paris, France, and moved the family there. They were unable to return to Afghanistan because of the April 1978 Saur Revolution in which the People's Democratic Party of Afghanistan (PDPA) seized power. In 1980, shortly after the start of the Soviet war in Afghanistan, they sought political asylum in the United States and made their residence in San Jose, California. Hosseini, then aged 15, did not speak English when he first arrived in the United States. He describes the experience as "a culture shock" and "very alienating." Hosseini did not return to Afghanistan until 2001 at the age of 36, where he "felt like a tourist in his own country." In interviews about the experience, he admitted to sometimes feeling survivor's guilt for having been able to leave the country before the Soviet invasion and subsequent wars.

Hosseini graduated from Independence High School in San Jose in 1984 and enrolled at Santa Clara University, where he earned a bachelor's degree in biology in 1988. The following year, he entered the University of California San Diego School of Medicine, where he earned his M.D. in 1993. He completed his residency in internal medicine at Cedars-Sinai Medical Center in Los Angeles in 1996. He practiced medicine for over ten years, until a year and a half after the release of *The Kite Runner*. After graduating from college, he worked as a doctor in California. Hosseini is married to Roya Hosseini, a lawyer. The couple have two children, Haris and Farah. He lives in Northern California with his family.

The Kite Runner, *A Thousand Splendid Suns*, *And the Mountains Echoed* and *Sea Prayer* are all the books Khaled Hosseini has written in his life. The first three became bestsellers: *The Kite Runner* (2003) spent 101 weeks on *The New York Times* Best Seller list. All of them are at least partially set in Afghanistan and feature an Afghan as the protagonist. Following the success of *The Kite Runner* he retired from medicine to write full-time. Hosseini's works are mainly about familial aspects. Hosseini has remarked that he regards the novel, *A Thousand Splendid Suns*, as a "mother-daughter story" in contrast to *The Kite Runner*, which he considers a "father-son story." Whereas *And the Mountains Echoed* tells its story through the prism of sibling relationships—a theme refracted through the lives of several pairs of brothers and sisters.

Khaled Hosseini is one of the most widely read and beloved novelists in the world, with more than ten million copies of *The Kite Runner* and *And the Mountains Echoed* in the Unites states, and more than thirty-eight million copies sold worldwide in more than seventy countries. Hosseini is also the founder of The Khaled Hosseini Foundation, a nonprofit that provides humanitarian assistance to the people of Afghanistan. According to *Library Journal*, Hosseini is possibly the only Afghan author writing in English. Because of him, a vivid picture of Afghanistan thirty years ago is presented to the world.

Theme

Hosseini's "very fond memories of his childhood" in peaceful pre-Soviet era Afghanistan, as well as his personal experiences with Afghanistan's Hazara people led to the writing of his first novel, *The Kite Runner*. One Hazara man, named Hossein Khan, worked for the Hosseinis when they were living in Iran. When Khaled Hosseini was in third grade, he taught Khan to read and write. Hosseini's fond memories of this relationship served as an inspiration for the relationship between Hassan and Amir in *The Kite Runner*. *The Kite Runner* tells the story of Amir, a young boy from the Wazir Akbar Khan district of Kabul, whose closest friend is Hassan. The story is set against a backdrop of tumultuous events, from the fall of Afghanistan's monarchy through the Soviet military intervention, the exodus of refugees to Pakistan and the United States, and the rise of the Taliban regime.

Term

Memoir: It's a history or narrative composed from or stressing personal experience and acquaintance with the events, scenes, or persons described. In the 20th century, many distinguished statesmen and military men have described their experiences in memoirs. Notable reminiscences of World War II include the memoirs of Dwight Eisenhower, Viscount Montgomery, and Charles de Gaulle. Closely related to, and often confused with, autobiography, a memoir usually differs chiefly in the degree of emphasis placed on external events; whereas writers of autobiography are concerned primarily with themselves as subject matter, writers of memoir are usually persons who have played roles in, or have been close observers of, historical events and whose main purpose is to describe or interpret those events.

Excerpt

Chapter 17

Rahim Khan slowly uncrossed his legs and leaned against the bare wall in the wary, deliberate way of a man whose every movement triggers spikes of pain. Outside, a donkey was braying and someone was shouting something in Urdu. The sun was beginning to set, glittering red through the cracks between the ramshackle buildings.

It hit me again, the enormity of what I had done that winter and that following summer. The names rang in my head: Hassan, Sohrab, Ali, Farzana, and Sanaubar. Hearing Rahim Khan speak Ali's name was like finding an old dusty music box that hadn't been opened in years; the melody began to play immediately: Who did you eat today, Babalu? Who did you eat, you slant-eyed Babalu? I tried to conjure Ali's frozen face, to really see his tranquil eyes, but time can be a greedy thing—sometimes it steals all the details for itself.

"Is Hassan still in that house now?" I asked.

Rahim Khan raised the teacup to his parched lips and took a sip. He then fished an envelope from the breast pocket of his vest and handed it to me. "For you."

I tore the sealed envelope. Inside, I found a Polaroid photograph and a folded letter. I stared at the photograph for a full minute.

A tall man dressed in a white turban and a green-striped *chapan* stood with a little boy in front of a set of wrought-iron gates. Sunlight slanted in from the left, casting a shadow on half of his rotund face. He was squinting and smiling at the camera, showing a pair of missing front teeth. Even in this blurry Polaroid, the man in the *chapan* exuded a sense of self-assuredness, of ease. It was in the way he stood, his feet slightly apart, his arms comfortably crossed on his chest, his head titled a little toward the sun. Mostly, it was in the way he smiled. Looking at the photo, one might have concluded that this was a man who thought the world had been good to him. Rahim Khan was right: I would have recognized him if I had bumped into him on the street. The little boy stood bare foot, one arm wrapped around the man's thigh, his shaved head resting against his father's hip. He too was grinning and squinting.

I unfolded the letter. It was written in Farsi. No dots were omitted, no crosses forgotten, no words blurred together—the handwriting was almost childlike in its neatness. I began to read:

> In the name of Allah the most beneficent,
> the most merciful,
> Amir agha, with my deepest respects,

Farzana jan, Sohrab, and I pray that this latest letter finds you in good health and in the lightof Allah's good graces. Please offer my warmest thanks to Rahim Khan sahib for carrying it to you. I am hopeful that one day I will hold one of your letters in my hands and read of your life in America. Perhaps a photograph of you will even grace our eyes. I have told much about you to Farzana jan and Sohrab, about us growing up together and playing games and running in the streets. They laugh at the stories of all the mischief you and I used to cause!

Amir agha,

Alas the Afghanistan of our youth is long dead. Kindness is gone from the land and you cannot escape the killings. Always the killings. In Kabul, fear is everywhere, in the streets, in the stadium, in the markets, it is a part of our lives here, Amir agha. The savages who rule our *watan* don't care about human decency. The other day, I accompanied Farzana Jan to the bazaar to buy some potatoes and *naan*. She asked the vendor how much the potatoes cost, but he did not hear her, I think he had a deaf ear. So she asked louder and suddenly a young Talib ran over and hit her on the thighs with his wooden stick. He struck her so hard she fell down. He was screaming at her and cursing and saying the Ministry of Vice and Virtue does not allow women to speak loudly. She had a large purple bruise on her leg for days but what could I do except stand and watch my wife get beaten? If I fought, that dog would have surely put a bullet in me, and gladly! Then what would happen to my Sohrab? The streets are full enough already of hungry orphans and every day I thank Allah that I am alive, not because I fear death, but because my wife has a husband and my son is not an orphan.

I wish you could see Sohrab. He is a good boy. Rahim Khan sahib and I have taught him to read and write so he does not grow up stupid like his father. And can he shoot with that slingshot! I take Sohrab around Kabul sometimes and buy him candy. There is still a monkey man in Shar-e-Nau and if we run into him, I pay him to make his monkey dance for Sohrab. You should see how he laughs! The two of us often walk up to the cemetery on the hill. Do you remember how we used to sit under the pomegranate tree there and read from the *Shahnamah*? The droughts have dried the hill and the tree hasn't borne fruit in years, but Sohrab and I still sit under its shade and I read to him from the *Shahnamah*. It is not necessary to tell you that his favorite part is the one with his namesake, Rostam and Sohrab. Soon he will be able to read from the book himself. I am a very proud and very lucky father.

Amir agha,

> Rahim Khan sahib is quite ill. He coughs all day and I see blood on his sleeve when he wipes his mouth. He has lost much weight and I wish he would eat a little of the *shorwa* and rice that Farzana Jan cooks for him. But he only takes a bite or two and even that I think is out of courtesy to Farzana jan. I am so worried about this dear man I pray for him every day. He is leaving for Pakistan in a few days to consult some doctors there and, *Inshallah*, he will return with good news. But in my heart I fear for him. Farzana jan and I have told little Sohrab that Rahim Khan sahib is going to be well. What can we do? He is only ten and he adores Rahim Khan sahib. They have grown so close to each other. Rahim Khan sahib used to take him to the bazaar for balloons and biscuits but he is too weak for that now.
>
> I have been dreaming a lot lately, Amir agha. Some of them are nightmares, like hanged corpses rotting in soccer fields with bloodred grass. I wake up from those short of breath and sweaty. Mostly, though, I dream of good things, and praise Allah for that. I dream that Rahim Khan sahib will be well. I dream that my son will grow up to be a good person, a free person, and an important person. I dream that *lawla* flowers will bloom in the streets of

Kabul again and *rubab* music will play in the samovar houses and kites will fly in the skies. And I dream that someday you will return to Kabul to revisit the land of our childhood. If you do, you will find an old faithful friend waiting for you.

May Allah be with you always.

Hassan

I read the letter twice. I folded the note and looked at the photograph for another minute. I pocketed both. "How is he?" I asked.

"That letter was written six months ago, a few days before I left for Peshawar," Rahim Khan said. "I took the Polaroid the day before I left. A month after I arrived in Peshawar, I received a telephone call from one of my neighbors in Kabul. He told me this story: Soon after I took my leave, a rumor spread that a Hazara family was living alone in the big house in Wazir Akbar Khan, or so the Taliban claim. A pair of Talib officials came to investigate and interrogated Hassan. They accused him of lying when Hassan told them he was living with me even though many of the neighbors, including the one who called me, supported Hassan's story. The Talibs said he was a liar and a thief like all Hazaras and ordered him to get his family out of the house by sundown. Hassan protested. But my neighbor said the Talibs were looking at the big house like—how did he say it? —yes, like 'wolves looking at a flock of sheep.' They told Hassan they would be moving in to supposedly keep it safe until I return. Hassan protested again. So they took him to the street—"

"No," I breathed.

"—and order him to kneel—"

"No. God, no."

"—and shot him in the back of the head."

"—Farzana came screaming and attacked them—"

"No."

"—shot her too. Self-defense, they claimed later—"

But all I could manage was to whisper "No. No. No." over and over again.

I KEPT THINKING OF THAT DAY in 1974, in the hospital room, Just after Hassan's harelip surgery. Baba, Rahim Khan, Ali, and I had huddled around Hassan's bed, watched him examine his new lip in a handheld mirror. Now everyone in that room was either dead or dying. Except for me.

Then I saw something else: a man dressed in a herringbone vest pressing the muzzle of his Kalashnikov to the back of Hassan's head. The blast echoes through the street of my father's house. Hassan slumps to the asphalt, his life of unrequited loyalty drifting from him like the windblown kites he used to chase.

"The Taliban moved into the house," Rahim Khan said. "The pretext was that they had evicted a trespasser. Hassan's and Farzana's murders were dismissed as a case of self-defense. No one said a word about it. Most of it was fear of the Taliban, I think. But no one was going to risk anything for a pair of Hazara servants."

"What did they do with Sohrab?" I asked. I felt tired, drained. A coughing fit gripped Rahim Khan and went on for a long time. When he finally looked up, his face was flushed and his eyes were bloodshot. "I heard he's in an orphanage somewhere in Karteh Seh. Amir jan—" then he was coughing again. When he stopped, he looked older than a few moments before, like he was aging with each coughing fit. "Amir jan, I summoned you here because I wanted to see you before I die, but that's not all."

I said nothing. I think I already knew what he was going to say.

"I want you to go to Kabul I want you to bring Sohrab here," he said.

I struggled to find the right words. I'd barely had time to deal with the fact that Hassan was dead.

"Please hear me. I know an American pair here in Peshawar, a husband and wife named Thomas and Betty Caldwell. They are Christians and they run a small charity organization that they manage with private donations. Mostly they house and feed Afghan children who have lost their parents. I have seen the place. It's clean and safe, the children are well cared for, and Mr. and Mrs. Caldwell are kind people. They have already told me that Sohrab would be welcome to their Home and—"

"Rahim Khan, you can't be serious."

"Children are fragile, Amir Jan. Kabul is already full of broken children and I don't want Sohrab to become another."

"Rahim Khan, I don't want to go to Kabul. I can't!" I said.

"Sohrab is a gifted little boy. We can give him a new life here, new hope, with people who would love him. Thomas agha is a good man and Betty khanum is so kind, you should see how she treats those orphans."

"Why me? Why can't you pay someone here to go? I'll pay for it if it's a matter of money."

"It isn't about money, Amir!" Rahim Khan roared. "I'm a dying man and I will not be insulted! It has never been about money with me, you know that. And why you? I think we both know why it has to be you, don't we?"

I didn't want to understand that comment, but I did. I understood it all too well. "I have a wife in America, a Home, a career, and a family. Kabul is a dangerous place, you know that, and you'd have me risk everything for ..." I stopped.

"You know," Rahim Khan said, "one time, when you weren't around, your father and I were talking. And you know how he always worried about you in those days. I remember he said to me, 'Rahim, a boy who won't stand up for himself becomes a man who can't stand up to anything.' I wonder, is that what you've become?"

I dropped my eyes.

"What I'm asking from you is to grant an old man his dying wish," he said gravely.

He had gambled with that comment. Played his best card. Or so I thought then. His words hung in limbo between us, but at least he'd known what to say. I was still searching for the right words, and I was the writer in the room. Finally, I settled for this:

"Maybe Baba was right."

"I'm sorry you think that, Amir."

I couldn't look at him. "And you don't?"

"If I did, I would not have asked you to come here."

I toyed with my wedding ring. "You've always thought too highly of me, Rahim Khan."

"And you've always been far too hard on yourself." He hesitated. "But there's something else. Something you don't know."

"Please, Rahim Khan—"

"Sanaubar wasn't Ali's first wife."

Now I looked up.

"He was married once before, to a Hazara woman from the Jaghori area. This was long before you were born. They were married for three years."

"What does this have to do with anything?"

"She left him childless after three years and married a man in Khost. She bore *him* three daughters. That's what I am trying to tell you."

I began to see where he was going. But I didn't want to hear the rest of it. I had a good life in California, pretty Victorian Home with a peaked roof, a good marriage, a promising writing career, in-laws who loved me. I didn't need any of this shit.

"Ali was sterile," Rahim Khan said.

"No he wasn't. He and Sanaubar had Hassan, didn't they? They had Hassan—"

"No they didn't," Rahim Khan said.

"Yes they did!"

"No they didn't, Amir. —"

"Then who—"

"I think you know who."

I felt like a man sliding down a steep cliff, clutching at shrubs and tangles of brambles and coming up empty-handed. The room was swooping up and down, swaying side to side. "Did Hassan know?" I said through lips that didn't feel like my own. Rahim Khan closed his eyes. Shook his head.

"You bastards," I muttered. Stood up. "You goddamn bastards!" I screamed. "All of you, you bunch of lying goddamn bastards!"

"Please sit down, " Rahim Khan said.

"How could you hide this from *me*? From *him*?" I bellowed. "Please think, Amir Jan. It was a shameful situation. People would talk. All that a man had back then, all that he was, was his honor, his name, and if people talked ... We couldn't tell anyone, surely you can see that." He reached for me, but I shed his hand. Headed for the door.

"Amir jan, please don't leave."

I opened the door and turned to him. "Why? What can you possibly say to me? I'm thirty-eight years old and I've Just found out my whole life is one big fucking lie! What can you possibly say to make things better? Nothing. Not a goddamn thing!"

And with that, I stormed out of the apartment.

Chapter 18

The sun had almost set and left the sky swathed in smothers of purple and red. I walked down the busy, narrow street that led away from Rahim Khan's building. The street was a noisy lane in a maze of alleyways choked with pedestrians, bicycles, and rickshaws. Billboards hung at its corners, advertising Coca-Cola and cigarettes; Hollywood movie posters displayed sultry actresses dancing with handsome, brown-skinned men in fields of marigolds.

I walked into a smoky little samovar house and ordered a cup of tea. I tilted back on the folding chair's rear legs and rubbed my face. That feeling of sliding toward a fall was fading. But in its stead, I felt like a man who awakens in his own house and finds all the furniture rearranged, so that every familiar nook and cranny looks foreign now. Disoriented, he has to reevaluate his surroundings, reorient himself.

How could I have been so blind? The signs had been there for me to see all along; they came flying back at me now: Baba hiring Dr. Kumar to fix Hassan's harelip. Baba never missing Hassan's birthday. I remembered the day we were planting tulips, when I had asked Baba if he'd ever consider getting new servants. *Hassan's not going anywhere*, he'd barked. *He's staying right here with us, where he belongs. This is his Home and we're his family*. He had wept, *wept*, when Ali announced he and Hassan were leaving us.

The waiter placed a teacup on the table before me. Where the table's legs crossed like an *X*, there was a ring of brass balls, each walnut-sized. One of the balls had come unscrewed. I stooped and tightened it. I wished I could fix my own life as easily. I took a gulp of the blackest tea I'd had in years and tried to think of Soraya, of the general and Khala Jamila, of the novel that needed finishing. I tried to watch the traffic bolting by on the street, the people milling in and out of the little sweetshops. Tried to listen to the *Qawali* music playing on the transistor radio at the next table. Anything. But I kept seeing Baba on the night of my graduation, sitting in the Ford he'd just given me, smelling of beer and saying, *I wish Hassan had been with us today*.

How could he have lied to me all those years? To Hassan? He had sat me on his lap when I was little, looked me straight in the eyes, and said, *There is only one sin. And that is theft ... When you tell a lie, you steal someone's right to the truth*. Hadn't he said those words to me? And now, fifteen years after I'd buried him, I was learning that Baba had been a thief. And a thief of the worst kind, because the things he'd stolen had been sacred: from me the right to know I had a brother, from Hassan his identity, and from Ali his honor. His *nang*. His *namoos*.

The questions kept coming at me: How had Baba brought himself to look Ali in the eye? How had Ali lived in that house, clay in and day out, knowing he had been dishonored by his master in the single worst way an Afghan man can be dishonored?

And how was I going to reconcile this new image of Baba with the one that had been imprinted on my mind for so long, that of him in his old brown suit, hobbling up the Taheris' driveway to ask for Soraya's hand?

Here is another cliché my creative writing teacher would have scoffed at; like father, like son. But it was true, wasn't it? As it turned out, Baba and I were more alike than I'd ever known. We had both betrayed the people who would have given their lives for us. And with that came this realization: that Rahim Khan had summoned me here to atone not just for my sins but for Baba's too.

Rahim Khan said I'd always been too hard on myself. But I wondered. True, I hadn't made Ali step on the land mine, and I hadn't brought the Taliban to the house to shoot Hassan. But I had driven Hassan and Ali out of the house. Was it too far-fetched to imagine that things might have turned out differently if I hadn't? Maybe Baba would have brought them along to America. Maybe Hassan would have had a Home of his own now, a job, a family, a life in a country where no one cared that he was a Hazara, where most people didn't even know what a Hazara was. Maybe not. But maybe so.

I *can't* go to *Kabul*, I had said to Rahim Khan. *I have a wife in America, a home, a career, and a family*. But how could I pack up and go back Home when my actions may have cost Hassan a chance at those very same things?

I wished Rahim Khan hadn't called me. I wished he had let me live on in my oblivion. But he had called me. And what Rahim Khan revealed to me changed things. Made me see how my entire life, long before the winter of 1975, dating back to when that singing Hazara woman was still nursing me, had been a cycle of lies, betrayals, and secrets.

There is a way to be good again, he'd said.

A way to end the cycle.

With a little boy. An orphan. Hassan's son. Somewhere in

Kabul.

ON THE RICKSHAW RIDE back to Rahim Khan's apartment, I remembered Baba saying that my problem was that someone had always done my fighting for me. I was thirty-eight flow. My hair was receding and streaked with gray, and lately I'd traced little crow's-feet etched around the corners of my eyes. I was older now, but maybe not yet too old to start doing my own fighting. Baba had lied about a lot of things as it turned out but he hadn't lied about that.

I looked at the round face in the Polaroid again, the way the sun fell on it. My brother's face. Hassan had loved me once, loved me in a way that no one ever had or ever would again. He was gone now, but a little part of him lived on. It was in Kabul.

Waiting.

I FOUND RAHIM KHAN praying *namaz* in a corner of the room. He was just a dark silhouette bowing eastward against a bloodred sky. I waited for him to finish.

Then I told him I was going to Kabul. Told him to call the Caldwells in the morning.

"I'll pray for you, Amir jan," he said.

（选自 Khaled Hosseini: *The Kite Runner*. New York: The Berkley Publishing Group, 2003. pp.214－227.）

Questions

1. What kind of person is Rahim Khan in the book?
2. Why Rahim Khan said that "There is a way to be good again"?
3. What does "kites" mean in the book?
4. What is the function of the letter?
5. How badly does the fact that "Hassan is Baba's son" hurt Amir?

Unit 8

Gabriel García Márquez: *One Hundred Years of Solitude*

Gabriel García Márquez (1927—2014) was born on 6 March 1927 in Aracataca, Colombia. Soon after García Márquez was born, his father became a pharmacist and moved to Barranquilla with his wife, leaving young Gabriel in Aracataca. He was raised by his maternal grandparents. In December 1936, his father took him and his brother to Sincé, while in March 1937, his grandfather died; the family then moved first (back) to Barranquilla and then on to Sucre, where his father started up a pharmacy. Since García Márquez's parents were more or less strangers to him for the first few years of his life, his grandparents influenced his early development very strongly. His grandfather, whom he called "Papalelo," was a Liberal veteran of the Thousand Days War. The Colonel was considered a hero by Colombian Liberals and was highly respected. He was well known for his refusal to remain silent about the banana massacres that took place the year after García Márquez was born. The Colonel, whom García Márquez described as his "umbilical cord with history and reality," was also an excellent storyteller. He taught García Márquez lessons from the dictionary, took him to the circus each year, and was the first to introduce his grandson to ice—a "miracle" found at the United Fruit Company store. He would also occasionally tell his young grandson "you can't imagine how much a dead man weighs," reminding him that there was no greater burden than to have killed a man, a lesson that García Márquez would later integrate into his novels. García Márquez's grandmother played an influential role in his upbringing. He was inspired by the way she "treated the extraordinary as something perfectly natural." The house was filled with stories of ghosts and premonitions, omens and portents, all of which were studiously ignored by her husband. According to García Márquez she was "the source of the magical, superstitious and supernatural view of reality." He enjoyed his grandmother's unique way of telling stories. No matter how fantastic or improbable her statements, she always delivered them as if they were the irrefutable truth. It was a deadpan style that, some thirty years later, heavily influenced her grandson's most popular novel, *One Hundred Years of Solitude*.

After arriving at Sucre, it was decided that García Márquez should start his formal education and he was sent to an internship in Barranquilla, a port on the mouth of the Río Magdalena. After his graduation in 1947, García Márquez stayed in Bogotá to study law at the Universidad Nacional de Colombia, where he had a special dedication to reading. He was excited with the idea of writing, not traditional literature, but a style similar to his grandfather's stories, in which they inserted extraordinary events and anomalies as if they were simply an aspect of everyday life.

Since García Márquez was eighteen, he had wanted to write a novel based on his grandparents' house where he grew up. However, he struggled with finding an appropriate tone and put off the idea until one day the answer hit him while driving his family to Acapulco. He turned the car around and the family returned home so he could begin writing. He sold his car so his family would have money to live on while he wrote, but writing the novel took far longer than he expected, and he wrote every day for eighteen months. His wife had to ask for food on credit from their butcher and their baker as well as nine months of rent on credit from their landlord. During the eighteen months of writing, García Márquez met with two couples, Eran Carmen and Álvaro Mutis, and María Luisa Elío and Jomí García Ascot, and discussed the progress of the novel, trying out different versions. Fortunately, when the book was finally published in 1967 it became his most commercially successful novel, *One Hundred Years of Solitude*, which sold more than 30 million copies.

This novel was widely popular and led to García Márquez's Nobel Prize as well as the Rómulo Gallegos Prize in 1972. William Kennedy has called it "the first piece of literature since the Book of Genesis that should be required reading for the entire human race," and hundreds of articles and books of literary critique have been published in response to it. García Márquez died of pneumonia at the age of 87 on 17 April 2014 in Mexico City.

Theme

The story chronicles several generations of the Buendía family from the time they founded the fictional South American village of Macondo, through their trials and tribulations, instances of incest, births and deaths. The most dominant theme in the story is that of solitude. Macondo was founded in the remote jungles of the Colombian rainforest. The solitude of the town was representative of the colonial period in Latin American history, where outposts and colonies were, for all intents and purposes, not interconnected. Isolated from the rest of the world, the Buendías grow to be increasingly solitary and selfish. With every member of the family living only for himself or herself, the Buendías became representative of the aristocratic, land-owning elite who came to dominate Latin America in keeping with the sense of Latin American history symbolized in the novel. This egocentricity is embodied, especially, in the characters of Aureliano, who lives in a private world of his own, and Remedios the Beauty, who innocently destroys the lives of four men enamored by her unbelievable beauty, because she is living in a different reality due to what some see as autism. Throughout the novel it seems as if no character can find true love or escape the destructiveness of their own egocentricity.

Term

Magic realism: It's a kind of modern fiction in which fabulous and fantastical events are included. It is a narrative that otherwise maintains the "reliable" tone of objective realistic report. The term was once applied to a trend in German fiction of the early 1950s, but is now associated chiefly with certain leading novelists of Central and South America. *One Hundred Years of Solitude* is often cited as a leading example, celebrated for the moment at which one character unexpectedly ascends to heaven while hanging her washing on a line. The term has also been extended to works from very different cultures, designating a tendency of the modern novel to reach beyond the confines of realism and draw upon the energies of fable, folktale, and myth while retaining a strong contemporary social relevance.

Excerpt

Chapter 1

MANY YEARS LATER as he faced the firing squad, Colonel Aureliano Buendía was to remember that distant afternoon when his father took him to discover ice. At that time Macondo was a village of twenty adobe houses, built on the bank of a river of clear water that ran along a bed of polished stones, which were white and enormous, like prehistoric eggs. The world was so recent that many things lacked names, and in order to indicate them it was necessary to point. Every year during the month of March a family of ragged gypsies would set up their tents near the village, and with a great uproar of pipes and kettledrums they would display new inventions. First they brought the magnet. A heavy gypsy with an untamed beard and sparrow hands, who introduced himself as Melquíades, put on a bold public demonstration of what he himself called the eighth wonder of the learned alchemists of Macedonia. He went from house to house dragging two metal ingots and everybody was amazed to see pots, pans, tongs, and braziers tumble down from their places and beams creak from the desperation of nails and screws trying to emerge, and even objects that had been lost for a long time appeared from where they had been searched for most and went dragging along in turbulent confusion behind Melquíades' magical irons. "Things have a life of their own," the gypsy proclaimed with a harsh accent. "It's simply a matter of waking up their souls." José Arcadio Buendía, whose unbridled imagination always went beyond the genius of nature and even beyond miracles and magic, thought that it would be possible to make use of that useless invention to extract gold from the bowels of the earth. Melquíades, who was an honest man, warned him: "It won't work for that." But José Arcadio Buendía at that time did not believe in the honesty of gypsies, so he traded his mule and a pair of goats for the two magnetized ingots. Úrsula Iguarán, his wife, who relied on those animals to increase their poor domestic holdings, was unable to dissuade him. "Very soon well have gold enough and more to pave the floors of the house," her husband replied. For several months he worked hard to demonstrate the truth of his idea. He explored every inch of the region, even the riverbed, dragging the two iron ingots along and reciting Melquíades' incantation aloud. The only thing he succeeded in doing was to unearth a suit of fifteenth-century armor which had all of its pieces soldered together with rust and inside of which there was the hollow resonance of an enormous stone-filled gourd. When José Arcadio Buendía and the four men of his expedition managed to take the armor apart, they found inside a calcified skeleton with a copper locket containing a woman's hair around its neck.

In March the gypsies returned. This time they brought a telescope and a magnifying glass the size of a drum, which they exhibited as the latest discovery of the Jews of Amsterdam. They placed a gypsy woman at one end of the village and set up the telescope at the entrance to the tent. For the price of five Úreales, people could look into the telescope and see the gypsy woman an arm's length away. "Science has eliminated distance," Melquíades proclaimed. "In a short time, man will be able to see what is happening in any place in the world without leaving his own house." A burning noonday sun brought out a startling demonstration with the gigantic magnifying glass: they put a pile of dry hay in the middle of the street and set it on fire by concentrating the sun's rays. José Arcadio Buendía, who had still not been consoled for the failure of big magnets, conceived the idea of using that invention as a weapon of war. Again Melquíades tried to dissuade him, but he finally accepted the two magnetized ingots and three colonial coins in exchange for the magnifying glass. Úrsula wept in consternation. That money was from a chest of gold coins that her father had put together ova an entire life of privation and that she had buried underneath her bed in hopes of a proper occasion to make use of it. José Arcadio Buendía made no at. tempt to console her, completely absorbed in his tactical experiments with the abnegation of a scientist and even at the risk of his own life. In an attempt to show the effects of the glass on enemy troops, he exposed himself to the concentration of the sun's rays and suffered burns which turned into sores that took a long time to heal. Over the protests of his wife, who was alarmed at such a dangerous invention, at one point he was ready to set the house on fire. He would spend hours on end in his room, calculating the strategic possibilities of his novel weapon until he succeeded in putting together a manual of startling instructional clarity and an irresistible power of conviction. He sent it to the government, accompanied by numerous descriptions of his experiments and several pages of explanatory sketches; by a messenger who crossed the mountains, got lost in measureless swamps, forded stormy rivers, and was on the point of perishing under the lash of despair, plague, and wild beasts until he found a route that joined the one used by the mules that carried the mail. In spite of the fact that a trip to the capital was little less than impossible at that time, José Arcadio Buendía promised to undertake it as soon as the government ordered him to so that he could put on some practical demonstrations of his invention for the military authorities and could train them himself in the complicated art of solar war. For several years he waited for an answer. Finally, tired of waiting, he bemoaned to Melquíades the failure of his project and the gypsy then gave him a convincing proof of his honesty: he gave him back the doubloons in exchange for the magnifying glass, and he left him in addition some Portuguese maps and several instruments of navigation. In his own handwriting he set down a concise synthesis of the studies by Monk Hermann. which he left José Arcadio so that he would be able to make use of the astrolabe, the compass, and the sextant. José Arcadio Buendía spent the long months of the rainy season shut up in a small room that he had built in the rear of the house so that no one would disturb his experiments. Having completely abandoned his domestic obligations, he spent entire nights in the courtyard watching the course of the stars and he almost contracted sunstroke from trying to establish an exact method to ascertain noon. When he became an expert in the use and manipulation of his instruments, he conceived a notion of space that allowed him to navigate across unknown seas, to visit uninhabited territories, and to establish relations with splendid beings without having to leave his study. That was the period in which he acquired the habit of talking to himself, of walking through the house without paying attention to anyone, as Úrsula and the children broke their backs in the garden, growing banana and caladium, cassava and yams, ahuyama roots and eggplants. Suddenly, without warning, his feverish activity was interrupted and was replaced by a kind of fascination. He spent several days as if he were bewitched, softly repeating to himself a string of fearful conjectures without giving credit to his own understanding. Finally, one Tuesday in December, at lunchtime, all at once he released the whole weight of his torment. The children would remember for the rest of their lives the august solemnity with which their father, devastated by his prolonged vigil and by the wrath of his imagination, revealed his discovery to them:

"The earth is round, like an orange."

Úrsula lost her patience. "If you have to go crazy, please go crazy all by yourself!" she shouted. "But don't try to put your gypsy ideas into the heads of the children." José Arcadio Buendía, impassive, did not let himself be frightened by the desperation of his wife, who, in a seizure of rage, mashed the astrolabe against the floor. He built another one, he gathered the men of the village in his little room, and he demonstrated to them, with theories that none of them could understand, the possibility of returning to where one had set out by consistently sailing east. The whole village was convinced that José Arcadio Buendía had lost his reason, when Melquíades returned to set things straight. He gave public praise to the intelligence of a man who from pure astronomical speculation had evolved a theory that had already been proved in practice, although unknown in Macondo until then, and as a proof of his admiration he made him a gift that was to have a profound influence on the future of the village: the laboratory of an alchemist.

By then Melquíades had aged with surprising rapidity. On his first trips he seemed to be the same age as José Arcadio Buendía. But while the latter had preserved his extraordinary strength, which permitted him to pull down a horse by grabbing its ears, the gypsy seemed to have been worn dowse by some tenacious illness. It was, in reality, the result of multiple and rare diseases contracted on his innumerable trips around the world. According to what he himself said as he spoke to José Arcadio Buendía while helping him set up the laboratory, death followed him everywhere, sniffing at the cuffs of his pants, but never deciding to give him the final clutch of its claws. He was a fugitive from all the plagues and catastrophes that had ever lashed mankind. He had survived pellagra in Persia, scurvy in the Malayan archipelago, leprosy in Alexandria, beriberi in Japan, bubonic plague in Madagascar, an earthquake in Sicily, and a disastrous shipwreck in the Strait of Magellan. That prodigious creature, said to possess the keys of Nostradamus, was a gloomy man, enveloped in a sad aura, with an Asiatic look that seemed to know what there was on the other side of things. He wore a large black hat that looked like a raven with widespread wings, and a velvet vest across which the patina of the centuries had skated. But in spite of his immense wisdom and his mysterious breadth, he had a human burden, an earthly condition that kept him involved in the small problems of daily life. He would complain of the ailments of old age, he suffered from the most insignificant economic difficulties, and he had stopped laughing a long time back because scurvy had made his teeth drop out. On that suffocating noontime when the gypsy revealed his secrets, José Arcadio Buendía had the certainty that it was the beginning of a great friendship. The children were startled by his fantastic stories. Aureliano, who could not have been more than five at the time, would remember him for the rest of his life as he saw him that afternoon, sitting against the metallic and quivering light from the window, lighting up with his deep organ voice the darkest reaches of the imagination, while down over his temples there flowed the grease that was being melted by the heat. José Arcadio, his older brother, would pass on that wonderful image as a hereditary memory to all of his descendants. Úrsula on the other hand, held a bad memory of that visit, for she had entered the room just as Melquíades had carelessly broken a flask of bichloride of mercury.

"It's the smell of the devil," she said.

"Not at all," Melquíades corrected her. "It has been proven that the devil has sulphuric properties and this is just a little corrosive sublimate."

Always didactic, he went into a learned exposition of the diabolical properties of cinnabar, but Úrsula paid no attention to him, although she took the children off to pray. That biting odor would stay forever in her mind linked to the memory of Melquíades.

The rudimentary laboratory-in addition to a profusion of pots, funnels, retorts, filters, and sieves-was made up of a primitive water pipe, a glass beaker with a long, thin neck, a reproduction of the philosopher's egg, and a still the gypsies themselves had built in accordance with modern descriptions of the three-armed alembic of Mary the Jew. Along with those items, Melquíades left samples of the seven metals that corresponded to the seven planets, the formulas of Moses and Zosimus for doubling the quantity of gold, and a set of notes and sketches concerning the processes of the Great Teaching that would permit those who could interpret them to undertake the manufacture of the philosopher's stone. Seduced by the simplicity of the formulas to double the quantity of gold, José Arcadio Buendía paid court to Úrsula for several weeks so that she would let him dig up her colonial coins and increase them by as many times as it was possible to subdivide mercury. Úrsula gave in, as always, to her husband's unyielding obstinacy. Then José Arcadio Buendía threw three doubloons into a pan and fused them with copper filings, orpiment, brimstone, and lead. He put it all to boil in a pot of castor oil until he got a thick and pestilential syrup which was more like common caramel than valuable gold. In risky and desperate processes of distillation, melted with the seven planetary metals, mixed with hermetic mercury and vitriol of Cyprus, and put back to cook in hog fat for lack of any radish oil, Úrsula's precious inheritance was reduced to a large piece of burnt hog cracklings that was firmly stuck to the bottom of the pot.

When the gypsies came back, Úrsula had turned the whole population of the village against them. But curiosity was greater than fear, for that time the gypsies went about the town making a deafening noise with all manner of musical instruments while a hawker announced the exhibition of the most fabulous discovery of the Naciancenes. So that everyone went to the tent and by paying one cent they saw a youthful Melquíades, recovered, unwrinkled, with a new and flashing set of teeth. Those who remembered his gums that had been destroyed by scurvy, his flaccid cheeks, and his withered lips trembled with fear at the final proof of the gypsy's supernatural power. The fear turned into panic when Melquíades took out his teeth, intact, encased in their gums, and showed them to the audience for an instant-a fleeting instant in which he went back to being the same decrepit man of years past-and put them back again and smiled once more with the full control of his restored youth. Even José Arcadio Buendía himself considered that Melquíades' knowledge had reached unbearable extremes, but he felt a healthy excitement when the gypsy explained to him atone the workings of his false teeth. It seemed so simple and so prodigious at the same time that overnight he lost all interest in his experiments in alchemy. He underwent a new crisis of bad humor. He did not go back to eating regularly, and he would spend the day walking through the house. "Incredible things are happening in the world," he said to Úrsula. "Right there across the river there are all kinds of magical instruments while we keep on living like donkeys." Those who had known him since the foundation of Macondo were startled at how much he had changed under Melquíades' influence.

At first José Arcadio Buendía had been a kind of youthful patriarch who would give instructions for planting and advice for the raising of children and animals, and who collaborated with everyone, even in the physical work, for the welfare of the community. Since his house from the very first had been the best in the village, the others had been built in its image and likeness. It had a small, well-lighted living roost, a dining room in the shape of a terrace with gaily colored flowers, two bedrooms, a courtyard with a gigantic chestnut tree, a well kept garden, and a corral where goats, pigs, and hens lived in peaceful communion. The only animals that were prohibited, not just in his house but in the entire settlement, were fighting cocks.

Úrsula's capacity for work was the same as that of her husband. Active, small, severe, that woman of unbreakable nerves who at no moment in her life had been heard to sing seemed to be everywhere, from dawn until quite late at night, always pursued by the soft whispering of her stiff, starched petticoats. Thanks to her the floors of tamped earth, the unwhitewashed mud walls, the rustic, wooden furniture they had built themselves were always dean, and the old chests where they kept their clothes exhaled the warm smell of basil.

José Arcadio Buendía, who was the most enterprising man ever to be seen in the village, had set up the placement of the houses in such a way that from all of them one could reach the river and draw water with the same effort, and he had lined up the streets with such good sense that no house got more sun than another during the hot time of day. Within a few years Macondo was a village that was more orderly and hard working than any known until then by its three hundred inhabitants. It was a truly happy village where no one was over thirty years of age and where no one had died.

Since the time of its founding, José Arcadio Buendía had built traps and cages. In a short time he filled not only his own house but all of those in the village with troupials, canaries, bee eaters, and redbreasts. The concert of so many different birds became so disturbing that Úrsula would plug her ears with beeswax so as not to lose her sense of reality. The first time that Melquíades' tribe arrived, selling glass balls for headaches, everyone was surprised that they had been able to find that village lost in the drowsiness of the swamp, and the gypsies confessed that they had found their way by the song of the birds.

That spirit of social initiative disappeared in a short time, pulled away by the fever of the magnets, the astronomical calculations, the dreams of transmutation, and the urge to discover the wonders of the world. From a clean and active man, José Arcadio Buendía changed into a man lazy in appearance, careless in his dress, with a wild beard that Úrsula managed to trim with great effort and a kitchen knife. There were many who considered him the victim of some strange spell. But even those most convinced of his madness left work and family to follow him when he brought out his tools to clear the land and asked the assembled group to open a way that would put Macondo in contact with the great inventions.

José Arcadio Buendía was completely ignorant of the geography of the region. He knew that to the east there lay an impenetrable mountain chain and that on the other side of the mountains there was the ardent city of Riohacha, where in times past—according to what he had been told by the first Aureliano Buendía, his grandfather—Sir Francis Drake had gone crocodile hunting with cannons and that he repaired hem and stuffed them with straw to bring to Queen Elizabeth. In his youth, José Arcadio Buendía and his men, with wives and children, animals and all kinds of domestic implements, had crossed the mountains in search of an outlet to the sea, and after twenty-six months they gave up the expedition and founded Macondo, so they would not have to go back. It was, therefore, a route that did not interest him, for it could lead only to the past. To the south lay the swamps, covered with an eternal vegetable scum and the whole vast universe of the great swamp, which, according to what the gypsies said, had no limits. The great swamp in the west mingled with a boundless extension of water where there were soft-skinned cetaceans that had the head and torso of a woman, causing the ruination of sailors with the charm of their extraordinary breasts. The gypsies sailed along that route for six months before they reached the strip of land over which the mules that carried the mail passed. According to José Arcadio Buendía's calculations, the only possibility of contact with civilization lay along the northern route. So he handed out clearing tools and hunting weapons to the same men who had been with him during the founding of Macondo. He threw his directional instruments and his maps into a knapsack, and he undertook the reckless adventure.

During the first days they did not come across any appreciable obstacle. They went down along the stony bank of the river to the place where years before they had found the soldier's armor, and from there they went into the woods along a path between wild orange trees. At the end of the first week they killed and roasted a deer, but they agreed to eat only half of it and salt the rest for the days that lay ahead. With that precaution they tried to postpone the necessity of having to eat macaws, whose blue flesh had a harsh and musky taste. Then, for more than ten days, they did not see the sun again. The ground became soft and damp, like volcanic ash, and the vegetation was thicker and thicker, and the cries of the birds and the uproar of the monkeys became more and more remote, and the world became eternally sad. The men on the expedition felt overwhelmed by their most ancient memories in that paradise of dampness and silence, going back to before original sin, as their boots sank into pools of steaming oil and their machetes destroyed bloody lilies and golden salamanders. For a week, almost without speaking, they went ahead like sleepwalkers through a universe of grief, lighted only by the tenuous reflection of luminous insects, and their lungs were overwhelmed by a suffocating smell of blood. They could not return because the strip that they were opening as they went along would soon close up with a new vegetation that. almost seemed to grow before their eyes. "It's all right," José Arcadio Buendía would say. "The main thing is not to lose our bearings." Always following his compass, he kept on guiding his men toward the invisible north so that they would be able to get out of that enchanted region. It was a thick night, starless, but the darkness was becoming impregnated with a fresh and clear air. Exhausted by the long crossing, they hung up their hammocks and slept deeply for the first time in two weeks. When they woke up, with the sun already high in the sky, they were speechless with fascination. Before them, surrounded by ferns and palm trees, white and powdery in the silent morning light, was an enormous Spanish galleon. Tilted slightly to the starboard, it had hanging from its intact masts the dirty rags of its sails in the midst of its rigging, which was adorned with orchids. The hull, covered with an armor of petrified barnacles and soft moss, was firmly fastened into a surface of stones. The whole structure seemed to occupy its own space, one of solitude and oblivion, protected from the vices of time and the habits of the birds. Inside, where the expeditionaries explored with careful intent, there was nothing but a thick forest of flowers.

The discovery of the galleon, an indication of the proximity of the sea, broke José Arcadio Buendía's drive. He considered it a trick of his whimsical fate to have searched for the sea without finding it, at the cost of countless sacrifices and suffering, and to have found it all of a sudden without looking for it, as if it lay across his path like an insurmountable object. Many years later Colonel Aureliano Buendía crossed the region again, when it was already a regular mail route, and the only part of the ship he found was its burned-out frame in the midst of a field of poppies. Only then, convinced that the story had not been some product of his father's imagination, did he wonder how the galleon had been able to get inland to that spot. But José Arcadio Buendía did not concern himself with that when he found the sea after another four days' journey from the galleon. His dreams ended as he faced that ashen, foamy, dirty sea, which had not merited the risks and sacrifices of the adventure.

"God damn it!" he shouted. "Macondo is surrounded by water on all sides."

The idea of a peninsular Macondo prevailed for a long time, inspired by the arbitrary map that José Arcadio Buendía sketched on his return from the expedition. He drew it in rage, evilly, exaggerating the difficulties of communication, as if to punish himself for the absolute lack of sense with which he had chosen the place. "We'll never get anywhere," he lamented to Úrsula. "We're going to rot our lives away here without receiving the benefits of science." That certainty, mulled over for several months in the small room he used as his laboratory, brought him to the conception of the plan to move Maeondo to a better place. But that time Úrsula had anticipated his feverish designs. With the secret and implacable labor of a small ant she predisposed the women of the village against the flightiness of their husbands, who were already preparing for the move. José Arcadio Buendía did not know at what moment or because of what adverse forces his plan had become enveloped in a web of pretexts, disappointments, and evasions until it turned into nothing but an illusion. Úrsula watched him with innocent attention and even felt some pity for him on the morning when she found him in the back room muttering about his plans for moving as he placed his laboratory pieces in their original boxes. She let him finish. She let him nail up the boxes and put his initials on them with an inked brush, without reproaching him, but knowing now that he knew (because she had heard him say so in his soft monologues) that the men of the village would not back him up in his undertaking. Only when he began to take down the door of the room did Úrsula dare ask him what he was doing, and he answered with a certain bitterness. "Since no one wants to leave, we'll leave all by ourselves." Úrsula did not become upset.

"We will not leave," she said. "We will stay here, because we have had a son here."

"We have still not had a death," he said. "A person does not belong to a place until there is someone dead under the ground."

Úrsula replied with a soft firmness:

"If I have to die for the rest of you to stay here, I will die."

José Arcadio Buendía had not thought that his wife's will was so firm. He tried to seduce her with the charm of his fantasy, with the promise of a prodigious world where all one had to do was sprinkle some magic liquid on the ground and the plants would bear fruit whenever a man wished, and where all manner of instruments against pain were sold at bargain prices. But Úrsula was insensible to his clairvoyance.

"Instead of going around thinking about your crazy inventions, you should be worrying about your sons," she replied. "Look at the state they're in, running wild just like donkeys."

José Arcadio Buendía took his wife's words literally. He looked out the window and saw the barefoot children in the sunny garden and he had the impression that only at that instant had they begun to exist, conceived by Úrsula's spell, Something occurred inside of him then, something mysterious and definitive that uprooted him from his own time and carried him adrift through an unexplored region of his memory. While Úrsula continued sweeping the house, which was safe now from being abandoned for the rest of her life, he stood there with an absorbed look, contemplating the children until his eyes became moist and he dried them with the back of his hand, exhaling a deep sigh of resignation.

"All right," he said. "Tell them to come help me take the things out of the boxes."

José Arcadio, the older of the children, was fourteen. He had a square head, thick hair, and his father's character. Although he had the same impulse for growth and physical strength, it was early evident that he lacked imagination. He had been conceived and born during the difficult crossing of the mountains, before the founding of Macondo, and his parents gave thanks to heaven when they saw he had no animal features. Aureliano, the first human being to be born in Macondo, would be six years old in March. He was silent and withdrawn. He had wept in his mother's womb and had been born with his eyes open. As they were cutting the umbilical cord, he moved his head from side to side, taking in the things in the room and examining the faces of the people with a fearless curiosity. Then, indifferent to those who came close to look at him, he kept his attention concentrated on the palm roof, which looked as if it were about to collapse under the tremendous pressure of the rain. Úrsula did not remember the intensity of that look again until one day when little Aureliano, at the age of three, went into the kitchen at the moment she was taking a pot of boiling soup from the stove and putting it on the table. The child, Perplexed, said from the doorway, "It's going to spill." The pot was firmly placed in the center of the table, but just as soon as the child made his announcement, it began an unmistakable movement toward the edge, as if impelled by some inner dynamism, and it fell and broke on the floor. Úrsula, alarmed, told her husband about the episode, but he interpreted it as a natural phenomenon. That was the way he always was alien to the existence of his sons, partly because he considered childhood as a period of mental insufficiency, and partly because he was always too absorbed in his fantastic speculations.

But since the afternoon when he called the children in to help him unpack the things in the laboratory, he gave them his best hours. In the small separate room, where the walls were gradually being covered by strange maps and fabulous drawings, he taught them to read and write and do sums, and he spoke to them about the wonders of the world, not only where his learning had extended, but forcing the limits of his imagination to extremes. It was in that way that the boys ended up learning that in the southern extremes of Africa there were men so intelligent and peaceful that their only pastime was to sit and think, and that it was possible to cross the Aegean Sea on foot by jumping from island to island all the way to the port of Salonika. Those hallucinating sessions remained printed on the memories of the boys in such a way that many years later, a second before the regular army officer gave the firing squad the command to fire, Colonel Aureliano Buendía saw once more that warm March afternoon on which his father had interrupted the lesson in physics and stood fascinated, with his hand in the air and his eyes motionless, listening to the distant pipes, drums, and jingles of the gypsies, who were coming to the village once more, announcing the latest and most startling discovery of the sages of Memphis.

They were new gypsies, young men and women who knew only their own language, handsome specimens with oily skins and intelligent hands, whose dances and music sowed a panic of uproarious joy through the streets, with parrots painted all colors reciting Italian arias, and a hen who laid a hundred golden eggs to the sound of a tambourine, and a trained monkey who read minds, and the multi-use machine that could be used at the same time to sew on buttons and reduce fevers, and the apparatus to make a person forget his bad memories, and a poultice to lose time, and a thousand more inventions so ingenious and unusual that José Arcadio Buendía must have wanted to invent a memory machine so that he could remember them all. In an instant they transformed the village. The inhabitants of Macondo found themselves lost is their own streets, confused by the crowded fair.

Holding a child by each hand so as not to lose them in the tumult, bumping into acrobats with gold-capped teeth and jugglers with six arms, suffocated by the mingled breath of manure and sandals that the crowd exhaled, José Arcadio Buendía went about everywhere like a madman, looking for Melquíades so that he could reveal to him the infinite secrets of that fabulous nightmare. He asked several gypsies, who did not understand his language. Finally he reached the place where Melquíades used to set up his tent and he found a taciturn Armenian who in Spanish was hawking a syrup to make oneself invisible. He had drunk down a glass of the amber substance in one gulp as José Arcadio Buendía elbowed his way through the absorbed group that was witnessing the spectacle, and was able to ask his question. The gypsy wrapped him in the frightful climate of his look before he turned into a puddle of pestilential and smoking pitch over which the echo of his reply still floated: "Melquíades is dead." Upset by the news, José Arcadio Buendía stood motionless, trying to rise above his affliction, until the group dispersed, called away by other artifices, and the puddle of the taciturn Armenian evaporated completely. Other gypsies confirmed later on that Melquíades had in fact succumbed to the fever on the beach at Singapore and that his body had been thrown into the deepest part of the Java Sea. The children had no interest in the news. They insisted that their father take them to see the overwhelming novelty of the sages of Memphis that was being advertised at the entrance of a tent that, according to what was said, had belonged to King Solomon. They insisted so much that José Arcadio Buendía paid the thirty reales and led them into the center of the tent, where there was a giant with a hairy torso and a shaved head, with a copper ring in his nose and a heavy iron chain on his ankle, watching over a pirate chest. When it was opened by the giant, the chest gave off a glacial exhalation. Inside there was only an enormous, transparent block with infinite internal needles in which the light of the sunset was broken up into colored stars. Disconcerted, knowing that the children were waiting for an immediate explanation, José Arcadio Buendía ventured a murmur:

"It's the largest diamond in the world."

"No," the gypsy countered. "It's ice."

José Arcadio Buendía, without understanding, stretched out his hand toward the cake, but the giant moved it away. "Five reales more to touch it," he said. José Arcadio Buendía paid them and put his hand on the ice and held it there for several minutes as his heart filled with fear and jubilation at the contact with mystery. Without knowing what to say, he paid ten reales more so that his sons could have that prodigious experience. Little José Arcadio refused to touch it. Aureliano, on the other hand, took a step forward and put his hand on it, withdrawing it immediately. "It's boiling," he exclaimed, startled. But his father paid no attention to him. Intoxicated by the evidence of the miracle, he forgot at that moment about the frustration of his delirious undertakings and Melquíades' body, abandoned to the appetite of the squids. He paid another five reales and with his hand on the cake, as if giving testimony on the holy scriptures, he exclaimed:

"This is the great invention of our time."

(选自 Gabriel Garcia Marquez. *One Hundred Years of Solitude*. New York: Avon Books, 1971. pp.8-15.)

Questions

1. Please describe the personality of José Arcadio Buendía.
2. What does the history of Maconda represent for?
3. How to understand the title of this book?
4. Why does writer create this imaginary town, Macondo?
5. How many main mythical elements are mentioned in this book?

Unit 9

Virginia Woolf: *Mrs Dalloway*

Adeline Virginia Woolf (1882—1941) was an English writer, who is considered one of the most important modernist authors in the 20th century and a pioneer in the use of stream of consciousness as a narrative device.

Virginia Woolf, was born into an affluent household in South Kensington, London. She was the seventh child in a blended family of eight. Her mother, Julia Stephen, celebrated as a Pre-Raphaelite artist's model, had three children from her first marriage, her father Leslie Stephen, a notable man of letters, had one previous daughter, and four children were born in her parents' second marriage, of whom the most well-known was the modernist painter Vanessa Stephen (later Vanessa Bell). While the boys in the family were educated at university, the girls were home-schooled in English classics and Victorian literature. An important influence in Woolf's early life was the summer home the family used in St Ives, Cornwall, where she first saw the Godrevy Lighthouse, which was to become iconic in her novel *To the Lighthouse* (1927). Virginia Woolf and her sisters were able to attend the Ladies' Department of King's College, where they studied classics and history (1897—1901) and came into contact with early reformers of women's higher education and the women's rights movement. Other important influences were their Cambridge-educated brothers and unfettered access to their father's vast library. Woolf's father encouraged her to become a writer and she began writing professionally in 1900. Their father's death in 1905 was a major turning point in their lives and the cause of another breakdown, following which the Stephens moved from Kensington to the more bohemian Bloomsbury, where they adopted a free-spirited lifestyle. It was there that, in conjunction with their brothers' intellectual friends, they formed the artistic and literary

Bloomsbury Group. With Vanessa's marriage in 1907, Virginia became more independent, marrying Leonard Woolf in 1912. With Leonard she founded the Hogarth Press in 1917, which published much of her work. In 1910, Woolf started to feel the need to have a retreat away from London, in Sussex, and following the destruction of their London home during the war, in 1940, the Woolfs moved there permanently.

During the interwar period, Virginia Woolf was an important part of London's literary and artistic society. She published her first novel, titled *The Voyage Out*, in 1915, through her half-brother's publishing house, Gerald Duckworth and Company. Her best-known works include the novels *Mrs. Dalloway* (1925), *To the Lighthouse* (1927) and *Orlando* (1928). She is also known for her essays, including *A Room of One's Own* (1929), where she wrote the much-quoted dictum, "A woman must have money and a room of her own if she is to write fiction." A major influence on Woolf from 1912 onward was Russian literature as Woolf adopted many of its aesthetic conventions. The style of Fyodor Dostoyevsky with his depiction of a fluid mind in operation helped to influence Woolf's writings about a "discontinuous writing process", though Woolf objected to Dostoyevsky's obsession with "psychological extremity" and the "tumultuous flux of emotions" in his characters together with his right-wing, monarchist politics as Dostoyevsky was an ardent supporter of the autocracy of the Russian Empire. In contrast to her objections to Dostoyevsky's "exaggerated emotional pitch," Woolf found much to admire in the work of Anton Chekhov and Leo Tolstoy. Woolf admired Chekhov for his stories of ordinary people living their lives, doing banal things and plots that had no neat endings. From Tolstoy, Woolf drew lessons about how a novelist should depict a character's psychological state and the interior tension within. From Ivan Turgenev, Woolf drew the lessons that the novelist needed to balance those multiple versions of him or herself to balance the "mundane facts" of a story vs. the writer's overreaching vision, which required a "total passion" for art. Throughout her life Woolf was troubled by bouts of mental illness and attempted suicide. Her illness is considered to be bipolar disorder, for which there was no effective intervention in her lifetime. Eventually in 1941 she drowned herself in a river at age 59.

VirginaWoolf became one of the central subjects of the 1970s movement of feminist criticism, and her works have since garnered much attention and widespread commentary for "inspiring feminism," an aspect of her writing that was unheralded earlier. Her works are widely read all over the world and have been translated into more than 50 languages. A large body of literature is dedicated to her life and work, and she has been the subject of many plays, novels, and films.

Theme

Mrs. Dalloway is a novel by Virginia Woolf that details a day in the life of Clarissa Dalloway, a fictional high-society woman in post-First World War England. Clarissa Dalloway goes around London in the morning, getting ready to host a party that evening. The nice day reminds her of her youth spent in the countryside in Bourton and makes her wonder about her choice of husband; she married the reliable Richard Dalloway instead of the enigmatic and demanding Peter Walsh, and she "had not the option" to be with Sally Seton. Peter reintroduces these conflicts by paying a visit that morning. Septimus Warren Smith, a First World War veteran suffering from deferred traumatic stress, spends his day in the park with his Italian-born wife Lucrezia, where Peter Walsh observes them. The novel has two main narrative lines involving two separate characters (Clarissa Dalloway and Septimus Smith); within each narrative there is a particular time and place in the past that the main characters keep returning to in their minds.

Term

Stream of Consciousness: is a narrative device with which the author makes an attempt to depict the exact process of mental workings of the character (mainly narrator), with all its illogical darts and dashes and sudden turns and free associations. Both Faulkner and Joyce employed this literary device in some of their works. It's the flow of sense perceptions, thoughts, feelings, and memories in the human mind; or a literary method of representing such a blending of mental processes in fictional characters, usually in an unpunctuated or disjointed form of *interior monologue*. While an interior monologue always presents a character's thoughts "directly", without the apparent intervention of a summarizing and selecting narrator, it does not necessarily mingle them with impressions and perceptions, nor does it necessarily violate the norms of grammar, syntax, and logic; but the steam-of-consciousness technique also does one or both of these things. An important device of modernist fiction and its later imitators, the technique was pioneered by Dorothy Richardson in *Pilgrimage* and by James Joyce in *Ulysses*, and further developed by Virginia Woolf in *Mrs. Dalloway* and William Faulkner in *The Sound and the Fury*.

Excerpt

Lucy came running full tilt downstairs, having just nipped in to the drawing-room to smooth a cover, to straighten a chair, to pause a moment and feel whoever came in must think how clean, how bright, how beautifully cared for, when they saw the beautiful silver, the brass fire-irons, the new chair-covers, and the curtains of yellow Ochintz: she appraised each; heard a roar of voices; people already coming up from dinner; she must fly!

The Prime Minister was coming, Agnes said: so she had heard them say in the dining-room, she said, coming in with a tray of glasses. Did it matter, did it matter in the least, one Prime Minister more or less? It made no difference at this hour of the night to Mrs. Walker among the plates, saucepans, cullenders, frying-pans, chicken in aspic, ice-cream freezers, pared crusts of bread, lemons, soup tureens, and pudding basins which, however hard they washed up in the scullery seemed to be all on top of her, on the kitchen table, on chairs, while the fire blared and roared, the electric lights glared, and still supper had to be laid. All she felt was, one Prime Minister more or less made not a scrap of difference to Mrs. Walker.

The ladies were going upstairs already, said Lucy; the ladies were going up, one by one, Mrs. Dalloway walking last and almost always sending back some message to the kitchen, "My love to Mrs. Walker," that was it one night. Next morning they would go over the dishes—the soup, the salmon; the salmon, Mrs. Walker knew, as usual underdone, for she always got nervous about the pudding and left it to Jenny; so it happened, the salmon was always underdone. But some lady with fair hair and silver ornaments had said, Lucy said, about the entrée, was it really made at home? But it was the salmon that bothered Mrs. Walker, as she spun the plates round and round, and pulled in dampers and pulled out dampers; and there came a burst of laughter from the dining-room; a voice speaking; then another burst of laughter—the gentlemen enjoying themselves when the ladies had gone. The tokay, said Lucy running in. Mr. Dalloway had sent for the tokay, from the Emperor's cellars, the Imperial Tokay.

It was borne through the kitchen. Over her shoulder Lucy reported how Miss Elizabeth looked quite lovely; she couldn't take her eyes off her; in her pink dress, wearing the necklace Mr. Dalloway had given her. Jenny must remember the dog, Miss Elizabeth's fox-terrier, which, since it bit, had to be shut up and might, Elizabeth thought, want something. Jenny must remember the dog. But Jenny was not going upstairs with all those people about. There was a motor at the door already! There was a ring at the bell—and the gentlemen still in the dining-room, drinking tokay!

There, they were going upstairs; that was the first to come, and now they would come faster and faster, so that Mrs. Parkinson (hired for parties) would leave the hall door ajar, and the hall would be full of gentlemen waiting (they stood waiting, sleeking down their hair) while the ladies took their cloaks off in the room along the passage; where Mrs. Barnet helped them, old Ellen Barnet, who had been with the family for forty years, and came every summer to help the ladies, and remembered mothers when they were girls, and though very unassuming did shake hands; said "milady" very respectfully, yet had a humorous way with her, looking at the young ladies, and ever so tactfully helping Lady Lovejoy, who had some trouble with her underbodice. And they could not help feeling, Lady Lovejoy and Miss Alice, that some little privilege in the matter of brush and comb, was awarded them having known Mrs. Barnet— "thirty years, milady," Mrs. Barnet supplied her. Young ladies did not use to rouge, said Lady Lovejoy, when they stayed at Bourton in the old days. And Miss Alice didn't need rouge, said Mrs. Barnet looking at her fondly. There Mrs. Barnet would sit, in the cloakroom patting down the furs, smoothing out the Spanish shawls, tidying the dressing-table, and knowing perfectly well, in spite of the furs and the embroideries, which were nice ladies, which were not. The dear old body, said Lady Lovejoy, mounting the stairs, Clarissa's old nurse.

And then Lady Lovejoy stiffened. "Lady and Miss Lovejoy," she said to Mr. Wilkins (hired for parties). He had an admirable manner, as he bent and straightened himself, bent and straightened himself and announced with perfect impartiality "Lady and Miss Lovejoy ... Sir John and Lady Needham ... Miss Weld ... Mr. Walsh." His manner was admirable; his family life must be irreproachable, except that it seemed impossible that a being with greenish lips and shaven cheeks could ever have blundered into the nuisance of children.

"How delightful to see you!" said Clarissa. She said it to everyone. How delightful to see you! She was at her worst—effusive, insincere. It was a great mistake to have come. He should have stayed at home and read his book, thought Peter Walsh; should have gone to a music hall; he should have stayed at home, for he knew no one.

Oh dear, it was going to be a failure; a complete failure, Clarissa felt it in her bones as dear old Lord Lexham stood there apologizing for his wife who had caught cold at the Buckingham Palace garden party. She could see Peter out of the tail of her eye, criticising her, there, in that corner. Why, after all, did she do these things? Why seek pinnacles and stand drenched in fire? Might it consume her anyhow! Burn her to cinders! Better anything, better brandish one's torch and hurl it to earth than taper and dwindle away like some Ellie Henderson! It was extraordinary how Peter put her into these states just by coming and standing in a corner. He made her see herself; exaggerate. It was idiotic. But why did he come, then, merely to criticise? Why always take, never give? Why not risk one's one little point of view? There he was wandering off, and she must speak to him. But she would not get the chance. Life was that—humiliation, renunciation. What Lord Lexham was saying was that his wife would not wear her furs at the garden party because "my dear, you ladies are all alike"—Lady Lexham being seventy-five at least! It was delicious, how they petted each other, that old couple. She did like old Lord Lexham. She did think it mattered, her party, and it made her feel quite sick to know that it was all going wrong, all falling flat. Anything, any explosion, any horror was better than people wandering aimlessly, standing in a bunch at a cornerlike Ellie Henderson, not even caring to hold themselves upright.

Gently the yellow curtain with all the birds of Paradise blew out and it seemed as if there were a flight of wings into the room, right out, then sucked back. (For the windows were open.) Was it draughty, Ellie Henderson wondered? She was subject to chills. But it did not matter that she should come down sneezing to-morrow; it was the girls with their naked shoulders she thought of, being trained to think of others by an old father, an invalid, late vicar of Bourton, but he was dead now; and her chills never went to her chest, never. It was the girls she thought of, the young girls with their baren shoulders, she herself having always been a wisp of a creature, with her thin hair and meagre profile; though now, past fifty, there was beginning to shine through some mild beam, something purified into distinction by years of self-abnegation but obscured again, perpetually, by her distressing gentility, her panic fear, which arose from three hundred pounds' income, and her weaponless state (she could not earn a penny) and it made her timid, and more and more disqualified year by year to meet well-dressed people who did this sort of thing every night of the season, merely telling their maids "I'll wear so and so," whereas Ellie Henderson ran out nervously and bought cheap pink flowers, half a dozen, and then threw a shawl over her old black dress. For her invitation to Clarissa's party had come at the last moment. She was not quite happy about it. She had a sort of feeling that

Clarissa had not meant to ask her this year.

Why should she? There was no reason really, except that they had always known each other. Indeed, they were cousins. But naturally they had rather drifted apart, Clarissa being so sought after. It was an event to her, going to a party. It was quite a treat just to see the lovely clothes. Wasn't that Elizabeth, grown up, with her hair done in the fashionable way, in the pink dress? Yet she could not be more than seventeen. She was very, very handsome. But girls when they first came out didn't seem to wear white as they used (She must remember everything to tell Edith.) Girls wore straight frocks, perfectly tight, with skirts well above the ankles. It was not becoming, she thought.

So, with her weak eyesight, Ellie Henderson craned rather forward, it wasn't so much she who minded not having any one to (she hardly knew anybody there), for she felt that they were all such interesting people to watch; politicians presumably; Richard Dalloway's friends; but it was Richard himself who felt that he could not let the poor creature go on standing there all the evening by herself.

"Well, Ellie, and how's the world treating *you*?" he said in his genial way, and Ellie Henderson, getting nervous and flushing and feeing that it was extraordinarily nice of him to come and talk to her, said that many people really felt the heat more than the cold.

"Yes, they do," said Richard Dalloway. "Yes."

But what more did one say?

"Hullo, Richard," said somebody, taking him by the elbow, and, good Lord, there was old Peter, old Peter Walsh. He was delighted to see him—ever so pleased to see him! He hadn't changed a bit. And off they went together walking right across the room, giving each other little pats, as if they hadn't met for a long time, Ellie Henderson thought, watching them go, certain she knew that man's face. A tall man, middle aged, rather fine eyes, dark, wearing spectacles, with a look of John Burrows. Edith would be sure to know.

The curtain with its flight of birds of Paradise blew out again. And Clarissa saw—she saw Ralph Lyon beat it back, and go on talking. So it wasn't a failure after all! it was going to be all right now—her party. It had begun. It had started. But it was still touch and go. She must stand there for the present. People seemed to come in a rush.

Colonel and Mrs. Garrod ... Mr. Hugh Whit-bread ... Mr. Bowley ... Mrs. Hilbery ... Lady Mary Maddox ... Mr. Quin ... intoned Wilkin. She had six or seven words with each, and they went on, they went into the rooms; into something now, not nothing, since Ralph Lyon had beat back the curtain.

And yet for her own part, it was too much of an effort. She was not enjoying it. It was too much like being—just anybody, standing there; anybody could do it; yet this anybody she did a little admire, couldn't help feeling that she had, anyhow, made this happen, that it marked a stage, this post that she felt herself to have become, for oddly enough she had quite forgotten what she looked like, but felt herself a stake driven in at the top of her stairs. Every time she gave a party she had this feeling of being something not herself, and that every one was unreal in one way; much more real in another. It was, she thought, partly their clothes, partly being taken out of their ordinary ways, partly the background, it was possible to say things you couldn't say anyhow else, things that needed an effort; possible to go much deeper. But not for her; not yet anyhow.

"How delightful to see you!" she said. Dear old Sir Harry! He would know every one.

And what was so odd about it was the sense one had as they came up the stairs one after another, Mrs. Mount and Celia, Herbert Ainsty, Mrs. Dakers—oh and Lady Bruton!

"How awfully good of you to come!" she said, and she meant it—it was odd how standing there one felt them going on, going on, some quite old, some ...

What name? Lady Rosseter? But who on earth was Lady Rosseter?

"Clarissa!" That voice! It was Sally Seton! Sally Seton! after all these years! She loomed through a mist. For she hadn't looked like that, Sally Seton, when Clarissa grasped the hot water can, to think of her under this roof, under this roof! Not like that!

All on top of each other, embarrassed, laughing, words tumbled out—passing through London; heard from Clara Haydon; what a chance of seeing you! So I thrust myself in—without an invitation ... .

One might put down the hot water can quite composedly. The lustre had gone out of her. Yet it was extraordinary to see her again, older, happier, less lovely. They kissed each other, first this cheek, then that, by the drawing-room door, and Clarissa turned, with Sally's hand in hers, and saw her rooms full, heard the roar of voices, saw the candlesticks, the blowing curtains, and the roses which Richard had given her.

"I have five enormous boys," said Sally.

She had the simplest egotism, the most open desire to be thought first always, and Clarissa loved her for being still like that. "I can't believe it!" she cried, kindling all over with pleasure at the thought of the past.

But alas, Wilkins; Wilkins wanted her; Wilkins was emitting in a voice of commanding authority as if the whole company must be admonished and the hostess reclaimed from frivolity, one name:

"The Prime Minister," said Peter Walsh.

The Prime Minister? Was it really? Ellie Henderson marvelled. What a thing to tell Edith!

One couldn't laugh at him. He looked so ordinary. You might have stood him behind a counter and bought biscuits—poor chap, all rigged up in gold lace. And to be fair, as he went his rounds, first with Clarissa then with Richard escorting him, he did it very well. He tried to look somebody. It was amusing to watch. Nobody looked him. They just went on talking, yet it was perfectly plain that they knew, felt to the marrow of their bones, this majesty passing; this symbol of what they all stood for, English society. Old Lady Bruto and she looked very fine too, very stalwart in her lace, swam up, and they withdrew into a little room which at once became spied upon, guarded, and a sort of stir and rustle rippled through everyone, openly: the Prime Minister!

Lord, lord, the snobbery of the English! thought Peter Walsh, standing in the corner. How they loved dressing up in gold lace and doing homage! There! That must be, by Jove it was, Hugh Whitbread, snuffing round the precincts of the great, grown rather fatter, rather whiter, the admirable Hugh!

He looked always as if he were on duty, thought Peter, a privileged, but secretive being, hoarding secrets which he would die to defend, though it was only some little piece of tittle-tattle dropped by a court footman, which would be in all the papers tomorrow. Such were his rattles, his baubles, in playing with which he had grown white, come to the verge of old age, enjoying the respect and affection of all who had the privilege of knowing this type of the English public-school man. Inevitably one made up things like that about Hugh; that was his style; the style of those admirable letters which Peter had read thousands of miles across the sea in the *Times*, and had thanked God he was out of that pernicious hubble-bubble if it were only to hear baboons chatter and coolies beat their wives. An olive-skinned youth from one of the Universities stood obsequiously by. Him he would patronise, initiate, teach how to get on. For he liked nothing better than doing kindnesses, making the hearts of old ladies palpitate with the joy of being thought of in their age, their affliction, thinking themselves quite forgotten, yet here was dear Hugh driving up and spending an hour talking of the past, remembering trifles, praising the home-made cake, though Hugh might eat cake with a Duchess any day of his life, and, to look at him, probably did spend a good deal of time in that agreeable occupation. The All-judging, the All-merciful, might excuse. Peter Walsh had no mercy. Villains there must be, and God knows the rascals who get hanged for battering the brains of a girl out in a train do less harm on the whole than Hugh Whitbread and his kindness. Look at him now, on tiptoe, dancing forward, bowing and scraping, as the Prime Minister and Lady Bruton emerged, intimating for all the world to see that he was privileged to say something, something private, to Lady Bruton as she passed. She stopped. She wagged her fine old head. She was thanking him presumably for some piece of servility. She had her toadies, minor officials in Government offices who ran about putting through little jobs on her behalf, in return for which she gave them luncheon. But she derived from the eighteenth century. She was all right.

And now Clarissa escorted her Prime Minister down the room, prancing, sparkling, with the stateliness of her grey hair. She wore ear-rings, and a silver-green mermaid's dress. Lolloping on the waves and braiding her tresses she seemed, having that gift still; to be; to exist; to sum it all up in the moment as she passed; turned, caught her scarf in some other woman's dress, unhitched it, laughed, all with the most perfect ease and air of a creature floating in its element. But age had brushed her; even as a mermaid might behold in her glass the setting sun on some very clear evening over the waves. There was a breath of tenderness; her severity, her prudery, her woodenness were all warmed through now, and she had about her as she said good-bye to the thick gold-laced man who was doing his best, and good luck to him, to look important, an inexpressible dignity; an exquisite cordiality; as if she wished the whole world well, and must now, being on the very verge and rim of things, take her leave. So she made him think. (But he was not in love.)

Indeed, Clarissa felt, the Prime Minister had been good to come. And, walking down the room with him, with Sally there and Peter there and Richard very pleased, with all those people rather inclined, perhaps, to envy, she had felt that intoxication of the moment, that dilatation of the nerves of the heart itself till it seemed to quiver, steeped, upright;—yes, but after all it was what other people felt, that; for, though she loved it and felt it tingle and sting, still these semblances, these triumphs (dear old Peter, for example, thinking her so brilliant), had a hollowness; at arm's length they were, not in the heart; and it might be that she was growing old but they satisfied her no longer as they used; and suddenly, as she saw the Prime Minister go down the stairs, the gilt rim of the Sir Joshua picture of the little girl with a muff brought back Kilman with a rush; Kilman her enemy. That was satisfying; that was real. Ah, how she hated her—hot, hypocritical, corrupt; with all that power; Elizabeth's seducer; the woman who had crept in to steal and defile (Richard would say, What nonsense!). She hated her: she loved her. It was enemies one wanted, not friends—not Mrs. Durrant and Clara, Sir William and Lady Bradshaw, Miss Truelock and Eleanor Gibson (whom she saw coming upstairs). They must find her if they wanted her. She was for the party!

There was her old friend Sir Harry.

"Dear Sir Harry!" she said, going up to the fine old fellow who had produced more bad pictures than any other two Academicians in the whole of St. John's Wood (they were always of cattle, standing in sunset pools absorbing moisture, or signifying, for he had a certain range of gesture, by the raising of one foreleg and the toss of the antlers, "the Approach of the Stranger"—all his activities, dining out, racing, were founded on cattle standing absorbing moisture in sunset pools).

"What are you laughing at?" she asked him. For Willie Titcomb and Sir Harry and Herbert Ainsty were all laughing. But no. Sir Harry could not tell Clarissa Dalloway (much though he liked her; of her type he thought her perfect, and threatened to paint her) his stories of the music hall stage. He chaffed her about her party. He missed his brandy. These circles, he said, were above him. But he liked her; respected her, in spite of her damnable, difficult upper-class refinement, which made it impossible to ask Clarissa Dalloway to sit on his knee. And up came that wandering will-o'-the-wisp, that vagous phosphorescence, old Mrs. Hilbery, stretching her hands to the blaze of his laughter (about the Duke and the Lady), which, as she heard it across the room, seemed to reassure her on a point which sometimes bothered her if she woke early in the morning and did not like to call her maid for a cup of tea; how it is certain we must die.

"They won't tell us their stories," said Clarissa.

"Dear Clarissa!" exclaimed Mrs. Hilbery. She looked to-night, she said, so like her mother as she first saw her walking in a garden in a grey hat.

And really Clarissa's eyes filled with tears. Her mother, walking in a garden! But alas, she must go.

For there was Professor Brierly, who lectured on Milton, talking to little Jim Hutton (who was unable even for a party like this to compass both tie and waistcoat or make his hair lie flat), and even at this distance they were quarrelling, she could see. For Professor Brierly was a very queer fish. With all those degrees, honours, lectureships between him and the scribblers he suspected instantly an atmosphere not favourable to his queer compound; his prodigious learning and timidity; his wintry charm without cordiality; his innocence blent with snobbery; he quivered if made conscious by a lady's unkempt hair, a youth's boots, of an underworld, very creditable doubtless, of rebels, of ardent young people; of would-be geniuses, and intimated with a little toss of the head, with a sniff—Humph! —the value of moderation; of some slight training in the classics in order to appreciate Milton. Professor Brierly (Clarissa could see) wasn't hitting it off with little Jim Hutton (who wore red socks, his black being at the laundry) about Milton. She interrupted.

She said she loved Bach. So did Hutton. That was the bond between them, and Hutton (a very bad poet) always felt that Mrs. Dalloway was far the best of the great ladies who took an interest in art. It was odd how strict she was. About music she was purely impersonal. She was rather a prig. But how charming to look at! She made her house so nice if it weren't for her Professors. Clarissa had half a mind to snatch him off and set him down at the piano in the back room. For he played divinely.

"But the noise!" she said. "The noise!"

"The sign of a successful party." Nodding urbanely, the Professor stepped delicately off.

"He knows everything in the whole world about Milton," said Clarissa.

"Does he indeed?" said Hutton, who would imitate the Professor throughout Hampstead; the Professor on Milton; the Professor on moderation; the Professor stepping delicately off.

But she must speak to that couple, said Clarissa, Lord Gayton and Nancy Blow.

Not that *they* added perceptibly to the noise of the party. They were not talking (perceptibly) as they stood side by side by the yellow curtains. They would soon be off elsewhere, together; and never had very much to say in any circumstances. They looked; that was all. That was enough. They looked so clean, so sound, she with an apricot bloom of powder and paint, but he scrubbed, rinsed, with the eyes of a bird, so that no ball could pass him or stroke surprise him. He struck, he leapt, accurately, on the spot. Ponies' mouths quivered at the end of his reins. He had his honours, ancestral monuments, banners hanging in the church at home. He had his duties; his tenants; a mother and sisters; had been all day at Lords, and that was what they were talking about—cricket, cousins, the movies—when Mrs. Dalloway came up. Lord Gayton liked her most awfully. So did Miss Blow. She had such charming manners.

"It is angelic—it is delicious of you to have come!" she said. She loved Lords; she loved youth, and Nancy, dressed at enormous expense by the greatest artists in Paris, stood there looking as if her body had merely put forth, of its own accord, a green frill.

"I had meant to have dancing," said Clarissa.

For the young people could not talk. And why should they? Shout, embrace, swing, be up at dawn; carry sugar to ponies; kiss and caress the snouts of adorable chows; and then all tingling and streaming, plunge and swim. But the enormous resources of the English language, the power it bestows, after all, of communicating feelings (at their age, she and Peter would have been arguing all the evening), was not for them. They would solidify young. They would be good beyond measure to the people on the estate, but alone, perhaps, rather dull.

"What a pity!" she said. "I had hoped to have dancing."

It was so extraordinarily nice of them to have come! But talk of dancing! The rooms were packed.

There was old Aunt Helena in her shawl. Alas, she must leave them—Lord Gayton and Nancy Blow. There was old Miss Parry, her aunt.

For Miss Helena Parry was not dead: Miss Parry was alive. She was past eighty. She ascended staircases slowly with a stick. She was placed in a chair (Richard had seen to it). People who had known Burma in the seventies were always led up to her. Where had Peter got to? They used to be such friends. For at the mention of India, or even Ceylon, her eyes (only one was glass) slowly deepened, became blue, beheld, not human beings—she had not ender memories, no proud illusions about Viceroys,

Generals, Mutinies—it was orchids she saw, and mountain passes and herself carried on the backs of coolies in the sixties over solitary peaks; or descending to uproot orchids (startling blossoms, never beheld before) which she painted in water-colour; an indomitable Englishwoman, fretful if disturbed by the War, say, which dropped a bomb at her very door, from her deep meditation over orchids and her own figure journeying in the sixties in India—but here was Peter.

"Come and talk to Aunt Helena about Burma," said Clarissa.

And yet he had not had a word with her all the evening!

"We will talk later," said Clarissa, leading him up to Aunt Helena, in her white shawl, with her stick.

"Peter Walsh," said Clarissa.

That meant nothing.

Clarissa had asked her. It was tiring; it was noisy; but Clarissa had asked her. So she had come. It was a pity that they lived in London—Richard and Clarissa. If only for Clarissa's health it would have been better to live in the country. But Clarissa had always been fond of society.

"He has been in Burma," said Clarissa.

Ah. She could not resist recalling what Charles Darwin had said about her little book on the orchids of Burma.

(Clarissa must speak to Lady Bruton.)

No doubt it was forgotten now, her book on the orchids of Burma, but it went into three editions before 1870, she told Peter. She remembered him now. He had been at Bourton (and he had left her, Peter Walsh remembered, without a word in the drawing-room that night when Clarissa had asked him to come boating). "Richard so much enjoyed his lunch party," said Clarissa to Lady Bruton.

"Richard was the greatest possible help," Lady Bruton replied. "He helped me to write a letter. And how are you?"

"Oh, perfectly well!" said Clarissa. (Lady Bruton detested illness in the wives of politicians.)

"And there's Peter Walsh!" said Lady Bruton (for she could never think of anything to say to Clarissa; though she liked her. She had lots of fine qualities; but they had nothing in common—she and Clarissa. It might have been better if Richard had married a woman with less charm, who would have helped him more in his work. He had lost his chance of the Cabinet). "There's Peter Walsh!" she said, shaking hands with that agreeable sinner, that very able fellow who should have made a name for himself but hadn't (always in difficulties with women), and, of course, old Miss Parry. Wonderful old lady!

Lady Bruton stood by Miss Parry's chair, a spectral grenadier, draped in black, inviting Peter Walsh to lunch; cordial; but without small talk, remembering nothing whatever about the flora or fauna of India. She had been there, of course; had stayed with three Viceroys; thought some of the Indian civilians uncommonly fine fellows; but what a tragedy it was—the state of India! The Prime Minister had just been telling her (old Miss Parry huddled up in her shawl, did not care what the Prime Minister had just been telling her), and Lady Bruton would like to have Peter Walsh's opinion, he being fresh from the centre, and she would get Sir Sampson to meet him, for really it prevented her from sleeping at night, the folly of it, the wickedness she might say, being a soldier's daughter. She was an old woman now, not good for much. But her house, her servants, her good friend Milly Brush—did he remember her? —were all there only asking to be used if—if they could be of help, in short. For she never spoke of England, but this isle of men, this dear, dear land, was in her blood (without reading Shakespeare), and if ever a woman could have worn the helmet and shot the arrow, could have led troops to attack, ruled with indomitable justice barbarian hordes and lain under a shield noseless in a church, or made a green grass mound on some primeval hillside, that woman was Millicent Bruton. Debarred by her sex and some truancy, too, of the logical faculty (she found it impossible to write a letter to the *Times*), she had the thought of Empire always at hand, and had acquired from her association with that armoured goddess her ramrod bearing, her robustness of demeanour, so that one could not figure her even in death parted from the earth or roaming territories over which, in some spiritual shape, the Union Jack had ceased to fly. To be not English even among the dead—no, no! Impossible!

But was it Lady Bruton (whom she used to know)? Was it Peter Walsh grown grey? Lady Rosseter asked herself (who had been Sally Seton). It was old Miss Parry certainly—the old aunt who usedto be so cross when she stayed at Bourton. Never should she forget running along the passage naked, and being sent for by Miss Parry! And Clarissa! oh Clarissa! Sally caught her by the arm.

Clarissa stopped beside them.

"But I can't stay," she said. "I shall come later. Wait," she said, looking at Peter and Sally. They must wait, she meant, until all these people had gone.

"I shall come back," she said, looking at her old friends, Sally and Peter, who were shaking hands, and Sally, remembering the past no doubt, was laughing.

But her voice was wrung of its old ravishing richness; her eyes not aglow as they used to be, when she smoked cigars, when she ran down the passage to fetch her sponge bag, without a stitch of clothing on her, and Ellen Atkins asked, What if the gentlemen had met her? But everybody forgave her. She stole a chicken from the larder because she was hungry in the night; she smoked cigars in her bedroom; she left a priceless book in the punt. But everybody adored her (except perhaps Papa). It was her warmth; her vitality—she would paint, she would write. Old women in the village never to this day forgot to ask after "your friend in the red cloak who seemed so bright." She accused Hugh Whitbread, of all people (and there he was, her old friend Hugh, talking to the Portuguese Ambassador), of kissing her in the smoking-room to punish her for saying that women should have votes. Vulgar men did, she said. And Clarissa remembered having to persuade her not to denounce him at family prayers—which she was capable of doing with her daring, her recklessness, her melodramatic love of being the centre of everything and creating scenes, and it was bound, Clarissa used to think, to end in some awful tragedy; her death; her martyrdom; instead of which she had married, quite unexpectedly, a bald man with a large buttonhole who owned, it was said, cotton mills at Manchester. And she had five boys!

She and Peter had settled down together. They were talking: it seemed so familiar—that they should be talking. They would discuss the past. With the two of them (more even than with Richard) she shared her past; the garden; the trees; old Joseph Breitko pf singing Brahms without any voice; the drawing-room wallpaper; the smell of the mats. A part of this Sally must always be; Peter must always be. But she must leave them. There were the Bradshaws, whom she disliked.

She must go up to Lady Bradshaw (in grey and silver, balancing like a sea-lion at the edge of its tank, barking for invitations, Duchesses, the typical successful man's wife), she must go up to Lady Bradshaw and say ...

But Lady Bradshaw anticipated her.

"We are shockingly late, dear Mrs. Dalloway, we hardly dared to come in," she said.

And Sir William, who looked very distinguished, with his grey hair and blue eyes, said yes; they had not been able to resist the temptation.

He was talking to Richard about that Bill probably, which they wanted to get through the Commons. Why did the sight of him, talking to Richard, curl her up? He looked what he was, a great doctor. A man absolutely at the head of his profession, very powerful, rather worn. For think what cases came before him—people in the uttermost depths of misery; people on the verge of insanity; husbands and wives. He had to decide questions of appalling difficulty. Yet—what she felt was, one wouldn't like Sir William to see one unhappy. No; not that man.

"How is your son at Eton?" she asked Lady Bradshaw.

He had just missed his eleven, said Lady Bradshaw, because of the mumps. His father minded even more than he did, she thought "being," she said, "nothing but a great boy himself."

Clarissa looked at Sir William, talking to Richard. He did not look like a boy—not in the least like a boy.

She had once gone with some one to ask his advice. He had been perfectly right; extremely sensible. But Heavens—what a relief to get out to the street again! There was some poor wretch sobbing, she remembered, in the waiting-room. But she did not know what it was—about Sir William; what exactly she disliked. Only Richard agreed with her, "didn't like his taste, didn't like his smell." But he was extraordinarily able. They were talking about this Bill. Some case, Sir William was mentioning, lowering his voice. It had its bearing upon what he was saying about the deferred effects of shell shock. There must be some provision in the Bill.

Sinking her voice, drawing Mrs. Dalloway into the shelter of a common femininity, a common pride in the illustrious qualities of husbands and their sad tendency to overwork, Lady Bradshaw (poor goose—one didn't dislike her) murmured how, "just as we were starting, my husband was called up on the telephone, a very sad case. A young man (that is what Sir William is telling Mr. Dalloway) had killed himself. He had been in the army." Oh! thought Clarissa, in the middle of my party, here's death, she thought.

She went on, into the little room where the Prime Minister had gone with Lady Bruton. Perhaps there was somebody there. But there was nobody. The chairs still kept the impress of the Prime Minister and Lady Bruton, she turned deferentially, he sitting four-square, authoritatively. They had been talking about India. There was nobody. The party's splendour fell to the floor, so strange it was to come in alone in her finery.

What business had the Bradshaws to talk of death at her party? A young man had killed himself. And they talked of it at her party—the Bradshaws, talked of death. He had killed himself—but how? Always her body went through it first, when she was told, suddenly, of an accident; her dress flamed, her body burnt. He had thrown himself from a window. Up had flashed the ground; through him, blundering, bruising, went the rusty spikes. There he lay with a thud, thud, thud in his brain, and then a suffocation of blackness. So she saw it. But why had he done it? And the Bradshaws talked of it at her party!

She had once thrown a shilling into the Serpentine, never anything more. But he had flung it away. They went on living (she would have to go back; the rooms were still crowded; people kept oncoming). They (all day she had been thinking of Bourton, of Peter, of Sally), they would grow old. A thing there was that mattered; a thing, wreathed about with chatter, defaced, obscured in her own life, let drop every day in corruption, lies, chatter. This he had preserved. Death was defiance. Death was an attempt to communicate; people feeling the impossibility of reaching the centre which, mystically, evaded them; closeness drew apart; rapture faded, one was alone. There was an embrace in death.

But this young man who had killed himself—had he plunged holding his treasure? "If it were now to die, it were now to be most happy," she had said to herself once, coming down in white.

Or there were the poets and thinkers. Suppose he had had that passion, and had gone to Sir William Bradshaw, a great doctor yet to her obscurely evil, without sex or lust, extremely polite to women, but capable of some indescribable outrage—forcing your soul, that was it—if this young man had gone to him, and Sir William had impressed him, like that, with his power, might he not then have said (indeed she felt it now), Life is made intolerable; they make life intolerable, men like that?

Then (she had felt it only this morning) there was the terror; the overwhelming incapacity, one's parents giving it into one's hands, this life, to be lived to the end, to be walked with serenely; there was in the depths of her heart an awful fear. Even now, quite often if Richard had not been there reading the Times, so that she could crouch like a bird and gradually revive, send roaring up that immeasurable delight, rubbing stick to stick, one thing with another, she must have perished. But that young man had killed himself.

Somehow it was her disaster—her disgrace. It was her punishment to see sink and disappear here a man, there a woman, in this profound darkness, and she forced to stand here in her evening dress. She had schemed; she had pilfered. She was never wholly admirable. She had wanted success. Lady Bexborough and the rest of it. And once she had walked on the terrace at Bourton.

Odd, incredible; she had never been so happy. Nothing could be slow enough; nothing last too long. No pleasure could equal, she thought, straightening the chairs, pushing in one book on the shelf, this having done with the triumphs of youth, lost herself in the process of living, to find it, with a shock of delight, as the sun rose, as the day sank. Many a time had she gone, at Bourton when they were all talking, to look at the sky; or seen it between people's shoulders at dinner; seen it in London when she could not sleep. She walked to the window.

It held, foolish as the idea was, something of her own in it, this country sky, this sky above Westminster. She parted the curtains; she looked. Oh, but how surprising! —In the room opposite the old lady stared straight at her! She was going to bed. And the sky. It will be a solemn sky, she had thought, it will be a dusky sky, turning away its cheek in beauty. But there it was—ashen pale, raced over quickly by tapering vast clouds. It was new to her. The wind must have risen. She was going to bed, in the room opposite. It was fascinating to watch her, moving about, that old lady, crossing the room, coming to the window. Could she see her? It was fascinating, with people still laughing and shouting in the drawing-room, to watch that old woman, quite quietly, going to bed. She pulled the blind now. The clock began striking. The young man had killed himself; but she did not pity him; with the clock striking the hour, one, two, three, she did not pity him, with all this going on. There! the old lady had put out her light! the whole house was dark now with this going on, she repeated, and the words came to her, Fear no more the heat of the sun. She must go back to them. But what an extraordinary night! She felt somehow very like him—the young man who had killed himself. She felt glad that he had done it; thrown it away. The clock was striking. The leaden circles dissolved in the air. He made her feel the beauty; made her feel the fun. But she must go back. She must assemble. She must find Sally and Peter. And she came in from the little room.

"But where is Clarissa?" said Peter. He was sitting on the sofa with Sally. (After all these years he really could not call her "Lady Rosseter.") "Where's the woman gone to?" he asked. "Where's

Clarissa?"

Sally supposed, and so did Peter for the matter of that, that there were people of importance, politicians, whom neither of them knew unless by sight in the picture papers, whom Clarissa had to be nice to, had to talk to. She was with them. Yet there was Richard Dalloway not in the Cabinet. He hadn't been a success, Sally supposed? For herself, she scarcely ever read the papers. She sometimes saw his name mentioned. But then—well, she lived a very solitary life, in the wilds, Clarissa would say, among great merchants, great manufacturers, men, after all, who did things. She had done things too!

"I have five sons!" she told him.

Lord, Lord, what a change had come over her! the softness of motherhood; its egotism too. Last time they met, Peter remembered, had been among the cauliflowers in the moonlight, the leaves "like rough bronze" she had said, with her literary turn; and she had picked a rose. She had marched him up and down that awful night, after the scene by the fountain; he was to catch the midnight train. Heavens, he had wept!

That was his old trick, opening a pocket-knife, thought Sally, always opening and shutting a knife when he got excited. They had been very, very intimate, she and Peter Walsh, when he was in love with Clarissa, and there was that dreadful, ridiculous scene over Richard Dalloway at lunch. She had called Richard "Wickham." Why not call Richard "Wickham"? Clarissa had flared up! and indeed they had never seen each other since, she and Clarissa, not more than half a dozen times perhaps in the last ten years. And Peter Walsh had gone off to India, and she had heard vaguely that he had made an unhappy marriage, and she didn't know whether he had any children, and she couldn't ask him, for he had changed. He was rather shrivelled-looking, but kinder, she felt, and she had a real affection for him, for he was connected with her youth, and she still had a little Emily Bront? he had given her, and he was to write, surely? In those days he was to write.

"Have you written?" she asked him, spreading her hand, her firm and shapely hand, on her knee in a way he recalled.

"Not a word!" said Peter Walsh, and she laughed. She was still attractive, still a personage, Sally Seton. But who was this Rosseter? He wore two camellias on his wedding day—that was all Peter knew of him. "They have myriads of servants, miles of conservatories," Clarissa wrote; something like that. Sally owned it with a shout of laughter.

"Yes, I have ten thousand a year"—whether before the tax was paid or after, she couldn't remember, for her husband, "whom you must meet," she said, "whom you would like," she said, did all that for her.

And Sally used to be in rags and tatters. She had pawned her grandmother's ring which Marie Antoinette had given her great-grandfather to come to Bourton.

Oh yes, Sally remembered; she had it still, a ruby ring which Marie Antoinette had given her great-grandfather. She never had a penny to her name in those days, and going to Bourton always meant some frightful pinch. But going to Bourton had meant so much to her—had kept her sane, she believed, so unhappy had she been at home. But that was all a thing of the past—all over now, she said. And Mr. Parry was dead; and Miss Parry was still alive. Never had he had such a shock in his life! said Peter. He had been quite certain she was dead. And the marriage had been, Sally supposed, a success? And that very handsome, very self-possessed young woman was Elizabeth, over there, by the curtains, in pink.

(She was like a poplar, she was like a river, she was like a hyacinth, Willie Titcomb was thinking. Oh how much nicer to be in the country and do what she liked! She could hear her poor dog howling, Elizabeth was certain.) She was not a bit like Clarissa, Peter Walsh said.

"Oh, Clarissa!" said Sally.

What Sally felt was simply this. She had owed Clarissa an enormous amount. They had been friends, not acquaintances, friends, and she still saw Clarissa all in white going about the house with her hands full of flowers—to this day tobacco plants made her think of Bourton. But—did Peter understand? —she lacked something. Lacked what was it? She had charm; she had extraordinary charm. But to be frank (and she felt that Peter was an old friend, a real friend—did absence matter? did distance matter? She had often wanted to write to him, but torn it up, yet felt he understood, for people understand without things being said, as one realises growing old, and old she was, had been that afternoon to see her sons at Eton, where they had the mumps), to be quite frank then, how could Clarissa have done it? —married Richard Dalloway? a sportsman, a man who cared only for dogs. Literally, when he came into the room he smelt of the stables. And then all this? She waved her hand.

Hugh Whitbread it was, strolling past in his white waistcoat, dim, fat, blind, past everything he looked, except self-esteem and comfort.

"He's not going to recognise *us*," said Sally, and really she hadn't the courage—so that was Hugh! the admirable Hugh!

"And what does he do?" she asked Peter.

He blacked the King's boots or counted bottles at Windsor, Peter told her. Peter kept his sharp tongue still! But Sally must be frank, Peter said. That kiss now, Hugh's.

On the lips, she assured him, in the smoking-room one evening. She went straight to Clarissa in a rage. Hugh didn't do such things! Clarissa said, the admirable Hugh! Hugh's socks were without exception the most beautiful she had ever seen—and now his evening dress. Perfect! And had he children?

"Everybody in the room has six sons at Eton," Peter told her, except himself. He, thank God, had none. No sons, no daughters, no wife. Well, he didn't seem to mind, said Sally. He looked younger, she thought, than any of them.

But it had been a silly thing to do, in many ways, Peter said, to marry like that; "a perfect goose she was," he said, but, he said, "we had a splendid time of it," but how could that be? Sally wondered; what did he mean? and how odd it was to know him and yet not know a single thing that had happened to him. And did he say it out of pride? Very likely, for after all it must be galling for him (though he was an oddity, a sort of sprite, not at all an ordinary man), it must be lonely at his age to have no home, nowhere to go to. But he must stay with them for weeks and weeks. Of course he would; he would love to stay with them, and that was how it came out. All these years the Dalloways had never been once. Time after time they had asked them. Clarissa (for it was Clarissa of course) would not come. For, said Sally, Clarissa was at heart a snob—one had to admit it, a snob. And it was that that was between them, she was convinced. Clarissa thought she had married beneath her, her husband being—she was proud of it—a miner's son. Every penny they had he had earned. As a little boy (her voice trembled) he had carried great sacks.

(And so she would go on, Peter felt, hour after hour; the miner's son; people thought she had married beneath her; her five sons; and what was the other thing—plants, hydrangeas, syringas, very very rare hibiscus lilies that never grow north of the Suez Canal, but she, with one gardener in a suburb near Manchester, had beds of them, positively beds! Now all that Clarissa had escaped, unmaternal as she was.)

A snob was she? Yes, in many ways. Where was she, all this time? It was getting late.

"Yet," said Sally, "when I heard Clarissa was giving a party, I felt I couldn't not come—must see her again (and I'm staying in Victoria Street, practically next door). So I just came without an invitation. But," she whispered, "tell me, do. Who is this?"

It was Mrs. Hilbery, looking for the door. For how late it was getting! And, she murmured, as the night grew later, as people went, one found old friends; quiet nooks and corners; and the loveliest views. Did they know, she asked, that they were surrounded by an enchanted garden? Lights and trees and wonderful gleaming lakes and the sky. Just a few fairy lamps, Clarissa Dalloway had said, in the back garden! But she was a magician! It was a park ... And she didn't know their names, but friends she knew they were, friends without names, songs without words, always the best. But there were so many doors, such unexpected places, she could not find her way.

"Old Mrs. Hilbery," said Peter; but who was that? that lady standing by the curtain all the evening, without speaking? He knew her face; connected her with Bourton. Surely she used to cut up underclothes at the large table in the window? Davidson, was that her name?

"Oh, that is Ellie Henderson," said Sally. Clarissa was really very hard on her. She was a cousin, very poor. Clarissa *was* hard on people.

She was rather, said Peter. Yet, said Sally, in her emotional way, with a rush of that enthusiasm which Peter used to love her for, yet dreaded a little now, so effusive she might become—how generous to her friends Clarissa was! and what a rare quality one found it, and how sometimes at night or on Christmas Day, when she counted up her blessings, she put that friendship first. They were young; that was it. Clarissa was pure-hearted; that was it Peter would think her sentimental. So she was. For she had come to feel that it was the only thing worth saying—what one felt. Cleverness was silly. One must say simply what one felt.

"But I do not know," said Peter Walsh, "what I feel."

Poor Peter, thought Sally. Why did not Clarissa come and talk to them? That was what he was longing for. She knew it. All the time he was thinking only of Clarissa, and was fidgeting with his knife.

He had not found life simple, Peter said. His relations with Clarissa had not been simple. It had spoilt his life, he said. (They had been so intimate—he and Sally Seton, it was absurd not to say it.) One could not be in love twice, he said. And what could she say? Still, it is better to have loved (but he would think her sentimental—he used to be so sharp). He must come and stay with them in Manchester. That is all very true, he said. All very true. He would love to come and stay with them, directly he had done what he had to do in London.

And Clarissa had cared for him more than she had ever cared for Richard. Sally was positive of that.

"No, no, no!" said Peter (Sally should not have said that—she went too far). That good fellow—there he was at the end of the room, holding forth, the same as ever, dear old Richard. Who was he talking to? Sally asked, that very distinguished-looking man? Living in the wilds as she did, she had an insatiable curiosity to know who people were. But Peter did not know. He did not like his looks, he said, probably a Cabinet Minister. Of them all, Richard seemed to him the best, he said—the most disinterested.

"But what has he done?" Sally asked. Public work, she supposed. And were they happy together? Sally asked (she herself was extremely happy); for, she admitted, she knew nothing about them, only jumped to conclusions, as one does, for what can one know even of the people one lives with every day? she asked Are we not all prisoners? She had read a wonderful play about a man who scratched on the wall of his cell, and she had felt that was true of life—one scratched on the wall. Despairing of human relationships (people were so difficult), she often went into her garden and got from her flowers a peace which men and women never gave her. But no; he did not like cabbages; he preferred human beings, Peter said. Indeed, the young are beautiful, Sally said, watching Elizabeth cross the room. How unlike Clarissa at her age! Could he make anything of her? She would not open her lips. Not much, not yet, Peter admitted. She was like a lily, Sally said, a lily by the side of a pool. But Peter did not agree that we know nothing. We know everything, he said; at least he did.

But these two, Sally whispered, these two coming now (and really she must go, if Clarissa did not come soon), this distinguished-looking man and his rather common-looking wife who had been talking to Richard—what could one know about people like that?

"That they're damnable humbugs," said Peter, looking at them casually. He made Sally laugh.

But Sir William Bradshaw stopped at the door to look at a picture. He looked in the corner for the engraver's name. His wife looked too. Sir William Bradshaw was so interested in art.

When one was young, said Peter, one was too much excited to know people. Now that one was old, fifty-two to be precise (Sally was fifty-five, in body, she said, but her heart was like a girl's of twenty); now that one was mature then, said Peter, one could watch, one could understand, and one did not lose the power of feeling, he said. No, that is true, said Sally. She felt more deeply, more passionately, every year. It increased, he said, alas, perhaps, but one should be glad of it—it went on increasing in his experience. There was some one in India. He would like to tell Sally about her. He would like Sally to know her. She was married, he said. She had two small children. They must all come to Manchester, said Sally—he must promise before they left.

There's Elizabeth, he said, she feels not half what we feel, not yet. But, said Sally, watching Elizabeth go to her father, one can see they are devoted to each other. She could feel it by the way Elizabeth went to her father.

For her father had been looking at her, as he stood talking to the Bradshaws, and he had thought to himself, Who is that lovely girl? And suddenly he realised that it was his Elizabeth, and he had not recognised her, she looked so lovely in her pink frock! Elizabeth had felt him looking at her as she talked to Willie Titcomb. So she went to him and they stood together, now that the party was almost over, looking at the people going, and the rooms getting emptier and emptier, with things scattered on the floor. Even Ellie Henderson was going, nearly last of all, though no one had spoken to her, but she had wanted to see everything, to tell Edith. And Richard and Elizabeth were rather glad it was over, but Richard was proud of his daughter. And he had not meant to tell her, but he could not help telling her. He had looked at her, he said, and he had wondered, Who is that lovely girl? and it was his daughter! That did make her happy. But her poor dog was howling.

"Richard has improved. You are right," said Sally. "I shall go and talk to him. I shall say goodnight. What does the brain matter," said Lady Rosseter, getting up, "compared with the heart?"

"I will come," said Peter, but he sat on for a moment. What is this terror? what is this ecstasy? he thought to himself. What is it that fills me with extraordinary excitement?

It is Clarissa, he said.

For there she was.

(选自 Virginia Woolf: *Mrs. Dalloway*. New York: Penguin Popular Classics, 1996. pp.181–213.)

Questions

1. What do you think about Clarissa's character?
2. Woolf creates Septimus as a double for Clarissa. In what ways are they similar?
3. What is the author's purpose for mentioning Septimus' death at Clarissa's party?
4. What is the significant role of Peter Walsh to Mrs. Dalloway?
5. What problems have been critiqued in *Mrs. Dalloway*?

Unit 10

William Somerset Maugham: *The Painted Veil*

William Somerset Maugham (1874—1965), better known as W. Somerset Maugham, was a British playwright, novelist and short story writer. He was among the most popular writers of his era and reputedly the highest-paid author during the 1930s.

Maugham's father, Robert Ormond Maugham, was a lawyer who handled the legal affairs of the British embassy in Paris. Since French law declared that all children born on French soil could be conscripted for military service, his father arranged for Maugham to be born at the embassy, technically on British soil. His grandfather, another Robert, was a prominent lawyer and co-founder of the Law Society of England and Wales. His family assumed Maugham and his brothers would be lawyers. His elder brother, Viscount Maugham, enjoyed a distinguished legal career and served as Lord Chancellor from 1938 to 1939.

Maugham's mother, Edith Mary died of tuberculosis on 31 January at the age of 41. The early death of his mother left Maugham traumatized. He kept his mother's photograph at his bedside for the rest of his life. Two years after Edith's death Maugham's father died of cancer in France. Maugham was sent to the UK to be cared for by his uncle. The move was damaging. Henry Maugham was cold and emotionally cruel. The boy attended The King's School, which was also difficult for him. He was teased for his bad English (French had been his first language) and his short stature, which he inherited from his father. Maugham developed a stammer that stayed with him all his life, although it was sporadic, being subject to his moods and circumstances. Miserable both at his uncle's vicarage and at school, the young Maugham developed a talent for making wounding remarks to those who displeased him. This ability is sometimes reflected in Maugham's literary characters. Not wanting to become a lawyer like other men in his family, Maugham eventually trained and qualified as a physician. The initial run of his first novel, *Liza of Lambeth* (1897) was about a tale of working-class adultery and its consequences, sold out so rapidly that Maugham gave up medicine to write full-time.

During the First World War he served with the Red Cross and in the ambulance corps, before being recruited into the British Secret Intelligence Service in 1916, for which he worked in Switzerland and Russia before the October Revolution of 1917. During and after the war, he travelled in India and Southeast Asia; these experiences were reflected in later short stories and novels.

Maugham is recognized as an Englishman deeply influenced by French literature. Maugham's words are not at loggerheads, and there is always a sort of British coldness that is aloof from the novel and the reader, and an acrid stroke that accurately depicts the social reality of what he sees and hears. Maugham described some individuals, but represented the whole human being in his eyes.

As a novelist, Maugham declared that fiction was storytelling, because "the desire to hear stories is as ingrained in human beings as the desire for wealth." Maugham's criticism of modern novels has a tendency to focus too much on portraying characters rather than on plot. Of course, it is important to portray characters because they are only concerned about what happens to them when they are familiar with and sympathetic to them. Focusing on portraying characters without paying attention to what happens between them is only a way of writing novels, but it is not the key. Maugham mocked many modern writers that "behavior is the same; the description is repetitive and verbose; it feels dull."

Theme

The title of *The Painted Veil* is taken from Percy Bysshe Shelley's sonnet, which begins with "Lift not the painted veil which those who live/Call Life." Maugham's view of love and marriage in his works is that there is no love in the world, and marriage is the yoke. Maugham himself does not believe in pure love. The so-called love, in fact, is only a thin "veil". It is impossible for man to really acquire it. If you obstinately, spare no effort to pursue, it will be empty. Maugham does not think that love is the only foundation of marriage, he sees more of the secular color of marriage. Like the themes of all Maugham's novels, *The Painted Veil* reveals that love and marriage are all untrue colored veils, which "will be a path to serenity."

Term

Interior monologue: It's the written representation of a character's inner thoughts, impressions, and memories as if directly "overheard" without the apparent intervention of a summarizing and selecting narrator. The term is often loosely used as a synonym for *stream of consciousness*. However, critics take *interior monologue* as the larger category, within which *stream of consciousness* is a specific technique emphasizing continuous "flow" by abandoning strict logic, syntax, and punctuation.

Excerpt

CHAPTER 23

SHE looked at him blankly. What he said was so unexpected that at the first moment she could hardly gather its sense.

"What on earth are you talking about?" she faltered.

Even to herself her reply rang false, and she saw the look of disdain which it called forth on Walter's stern face.

"I'm afraid you've thought me a bigger fool than I am."

She did not quite know what to say. She was undecided whether indignantly to assert her innocence or to break out into angry reproaches. He seemed to read her thoughts.

"I've got all the proof necessary."

She began to cry. The tears flowed from her eyes without any particular anguish and she did not dry them: to weep gave her a little time to collect herself. But her mind was blank. He watched her without concern, and his calmness frightened her. He grew impatient.

"You're not going to do much good by crying, you know."

His voice, so cold and hard, had the effect of exciting in her a certain indignation. She was recovering her nerve.

"I don't care. I suppose you have no objection to my divorcing you. It means nothing to a man."

"Will you allow me to ask why I should put myself to the smallest inconvenience on your account?"

"It can't make any difference to you. It's not much to ask you to behave like a gentleman."

"I have much too great a regard for your welfare."

She sat up now and dried her eyes.

"What do you mean?" she asked him.

"Townsend will marry you only if he is co-respondent and the case is so shameless that his wife is forced to divorce him."

"You don't know what you're talking about," she cried.

"You stupid fool."

His tone was so contemptuous that she flushed with anger. And perhaps her anger was greater because she had never before heard him say to her any but sweet, flattering and delightful things. She had been accustomed to find him subservient to all her whims.

"If you want the truth you can have it. He's only too anxious to marry me. Dorothy Townsend is perfect willing to divorce him and we shall be married the moment we're free."

"Did he tell you that in so many words or is that the impression you have gained from his manner?"

Walter's eyes shone with bitter mockery. They made Kitty a trifle uneasy. She was not quite sure that Charlie had ever said exactly that in so many words.

"He's said it over and over again."

"That's a lie and you know it's a lie."

"He loves me with all his heart and soul. He loves me as passionately as I love him. You've found out. I'm not going to deny anything. Why should I? we've been lovers for a year and I'm proud of it. He means everything in the world to me and I'm glad that you know at last. We're sick to death of secrecy and compromise and all the rest of it. It was a mistake that I ever married you, I never should have done it, I was a fool. I never cared for you. We never had anything in common. I don't like the people you like and I'm bored by the things that interest you. I'm thankful it's finished."

He watched her without a gesture and without a movement of his face. He listened attentively and no change in his expression showed that what she said affected him.

"Do you know why I married you?"

"Because you wanted to be married before your sister Doris."

It was true, but it gave her a funny little tum to realise that he knew it. Oddly enough, even in that moment of fear and anger, it excited her compassion. He faintly smiled.

"I had no illusions about you," he said. "I knew you were silly and frivolous and empty-headed. But I loved you. I knew that your aims and ideals were vulgar and commonplace. But I loved you. I knew that you were second-rate. But I loved you. It's comic when I think how hard I tried to be amused by the things that amused you and how anxious I was to hide from you that I wasn't ignorant and vulgar and scandal-mongering and stupid. I knew how frightened you were of intelligence and I did everything I could to make you think me as big a fool as the rest of the men you knew. I knew that you'd only married me for convenience. I loved you so much, I didn't care. Most people, as far as I can see, when they're in love with someone and love isn't returned feel that they have a grievance. They grow angry and bitter. I wasn't like that. I never expected you to love me, I didn't see any reason that you should, I never thought myself very lovable. I was thankful to be allowed to love you and I was enraptured when now and then I thought you were pleased with me or when I noticed in your eyes a gleam of good-humoured affection. I tried nor to bore you with my love; I knew I couldn't afford to do that and I was always on the lookout for the first sign that you were impatient with my affection. What most husbands expect as a right I was prepared to receive as a favour."

Kitty, accustomed to flattery all her life, had never heard such things said to her before. Blind wrath, driving out tear, arose in her heart: it seemed to choke her, and she felt the blood-vessels in her temples swell and throb. Wounded vanity can make a woman more vindictive than a lioness robbed of her cubs. Kitty's jaw, always a little too square, protruded with an apish hideousness and her beautiful eyes were black with malice. But she kept her temper in check.

"If a man hasn't what's necessary to make a woman love him, it's his fault, not hers."

"Evidently."

His derisive tone increased her irritation. She felt that she could wound him more by maintaining her calm.

"I'm not very well-educated and I'm not very clever. I'm just a perfectly ordinary young woman. I like the things that the people like among whom I've lived all my life. I like dancing and tennis and theatres and I like the men who play games. It's quite true that I've always been bored by you and by the things you like. They mean nothing to me and I don't want them too. You dragged me round those interminable galleries in Venice: I should have enjoyed myself much more playing golf at Sandwich."

"I know."

"I'm sorry if I haven't been all that you expected me to be. Unfortunately I always found you physically repulsive. You can hardly blame me for that."

"I don't."

Kitty could more easily have coped with the situation if he had raved and stormed. she could have met violence with violence. His self-control was inhuman and she hated him now as she had never hated him before.

"I don't think you're a man at all. Why didn't you break into the room when you knew was there with Charlie? You might at least have tried to thrash him. Were you afraid?"

But the moment she had said this she flushed, for she was ashamed. He did not answer, but in his eyes she read an icy disdain. The shadow of a smile flickered on his lips.

"It may be that, like a historical character, I am too proud to fight."

Kitty, unable to think of anything to answer, shrugged her shoulders. For a moment longer he held her in his immobile gaze.

"I think I've said all I had to say: if you refuse to come to Mei-Tan-Fu I shall file my petition."

"Why won' t you consent to let me divorce you?"

He took his eyes off her at last. He leaned back in his chair and lit a cigarette. He smoked it to the end without saying a word. Then, throwing away the butt, he gave a little smile. He looked at her once more.

"If Mrs. Townsend will give her assurance that she will divorce her husband and if he will give me his written promise to marry you within a week of the two decrees being made absolute, I will do that."

There was something in the way he spoke which disconcerted her. But her self-respect obliged her to accept his offer in the grand manner.

"That is very generous of you, Walter."

To her astonishment he burst suddenly into a shout of laughter. She flushed angrily.

"What are you laughing at? I see nothing to laugh at."

"I beg your pardon. I daresay my sense of humour is peculiar."

She looked at him frowning. she would have liked to say something bitter and wounding, but no rejoinder occurred to her. He looked at his watch.

"You had better look sharp if you want to catch Townsend at his office. If you decide to come with me to Mei-Tan-Fu it would be necessary to start the day after to-morrow."

"Do you want me to tell him to-day?"

"They say there is no time like the present."

Her heart began to beat a little faster. It was not uneasiness that she felt, it was, she didn't quite know what it was. She wished she could have had a little longer she would have liked to prepare Charlie. But she had the fullest confidence in him, he loved her as much as she loved him, and it was treacherous even to let the thought cross her mind that he would not welcome the necessity that was forced upon them. She turned to Walter gravely.

"I don't think you know what love is. You have no conception how desperately in love Charlie and I are with one another. It really is the only thing that matters and every sacrifice that our love calls for will be as easy as falling off a log."

He gave a little bow, but said nothing, and his eyes followed her as she walked with measured step from the room.

CHAPTER 63

Suddenly, walking along a blank long wall they came to a gateway flanked by sentry boxes, and the bearers set down the chairs. Waddington hurried up to Kitty. She had already jumped out. The officer knocked loudly on the door and shouted. A postern was opened and they passed into a courtyard. It was large and square. Huddled against the walls, under the eaves of the overhanging roofs, soldiers wrapped in their blankets were lying in huddled groups. They stopped for a moment while the officer spoke to a man who might have been a sergeant on guard. He turned and said something to Waddington.

"He's still alive," said Waddington in a low voice. "Take care how you walk."

Still preceded by the men with lanterns they made their way across the yard, up some steps, through a great doorway and then down into another wide court. On one side of this was a long chamber with lights in it; the lights within shining through the rice paper silhouetted the elaborate pattern of the lattice. The lantern-bearer sled them across the yard towards this room and at the door the officer knocked. It was opened immediately and the officer with a glance at Kitty stepped back.

"Will you walk in," said Waddington.

It was a long, low room and the smoky lamps that lit it made the gloom ominous. Three or four orderlies stood about. On a pallet against the wall opposite the door a man was lying huddled under a blanket. An officer was standing motionless at the foot.

Kitty hurried up and leaned over the pallet. Walter lay with his eyes closed and in that sombre light his face had the greyness of death. He was horribly still.

"Walter, Walter," she gasped, in a low, terrified tone.

There was a slight movement in the body, or the shadow of a movement; it was so slight it was like a breath of air which you cannot feel and yet for an instant ruffles the surface of still water.

"Walter, Walter, speak to me." The eyes were opened slowly, as though it were an infinite effort to raise those heavy lids, but he did not look, he stared at the wall a few inches from his face. He spoke; his voice, low and weak, had the hint of a smile in it.

"This is a pretty kettle of fish," he said.

Kitty dared not breathe. He made no further sound, no beginning of a gesture, but his eyes, those dark, cold eyes of his (seeing now what mysteries?) stared at the white washed wall. Kitty raised herself to her feet. With haggard gaze she faced the man who stood there.

"Surely something can be done. You're not going to stand there and do nothing?"

She clasped her hands. Waddington spoke to the officer who stood at the end of the bed.

"I'm afraid they've done everything that was possible. The regimental surgeon has been treating him. Your husband has trained him and he's done all that your husband could do himself."

"Is that the surgeon?"

"No, that is Colonel Yü. He's never left your husband's side."

Distracted, Kitty gave him a glance. He was a tallish man, but stockily built, and he seemed ill at ease in his khaki uniform. He was looking at Walter and she saw that his eyes were wet with tears. It gave her a pang. Why should that man with his yellow, flat face have tears in his eyes? It exasperated her.

"It's awful to be able to do nothing."

"At least he's not in pain any more," said Waddington.

She leaned once more over her husband. Those ghastly eyes of his still stared vacantly in front of him. She could not tell if he saw with them. She did not know whether he had heard what was said. She put her lips close to his ears.

"Walter, isn't there something we can do?"

She thought that there must be some drug they could give him which would stay the dreadful ebbing of his life. Now that her eyes were more accustomed to the dimness she saw with horror that his face had fallen. She would hardly have recognised him. It was unthinkable that in a few short hours he should look like another man; he hardly looked like a man at all; he looked like death.

She thought that he was making an effort to speak. She put her ear close.

"Don't fuss. I've had a rough passage, but I'm all right now."

Kitty waited for a moment, but he was silent. His immobility rent her heart with anguish; it was terrifying that he should lie so still. He seemed prepared already for the stillness of the grave. Someone, the surgeon or a dresser, came forward and with a gesture motioned her aside; he leaned over the dying man and with a dirty ragwet his lips. Kitty stood up once more and turned to Waddington despairingly.

"Is there no hope at all?" she whispered.

He shook his head. "How much longer can he live?"

"No one can tell. An hour perhaps."

Kitty looked round the bare chamber and her eyes rested for an instant on the substantial form of Colonel Yü.

"Can I be left alone with him for a little while?" she asked. "Only for a minute."

"Certainly, if you wish it."

Waddington stepped over to the Colonel and spoke to him. The Colonel gave a little bow and then in a low tone an order.

"We shall wait on the steps," said Waddington as they trooped out. "You have only to call."

Now that the incredible had overwhelmed her consciousness, like a drug coursing through her veins, and she realised that Walter was going to die she had but one thought, and that was to make his end easier for him by dragging from his soul the rancour which poisoned it. If he could die at peace with her it seemed to her that he would die at peace with himself. She thought now not of herself at all but only of him.

"Walter, I beseech you to forgive me," she said, leaning over him. For fear that he could not bear the pressure she took care not to touch him. "I'm so desperately sorry for the wrong I did you. I so bitterly regret it."

He said nothing. He did not seem to hear. She was obliged to insist. It seemed to her strangely that his soul was a fluttering moth and its wings were heavy with hatred.

"Darling."

A shadow passed over his wan and sunken face. It was less than a movement, and yet it gave all the effect of a terrifying convulsion. She had never used that word to him before. Perhaps in his dying brain there passed the thought, confused and difficultly grasped, that he had only heard her use it, a commonplace of her vocabulary, to dogs and babies and motor-cars. Then something horrible occurred. She clenched her hands, trying with all her might to control herself, for she saw two tears run slowly down his wasted cheeks.

"Oh, my precious, my dear, if you ever loved me—I know you loved me and I was hateful—I beg you to forgive me. I've no chance now to show my repentance. Have mercy on me. I beseech you to forgive."

She stopped. She looked at him, all breathless, waiting passionately for a reply. She saw that he tried to speak. Her heart gave a great bound. It seemed to her that it would be in a manner a reparation for the suffering she had caused him if at this last moment she could effect his deliverance from that load of bitterness. His lips moved. He did not look at her. His eyes stared unseeing at the white-washed wall. She leaned over him so that she might hear. But he spoke quite clearly.

"The dog it was that died."

She stayed as still as though she were turned to stone. She could not understand and gazed at him in terrified perplexity. It was meaningless. Delirium. He had not understood a word she said. It was impossible to be so still and yet to live. She stared and stared. His eyes were open. She could not tell if he breathed. She began to grow frightened. "Walter," she whispered. "Walter." At last, suddenly, she raised herself. A sudden fear seized her. She turned and went to the door. "Will you come, please. He doesn't seem to ..."

They stepped in. The Chinese surgeon went up to the bed. He had an electric torch in his hand and he lit it and looked at Walter's eyes. Then he closed them. He said something in Chinese. Waddington put his arm round Kitty.

"I'm afraid he's dead."

Kitty gave a deep sigh. A few tears fell from her eyes. She felt dazed rather than overcome. The Chinese stood about, round the bed, helplessly, as though they did not quite know what to do next. Waddington was silent. In a minute the Chinese began to speak in a low tone among themselves.

"You'd better let me take you back to the bungalow," said Waddington. "He'll be brought there."

Kitty passed her hand wearily across her forehead. She went up to the pallet bed and leaned over it. She kissed Walter gently on the lips. She was not crying now.

"I'm sorry to give you so much trouble."

The officers saluted as she passed and she gravely bowed. They walked back across the courtyard and got into their chairs. She saw Waddington light a cigarette. A little smoke lost in the air, that was the life of man.

(选自 William Somerset Maugham. *The Painted Veil*. London: Heinemann, 1949. pp.65-70, 187-191.)

Questions

1. What does the "veil" mean?

2. Why did Kitty answer she didn't know when Walter asked Kitty if the baby belongs to her?

3. How Walter's death influenced Kitty?

4. After Kitty went back to London, what kind of change did she make?

5. Why did the writer choose China as the background of this novel?

Unit 11

Colleen McCullough: *The Thorn Birds*

Colleen McCullough (1937—2015), a native Australian born in Wellington, New South Wales. McCullough spent most of her childhood in Sydney, where her family settled after a series of relocations in the Outback. Her mother Laurie was a New Zealander of Maori ancestry and her father Jim was an Irish immigrant who worked as a cane cutter and spent long periods away from the family. She taught herself to read by the time she was three. She had a younger brother, Carl, who drowned off the coast of Crete when he was 25 while trying to rescue tourists in difficulty. She based a character in *The Thorn Birds* on him, and also wrote about him in *Life Without the Boring Bits*.

As a child, McCullough was an avid reader and took an early interest in literature and history; she also displayed an aptitude for science while in high school. Choosing science over the humanities for practical reasons, McCullough attended Holy Cross College and the University of Sydney intending to enter the medical profession, but an allergy to soap precluded a surgical career. McCullough eventually settled into work as a neurophysiology researcher in Sydney and London, and finally the Yale University School of Internal Medicine, where she remained from 1967 to 1976. While at Yale she wrote her first two books. Colleen McCullough's first novel, *Tim*, describes the romance and marriage of a wealthy, middle-aged woman and a much younger, mentally retarded man endowed with striking classical beauty. Their uncommon attachment blossoms as the woman teaches the man to read and function independently in the world. Through the realistic depiction of their tender relationship, McCullough conveys the profound power of love to bring meaning into solitary lives and to defy social expectations. *The Thorn Birds*, became an international best seller and one of the best-selling books in history, with sales of over 30 million copies worldwide, that in

1983 inspired one of the most-watched television miniseries of all time. With the enormous success of *The Thorn Birds*, McCullough abandoned her scientific employment to devote her full attention to writing. She soon left the United States for the quiet isolation of Norfolk Island, an idyllic locale in the remote South Pacific. There she met Ric Robinson, a former house painter; they married in April 1984.

Since McCullough's resettlement to Norfolk Island, she has produced additional best-selling novels, including *An Indecent Obsession*, *A Creed for the Third Millennium*, *The Ladies of Missalonghi* (1987), and the first four volumes of her "Masters of Rome" series—*The First Man in Rome*, *The Grass Crown* (1991), *Fortune's Favorites* (1993), and *Caesar's Women* (1996). McCullough is a versatile novelist who has written in a variety of genres and her works show the persistence in the creation journey of "lonely" and "self."

McCullough describes love as a transformative force, though adds a more pronounced moral and ethical dimension. With *The First Man in Rome* McCullough initiated an expansive series of epic historical novels set in ancient Rome during the first century B. C. *The First Man in Rome*, along with *The Grass Crown*, *Fortune's Favorites*, and *Caesar's Women*, are the first four installments of McCullough's projected six-volume "Masters of Rome" series and recount in prodigious detail the political and personal intrigue behind the decline of the Roman Republic and the ascendancy of Julius Caesar. Each of these massive volumes includes a large cast of characters and complex plots supported by meticulous historical research.

McCullough died on 29 January 2015, at the age of 77, in the Norfolk Island Hospital from apparent renal failure after suffering from a series of small strokes. She had suffered from failing eyesight due to hemorrhagic macular degeneration, osteoporosis, trigeminal neuralgia, diabetes and uterine cancer, and was confined to a wheelchair. She was buried in a traditional Norfolk Island funeral ceremony at the Emily Bay cemetery on the island.

Theme

The Thorn Birds is a family saga that spans the Australian continent and three generations of Cleary descendants between 1915 and 1969. The central character is Meggie Cleary, whose frustrating lifelong love for a handsome Roman Catholic priest, Ralph de Bricassart, dominates the plot and underscores the theme of female suffering in the novel. Meggie's futile longing for Ralph is suggested by the title, which refers to a legendary bird that impales itself on a thorn and sings stoically as it dies. Meggie subsequently enters into an unhappy marriage to another man with whom she has a daughter, Justine. During a brief adulterous affair, Ralph fathers an illegitimate son with Meggie but remains devoted to his religious calling and resists commitment to her in favor of a promising career in the church hierarchy. The son, Dane, eventually enters the priesthood under the tutelage of Ralph, unaware that his teacher is also his father. The novel culminates with Dane's tragic drowning in Greece shortly after his ordination.

Term

Feminism: Feminism incorporates both a doctrine of equal rights for women and an ideology of social transformation aiming to create a world for women beyond simple social equality. Feminism focuses on women's rights and women's emancipation. In general, feminism is the ideology of women's liberation, believing that women suffer injustice because of their sex. Consciousness raising is the quintessential concern of feminism. For example, feminism challenges universalisms and uses the pursuit of consciousness itself as a form of political theory and practice.

Excerpt

18

If they applied themselves to it, the Drogheda people could imagine that Rome and London were no farther away than Sydney, and that the grown-up Dane and Justine were still children going to boarding school. Admittedly they couldn't come home for all the shorter vacations of other days, but once a year they turned up for a month at least. Usually in August or September, and looking much as always. Very young. Did it matter whether they were fifteen and sixteen or twenty-two and twenty-three? And if the Drogheda people lived for that month in early spring, they most definitely never went round saying things like, Well, only a few weeks to go! or, Dear heaven, it's not a month since they left! But around July everyone's step became brisker, and permanent smiles settled on every face. From the cookhouse to the paddocks to the drawing room, treats and gifts were planned.

In the meantime there were letters. Mostly these reflected the personalities of their authors, but sometimes they contradicted. One would have thought, for instance, that Dane would be a meticulously regular correspondent and Justine a scrappy one. That Fee would never write at all. That the Cleary men would write twice a year. That Meggie would enrich the postal service with letters every day, at least to Dane. That Mrs. Smith, Minnie and Cat would send birthday and Christmas cards. That Anne Mueller would write often to Justine, never to Dane.

Dane's intentions were good, and he did indeed write regularly. The only trouble was he forgot to post his efforts, with the result that two or three months would go by without a word, and then Drogheda would receive dozens on the same mail run. The loquacious Justine wrote lengthy missives which were pure stream of-consciousness, rude enough to evoke blushes and clucks of alarm, and entirely fascinating. Meggie wrote once every two weeks only, to both her children. Though Justine never received letters from her grand-mother, Dane did quite often. He also got word regularly from all his uncles, about the land and the sheep and the health of the Drogheda women, for they seemed to think it was their duty to assure him all was truly well at home. However, they didn't extend this to Justine, who would have been flabbergasted by it anyway. For the rest, Mrs. Smith, Minnie, Cat and Anne Mueller, correspondence went as might be expected.

It was lovely reading letters, and a burden writing them. That is, for all save Justine, who experienced twinges of exasperation because no one ever sent her the kind she desired-fat, wordy and frank. It was from Justine the Drogheda people got most of their information about Dane, for his letters never plunged his readers right into the middle of a scene. Whereas Justine's did.

Rain flew into London today [she wrote once], and he was telling me he saw Dane in Rome last week. Well, he sees a lot more of Dane than of me, since Rome is at the top of his travel agenda and London is rock bottom. So I must confess Rain is one of the prime reasons why I meet Dane in Rome every year before we come home. Dane likes coming to London, only I won't let him if Rain is in Rome. Selfish. But you've no idea how I enjoy Rain. He's one of the few people I know who gives me a run for my money, and I wish we met more often.

In one respect Rain's luckier than I am. He gets to meet Dane's fellow students where I don't. I think Dane thinks I'm going to rape them on the spot. Or maybe he thinks they'll rape me. Hah. Only happen if they saw me in my Charmian costume. It's a stunner, people, it really is. Sort of up-to-date Theda Bara. Two little round bronze shields for the old tits, lots and lots of chains and what I reckon is a chastity belt you'd need a pair of tin-cutters to get inside it, anyway. In a long black wig, tan body paint and my few scraps of metal I look a smasher.

... Where was I Oh, yes, Rain in Rome last week meeting Dane and his pals. They all went out on the tiles. Rain insists on paying, saves Dane embarrassment. It was some night. No women, natch, but everything else. Can you imagine Dane down on his knees in some seedy Roman bar saying "Fair daffodils, we haste to see thee weep so soon away" to a vase of daffodils? He tried for ten minutes to get the words of the quotation in their right order and couldn't, then he gave up, put one of the daffodils between his teeth instead and did a dance. Can you ever imagine Dane doing that? Rain says it's harmless and necessary, all work and no play, etc. Women being out, the next best thing is a skinful of grog. Or so Rain insists. Don't get the idea it happens often, it doesn't, and I gather when it does Rain is the ringleader, so he's along to watch out for them, the naive lot of raw prawns. But I did laugh to think of Dane's halo slipping during the course of a flamenco dance with a daffodil.

It took Dane eight years in Rome to attain his priesthood, and at their beginning no one thought they could ever end. Yet those eight years used themselves up faster than any of the Drogheda people had imagined. Just what they thought he was going to do after he was ordained they didn't know, except that they did assume he would return to Australia. Only Meggie and Justine suspected he would want to remain in Italy, and Meggie at any rate could lull her doubts with memories of his content when he came back each year to his home. He was an Australian, he would want to come home. With Justine it was different. No one dreamed she would come home for good. She was an actress; her career would founder in Australia. Where Dane's career could be pursued with equal zeal anywhere at all.

Thus in the eighth year there were no plans as to what the children would do when they came for their annual holiday; instead the Drogheda people were planning their trip to Rome, to see Dane ordained a priest.

"We fizzled out," said Meggie.

"I beg your pardon, dear?" asked Anne.

They were sitting in a warm corner of the veranda reading, but Meggie's book had fallen neglected into her lap, and she was absently watching the antics of two willy-wagtails on the lawn. It had been a wet year; there were worms everywhere and the fattest, happiest birds anyone ever remembered. Bird songs filled the air from dawn to the last of dusk.

"I said we fizzled out," repeated Meggie, crowlike. "A damp squib. All that promise! Whoever would have guessed it in 1921, when we arrived on Drogheda?"

"How do you mean?"

"A total of six sons, plus me. And a year later, two more sons. What would you think? Dozens of children, half a hundred grandchildren? So look at us now. Hal and Stu are dead, none of the ones left alive seem to have any intention of ever getting married, and I, the only one not entitled to pass on the name, have been the only one to give Drogheda its heirs. And even then the gods weren't happy, were they? A son and a daughter. Several grandchildren at least, you might think. But what happens? My son embraces the priesthood and my daughter's an old maid career woman. Another dead end for Drogheda."

"I don't see what's so strange about it," said Anne. "After all, what could you expect from the men? Stuck out here as shy as kangas, never meeting the girls they might have married. And with Jims and Patsy, the war to boot. Could you see Jims marrying when he knows Patsy can't? They're far too fond of each other for that. And besides, the land's demanding in a neutered way. It takes just about all they've got to give, because I don't think they have a great deal. In a physical sense, I mean. Hasn't it ever struck you, Meggie? Yours isn't a very highly sexed family, to put it bluntly. And that goes for Dane and Justine, too. I mean, there are some people who compulsively hunt it like tomcats, but not your lot. Though perhaps Justine will marry. There's this German chap Rainer; she seems terribly fond of him."

"You've hit the nail on the head," said Meggie, in no mood to be comforted. "She seems terribly fond of him. Just that. After all, she's known him for seven years. If she wanted to marry him, it would have happened ages ago."

"Would it? I know Justine pretty well," answered Anne truthfully, for she did; better than anyone else on Drogheda, including Meggie and Fee. "I think she's terrified of committing herself to the kind of love marriage would entail, and I must say I admire Rainer. He seems to understand her very well. Oh, I don't say he's in love with her for sure, but if he is, at least he's got the sense to wait until she's ready to take the plunge." She leaned forward, her book falling forgotten to the tiles. "Oh, will you listen to that bird? I'm sure even a nightingale couldn't match it." Then she said what she had been wanting to say for weeks. "Meggie, why won't you go to Rome to see Dane ordained? Isn't that peculiar? Dane-ordain."

"I'm not going to Rome!" said Meggie between clenched teeth. "I shall never leave Drogheda again."

"Meggie, don't! You can't disappoint him so! Go, please! If you don't, Drogheda won't have a single woman there, because you're the only woman young enough to take the flight. But I tell you, if I thought for one minute my body would survive I'd be right on that plane."

"Go to Rome and see Ralph de Bricassart smirking? I'd rather be dead!"

"Oh, Meggie, Meggie! Why must you take out your frustrations on him, and on your son? You said it once yourself—it's your own fault. So beggar your pride, and go to Rome. Please!"

"It isn't a question of pride." She shivered. "Oh, Anne, I'm frightened to go! Because I don't believe it, I just don't! My flesh creeps when I think about it."

"And what about the fact he mightn't come home after he's a priest? Did that ever occur to you? He won't be given huge chunks of leave the way he was in the seminary, so if he decides to remain in Rome you may well have to take yourself there if you ever want to see him at all. Go to Rome, Meggie!"

"I can't. If you knew how frightened I am! It's not pride, or Ralph scoring one over on me, or any of the things I say it is to stop people asking me questions. Lord knows, I miss both my men so much I'd crawl on my knees to see them if I thought for a minute they wanted me. Oh, Dane would be glad to see me, but Ralph? He's forgotten I ever existed. I'm frightened, I tell you. I know in my bones that if I go to Rome something will happen. So I'm not going."

"What could happen, for pity's sake?" "I don't know ... If I did, I'd have something to battle. A feeling, how can I battle a feeling? Because that's all it is. A premonition. As if the gods are gathering."

Anne laughed. "You're becoming a real old woman, Meggie. Stop!"

"I can't, I can't! And I am an old woman." "Nonsense, you're just in brisk middle age. Well and truly young enough to hop on that plane."

"Oh, leave me alone!" said Meggie savagely, and picked up her book.

Occasionally a crowd with a purpose converges upon Rome. Not tourism, the voyeuristic sampling of past glories in present relics; not the filling in of a little slice of time between A and B, with Rome a point on the line between those two places. This is a crowd with a single uniting emotion; it bursts with pride, for it is coming to see its son, nephew, cousin, friend ordained a priest in the great basilica which is the most venerated church in the world. Its members put up in humble pensions, luxury hotels, the homes of friends or relatives. But they are totally united, at peace with each other and with the world. They do the rounds dutifully; the Vatican Museum with the Sistine Chapel at its end like a prize for endurance; the Forum, the Colosseum, the Appian Way, the

Spanish Steps, the greedy Trevi Fountain, the *son et lumiere*. Waiting for the day, filling in time. They will be accorded the special privilege of a private audience with the Holy Father, and for them Rome will find nothing too good.

This time it wasn't Dane waiting on the platform to meet Justine, as it had been every other time; he was in retreat. Instead, Rainer Moerling Hartheim prowled the dirty paving like some great animal. He didn't greet her with a kiss, he never did; he just put an arm about her shoulders and squeezed.

"Rather like a bear," said Justine.

"A bear?"

"I used to think when I first met you that you were some sort of missing link, but I've finally decided you're more of a bear than a gorilla. It was an unkind comparison, the gorilla."

"And bears are kind?"

"Well, perhaps they do one to death just as quickly, but they're more cuddly." She linked her arm through his and matched his stride, for she was almost as tall as he. "How's Dane? Did you see him before he went into retreat? I could kill Clyde, not letting me go sooner."

"Dane is as always."

"You haven't been leading him astray?"

"Me? Certainly not. You look very nice, Herzchen."

"I'm on my very best behavior, and I bought out every couturier in London. Do you like my new short skirt? They call it the mini."

"Walk ahead of me, and I'll tell you."

The hem of the full silk skirt was about midthigh; it swirled as she turned and came back to him. "What do you think, Rain? Is it scandalous? I noticed no one in Paris is wearing this length yet."

"It proves a point, Herzchen—that with legs as good as yours, to wear a skirt one millimeter longer is scandalous. I'm sure the Romans will agree with me."

"Which means my arse will be black and blue in an hour instead of a day. Damn them! Though do you know something, Rain?"

"What?"

"I've never been pinched by a priest. All these years I've been flipping in and out of the Vatican with nary a pinch to my credit. So I thought maybe if I wore a miniskirt, I might be the undoing of some poor prelate yet."

"You might be my undoing." He smiled.

"No, really? In orange? I thought you hated me in orange, when I've got orange hair."

"It inflames the senses, such a busy color."

"You're teasing me," she said, disgusted, climbing into his Mercedes limousine, which had a German pennant fluttering from its bonnet talisman. "When did you get the little flag?"

"When I got my new post in the government."

"No wonder I rated a mention in the News of the World! Did you see it?"

"You know I never read rags, Justine."

"Well, nor do I; someone showed it to me," she said, then pitched her voice higher and endowed it with a shabby-genteel, frightfully nice accent. "What up-and-coming carrot-topped Australian actress is cementing very cordial relations with what member of the West German cabinet?"

"They can't be aware how long we've known each other," he said tranquilly, stretching out his legs and making himself comfortable.

Justine ran her eyes over his clothes with approval; very casual, very Italian. He was rather in the European fashion swim himself, daring to wear one of the fishing-net shirts which enabled Italian males to demonstrate the hairiness of their chests.

"You should never wear a suit and collar and tie," she said suddenly.

"No? Why not?"

"Machismo is definitely your style-you know, what you've got on now, the gold medallion and chain on the hairy chest. A suit makes you look as if your waistline is bulging, when it really isn't at all."

For a moment he gazed at her in surprise, then the expression in his eyes became alert, in what she called his "concentrated thinking look." "A first," he said.

"What's a first?"

"In the seven years I've known you, you've never before commented upon my appearance except perhaps to disparage it."

"Oh, dear, haven't I?" she asked, looking a little ashamed. "Heavens, I've thought of it often enough, and never disparagingly." For some reason she added hastily, "I mean, about things like the way you look in a suit."

He didn't answer, but he was smiling, as at a very pleasant thought.

That ride with Rainer seemed to be the last quiet thing to happen for days. Shortly after they returned from visiting Cardinal de Bricassart and

Cardinal di Contini-Verchese, the limousine Rainer had hired deposited the Drogheda contingent at their hotel. Out of the corner of her eye Justine watched Rain's reaction to her family, entirely uncles. Right until the moment her eyes didn't find her mother's face, Justine had been convinced she would change her mind and come to Rome. That she hadn't was a cruel blow; Justine didn't know whether she ached more on Dane's behalf or on her own. But in the meantime here were the Unks, and she was undoubtedly their hostess.

Oh, they were so shy! Which one of them was which? The older they got, the more alike they looked. And in Rome they stuck out like-well, like Australian graziers on holiday in Rome. Each one was clad in the city going uniform of affluent squatters: tan elastic-sided riding boots, neutral trousers, tan sports jackets of very heavy, fuzzy wool with side vents and plenty of leather patches, white shirts, knitted wool ties, flat-crowned grey hats with broad brims. No novelty on the streets of Sydney during Royal Easter Show time, but in a late Roman summer, extraordinary.

And I can say with double sincerity, thank God for Rain! How good he is with them. I wouldn't have believed anyone could stimulate Patsy into speech, but he's doing it, bless him. They're talking away like old hens, and where did he get Australian beer for them? He likes them, and he's interested, I suppose. Everything is grist to the mill of a German industrialist-politician, isn't it? How can he stick to his faith, being what he is? An enigma, that's what you are, Rainer Moerling Hartheim. Friend of popes and cardinals, friend of Justine O'neill. Oh, if you weren't sougly I'd kiss you, I'm so terribly grateful. Lord, fancy being stuck in Rome with the Unks and no Rain! You are well named.

He was sitting back in his chair, listening while Bob told him about shearing, and having nothing better to do because he had so completely taken charge, Justine watched him curiously. Mostly she noticed everything physical about people immediately, but just occasionally that vigilance slipped and people stole up on her, carved a niche in her life without her having made that vital initial assessment. For if it wasn't made, sometimes years would go by before they intruded into her thoughts again as strangers. Like now, watching Rain. That first meeting had been responsible, of course; surrounded by churchmen, awed, frightened, brazening it out. She had noticed only the obvious things: his powerful build, his hair, how dark he was. Then when he had taken her off to dinner the chance to rectify things had been lost, for he had forced an awareness of himself on her far beyond his physical attributes; she had been too interested in what the mouth was saying to look at the mouth.

He wasn't really ugly at all, she decided now. He looked what he was, perhaps, a mixture of the best and the worst. Like a Roman emperor. No wonder he loved the city. It was his spiritual home. A broad face with high, wide cheekbones and a small yet aquiline nose. Thick black brows, straight instead of following the curve of the orbits. Very long, feminine black lashes and quite lovely dark eyes, mostly hooded to hide his thoughts. By far his most beautiful possession was his mouth, neither full nor thin-lipped, neither small nor large, but very well shaped, with a distinct cut to the boundaries of its lips and a peculiar firmness in the way he held it; as if perhaps were he to relax his hold upon it, it might give away secrets about what he was really like. Interesting, to take a face apart which was already so well known, yet not known at all.

She came out of her reverie to find him watching her watch him, which was like being stripped naked in front of a crowd armed with stones. For a moment his eyes held hers, wide open and alert, not exactly startled, rather arrested. Then he transferred his gaze calmly to Bob, and asked a pertinent question about bogg is. Justine gave herself a mental shake, told herself not to go imagining things. But it was fascinating, suddenly to see a man who had been a friend for years as a possible lover. And not finding the thought at all repulsive.

There had been a number of successors to Arthur Lestrange, and she hadn't wanted to laugh. Oh, I've come along way since that memorable night. But I wonder have I actually progressed at all? It's very nice to have a man, and the hell with what Dane said about it being the one man. I'm not going to make it one man, so I'm not going to sleep with Rain; oh, no. It would change too many things, and I'd lose my friend. I need my friend, I can't afford to be without my friend. I shall keep him as I keep Dane, a male human being without any physical significance for me.

The church could hold twenty thousand people, so it wasn't crowded. Nowhere in the world had so much time and thought and genius been put into the creation of a temple of God; it paled the pagan works of antiquity to insignificance. It did. So much love, so much sweat. Bramante's basilica, Michelangelo's dome, Bernini's colonnade. A monument not only to God, but to Man. Deep under the confession in a little stone room Saint Peter himself was buried; here the Emperor Charlemagne had been crowned. The echoes of old voices seemed to whisper among the pouring slivers of light, dead fingers polished the bronze rays behind the high altar and caressed the twisted bronze columns of the *baldacchino*.

He was lying on the steps, face down, as though dead. What was he thinking? Was there a pain in him that had no right to be there, because his mother had not come? Cardinal Ralph looked through his tears, and knew there was no pain. Beforehand, yes; afterward, certainly. But now, no pain. Everything in him was projected into the moment, the miracle. No room in him for anything which was not God. It was his day of days, and nothing mattered save the task at hand, the vowing of his life and soul to God. He could probably do it, but how many others actually had? Not Cardinal Ralph, though he still remembered his own ordination as filled with holy wonder. With every part of him he had tried, yet something he had withheld.

Not so august as this, my ordination, but I live it again through him. And wonder what he truly is, that in spite of our fears for him he could have passed among us so many years and not made an unfriend, let alone a real enemy. He is loved by all, and he loves all. It never crosses his mind for an instant that this state of affairs is extraordinary. And yet, when he came to us first he was not so sure of himself; we have given him that, for which perhaps our existences are vindicated. There have been many priests made here, thousands upon thousands, yet for him there is something special. Oh, Meggie! Why wouldn't you come to see the gift you've given Our Lord-the gift I could not, having given Him myself? And I suppose that's it, how he can be here today free of pain. Because for today I've been empowered to take his pain to myself, free him from it. I weep his tears, I mourn in his place. And that is how it should be.

Later he turned his head, looked at the row of Drogheda people in alien dark suits. Bob, Jack, Hughie, Jims, Patsy. A vacant chair for Meggie, then Frank. Justine's fiery hair dimmed under a black lace veil, the only female Cleary present. Rainer next to her. And then a lot of people he didn't know, but who shared in today as fully as the Drogheda people did. Only today it was different, today it was special for him. Today he felt almost as if he, too, had had a son to give. He smiled, and sighed. How must Vittorio feel, bestowing Dane's priesthood upon him?

Perhaps because he missed his mother's presence so acutely, Justine was the first person Dane managed to take aside at the reception Cardinal Vittorio and Cardinal Ralph gave for him. In his black soutane with the high white collar he looked magnificent, she thought; only not like a priest at all. Like an actor playing a priest, until one looked into the eyes. And there it was, the inner light, that something which transformed him from a very good-looking man into one unique.

"Father O'neill," she said.

"I haven't assimilated it yet, Jus."

"That isn't hard to understand. I've never felt quite the way I did in Saint Peter's, so what it must have been like for you I can't imagine."

"Oh, I think you can, somewhere inside. If you truly couldn't, you wouldn't be such a fine actress. But with you, Jus, it comes from the unconscious; it doesn't erupt into thought until you need to use it."

They were sitting on a small couch in a far corner of the room, and no one came to disturb them.

After a while he said, "I'm so pleased Frank came," looking to where Frank was talking with Rainer, more animation in his face than his niece and nephew had ever seen. "There's an old Rumanian refugee priest I know," Dane went on, "who has a way of saying, 'Oh, the poor one!' with such compassion in his voice .... I don't know, somehow that's what I always find myself saying about our Frank. And yet, Jus, why?"

But Justine ignored the gambit, went straight to the crux. "I could kill Mum!" she said through her teeth. "She had no right to do this to you!"

"Oh, Jus! I understand. You've got to try, too. If it had been done in malice or to get back at me I might be hurt, but you know her as well as I do, you know it's neither of those. I'm going down to Drogheda soon. I'll talk to her then, find out what's the matter."

"I suppose daughters are never as patient with their mothers as sons are." She drew down the corners of her mouth ruefully, shrugged. "Maybe it's just as well I'm too much of a loner ever to inflict myself on anyone in the mother role."

The blue eyes were very kind, tender; Justine felt her hackles rising, thinking Dane pitied her.

"Why don't you marry Rainer?" he asked suddenly.

Her jaw dropped, she gasped. "He's never asked me," she said feebly.

"Only because he thinks you'd say no. But it might be arranged."

Without thinking, she grabbed him by the ear, as she used to do when they were children. "Don't you dare, you dog-collared prawn! Not one word, do you hear? I don't love Rain. He's just a friend, and I want to keep it that way. If you so much as light a candle for it, I swear I'll sit down, cross my eyes and put a curse on you, and you remember how that used to scare the living daylights out of you, don't you?"

He threw back his head and laughed. "It wouldn't work, Justine! My magic is stronger than yours these days. But there's no need to get so worked up about it, you twit. I was wrong, that's all. I assumed there was a case between you and Rain."

"No, there isn't. After seven years? Break it down, pigs might fly." Pausing, she seemed to seek for words, then looked at him almost shyly. "Dane, I'm so happy for you. I think if Mum was here she'd feel the same. That's all it needs, for her to see you now, like this. You wait, she'll come around."

Very gently he took her pointed face between his hands, smiling down at her with so much love that her own hands came up to clutch at his wrists, soak it in through every pore. As if all those childhood years were remembered, treasured.

Yet behind what she saw in his eyes on her behalf she sensed a shadowy doubt, only perhaps doubt was too strong a word; more like anxiety. Mostly he was sure Mum would understand eventually, but he was human, though all save he tended to forget the fact.

"Jus, will you do something for me?" he asked as he let her go.

"Anything," she said, meaning it.

"I've got a sort of respite, to think about what I'm going to do. Two months. And I'm going to do the heavy thinking on a Drogheda horse after I've talked to Mum—somehow I feel I can't sort anything out until after I've talked to her. But first, well ... I've got to get up my courage to go home. So if you could manage it, come down to the Peloponnese with me for a couple of weeks, tick me off good and proper about being a coward until I get so sick of your voice I put myself on a plane to get away from it." He smiled at her. "Besides, Jussy, I don't want you to think I'm going to exclude you from my life absolutely, any more than I will Mum. You need your old conscience around occasionally."

"Oh, Dane, of course I'll go!"

"Good," he said, then grinned, eyed her mischievously. "I really do need you, Jus. Having you bitching in my ear will be just like old times."

"Uh-uh-uh! No obscenities, Father O'neill!"

His arms went behind his head, he leaned back on the couch contentedly. "I am! Isn't it marvelous? And may be after I've seen Mum, I can concentrate on Our Lord. I think that's where my inclinations lie, you know. Simply thinking about Our Lord."

"You ought to have espoused an order, Dane."

"I still can, and I probably will. I have a whole lifetime; there's no hurry."

Justine left the party with Rainer, and after she talked of going to Greece with Dane, he talked of going to his office in Bonn. "About bloody time," she said. "For a cabinet minister you don't seem to do much work, do you?

All the papers call you a playboy, fooling around with carrot-topped Australian actresses, you old dog, you." He shook his big fist at her. "I pay for my few pleasures in more ways than you'll ever know." "Do you mind if we walk, Rain?" "Not if you keep your shoes on." "I have to these days. Miniskirts have their disadvantages; the days of stockings one could peel off easily are over. They've invented a sheer version of theatrical tights, and one can't shed those in public without causing the biggest furor since Lady Godiva. So unless I want to ruin a five-guinea pair of tights, I'm imprisoned in my shoes." "At least you improve my education in feminine garb, under as well as over," he said mildly.

"Go on! I'll bet you've got a dozen mistresses, and undress them all."

"Only one, and like all good mistresses she waits for me in her negligee."

"Do you know, I believe we've never discussed your sex life before? Fascinating! What's she like?"

"Fair, fat, forty and flatulent."

She stopped dead. "Oh, you're kidding me," she said slowly. "I can't see you with a woman like that."

"Why not?"

"You've got too much taste."

"*Chacun a son gout*, my dear. I'm nothing much to look at, myself-why should you assume I could charm a young and beautiful woman into being my mistress?"

"Because you could!" she said indignantly. "Oh, of course you could!"

"My money, you mean?"

"Not, not your money! You're teasing me, you always do! Rainer

Moerling Hartheim, you're very well aware how attractive you are, otherwise you wouldn't wear gold medallions and netting shirts. Looks aren't everything—if they were, I'd still be wondering."

"Your concern for me is touching, *Herzchen*."

"Why is it that when I'm with you I feel as if I'm forever running to catch up with you, and I never do?" Her spurt of temper died; she stood looking at him uncertainly. "You're not serious, are you?"

"Do you think I am?"

"No! You're not conceited, but you do know how very attractive you are."

"Whether I do or not isn't important. The important thing is that you think I'm attractive."

She was going to say: Of course I do; I was mentally trying you on as a lover not long ago, but then I decided it wouldn't work, I'd rather keep on having you for my friend. Had he let her say it, he might have concluded his time hadn't come, and acted differently. As it was, before she could shape the words he had her in his arms, and was kissing her. For at least sixty seconds she stood, dying, split open, smashed, the power in her screaming in wild elation to find a matching power. His mouth—it was beautiful! And his hair, incredibly thick, vital, something to seize in her fingers fiercely. Then he took her face between his hands and looked at her, smiling.

"I love you," he said.

Her hands had gone up to his wrists, but not to enclose them gently, as with Dane; the nails bit in, scored down to meat savagely. She stepped back two paces and stood rubbing her arm across her mouth, eyes huge with fright, breasts heaving.

"It couldn't work," she panted. "It could never work, Rain!"

Off came the shoes; she bent to pick them up, then turned and ran, and within three seconds the soft quick pad of her feet had vanished.

Not that he had any intention of following her, though apparently she had thought he might. Both his wrists were bleeding, and they hurt. He pressed his handkerchief first to one and then to the other, shrugged, put the stained cloth away, and stood concentrating on the pain. After a while he unearthed his cigarette case, took out a cigarette, lit it, and began to walk slowly. No one passing by could have told from his face what he felt. Everything he wanted within his grasp, reached for, lost. Idiot girl. When would she grow up? To feel it, respond to it, and deny it.

But he was a gambler, of the win-a-few, lose-a-few kind. He had waited seven long years before trying his luck, feeling the change in her at this ordination time. Yet apparently he had moved too soon. Ah, well. There was always tomorrow—or knowing Justine, next year, the year after that. Certainly he wasn't about to give up. If he watched her carefully, one day he'd get lucky.

The soundless laugh quivered in him; fair, fat, forty and flatulent. What had brought it to his lips he didn't know, except that a long-time ago his ex-wife had said it to him. The four F's, describing the typical victim of gall stones. She had been a martyr to them, poor Annelise, even though she was dark, skinny, fifty and as well corked as a genie in a bottle. What am I thinking of Annelise for, now? My patient campaign of years turned in to a rout, and I can do no better than poor Annelise. So, *Fraulein Justine O'neill*! We shall see.

There were lights in the palace windows; he would go up for a few minutes, talk to Cardinal Ralph, who was looking old. Not well. Perhaps he ought to be persuaded into a medical examination. Rainer ached, but not for Justine; she was young, there was time. For Cardinal Ralph, who had seen his own son ordained, and not known it.

It was still early, so the hotel foyer was crowded. Shoes on, Justine crossed quickly to the stairs and ran up them, head bent. Then for some time her trembling hands couldn't find the room key in her bag and she thought she would have to go down again, brave the crowd about the desk. But it was there; she must have passed her fingers over it a dozen times.

Inside at last, she groped her way to the bed; sat down on its edge and let coherent thought gradually return. Telling herself she was revolted, horrified, disillusioned; all the while staring drearily at the wide rectangle of pale light which was the night sky through the window, wanting to curse, wanting to weep. It could never be the same again, and that was a tragedy. The loss of the dearest friend. Betrayal.

Empty words, untrue; suddenly she knew very well what had frightened her so, made her flee from Rain as if he had attempted murder, not a kiss. The rightness of it! The feeling of coming home, when she didn't want to come home any more than she wanted the liability of love. Home was frustration, so was love. Not only that, even if the admission was humiliating; she wasn't sure she could love. If she was capable of it, surely once or twice her guard would have slipped; surely once or twice she would have experienced a pang of something more than tolerant affection for her infrequent lovers. It didn't occur to her that she deliberately chose lovers who would never threaten her self-imposed detachment, so much a part of herself by now that she regarded it as completely natural. For the first time in her life she had no reference point to assist her. There was no time in the past she could take comfort from, no once-deep involvement, either for herself or for those shadowy lovers. Nor could the Drogheda people help, because she had always withheld herself from them, too.

She had had to run from Rain. To say yes, commit herself to him, and then have to watch him recoil when he found out the extent of her inadequacy? Unbearable! He would learn what she was really like, and the knowledge would kill his love for her. Unbearable to say yes, and end in being rebuffed for all time. Far better to do any rebuffing herself. That way at least pride would be satisfied, and Justine owned all her mother's pride. Rain must never discover what she was like beneath all that brick flippancy.

He had fallen in love with the Justine he saw; she had not allowed him any opportunity to suspect the sea of doubts beneath. Those only Dane suspected—no, knew.

She bent forward to put her forehead against the cool bedside table, tears running down her face. That was why she loved. Dane so, of course. Knowing what the real Justine was like, and still loving her. Blood helped, so did a lifetime of shared memories, problems, pains, joys. Whereas Rain was a stranger, not committed to her the way Dane was, or even the other members of her family. Nothing obliged him to love her.

She sniffled, wiped her palm around her face, shrugged her shoulders and began the difficult business of pushing her trouble back into some corner of her mind where it could lie peacefully, unremembered. She knew she could do it; she had spent all her life perfecting the technique. Only it meant ceaseless activity, continuous absorption in things outside herself. She reached over and switched on the bedside lamp.

One of the Unks must have delivered the letter to her room, for it was lying on the bedside table, a pale-blue airletter with Queen Elizabeth in its upper corner.

"Darling Justine," wrote Clyde Daltinham-Roberts, "Come back to the fold, you're needed! At once! There's apart going begging in the new season's repertoire, and a tiny little dicky-bird told me you just might want it. Desdemona, darling? With Marc Simpson as your Othello? Rehearsals for the principals start neat week, if you're interested"

If she was interested! Desdemona! Desdemona in London! And with Marc Simpson as Othello! The opportunity of a lifetime. Her mood skyrocketed to a point where the scene with Rain lost significance, or rather assumed a different significance. Perhaps if she was very, very careful she might be able to keep Rain's love; a highly acclaimed, successful actress was too busy to share much of her life with her lovers. It was worth a try. If he looked as if he were getting too close to the truth, she could always back off again. To keep Rain in her life, but especially this new Rain, she would be prepared to do anything save strip off the mask.

In the meantime, news like this deserved some sort of celebration. She didn't feel up to facing Rain yet, but there were other people on hand to share her triumph. So she put on her shoes, walked down the corridor to the Unks' communal sitting room, and when Patsy let her in she stood with arms spread wide, beaming.

"Break out the beer, I'm going to be Desdemona!" she announced in ringing tones.

For a moment no one answered, then Bob said warmly, "That's nice, Justine."

Her pleasure didn't evaporate; instead it built up to an uncontrollable elation. Laughing, she flopped into a chair and stared at her uncles. What truly lovely men they were! Of course her news meant nothing to them! They didn't have a clue who Desdemona was. If she had come to tell them she was getting married, Bob's answer would have been much the same.

Since the beginning of memory they had been a part of her life, and sadly she had dismissed them as contemptuously as she did everything about Drogheda. The Unks, a plurality having nothing to do with Justine O'neill. Simply members of a conglomerate who drifted in and out of the homestead, smiled at her shyly, avoided her if it meant conversation. Not that they didn't like her, she realized now; only that they sensed how foreign she was, and it made them uncomfortable. But in this Roman world which was alien to them and familiar to her, she was beginning to understand them better.

Feeling a glow of something for them which might have been called love, Justine stared from one creased, smiling face to the next. Bob, who was the life force of the unit, the Boss of Drogheda, but in such an unobtrusive way; Jack, who merely seemed to follow Bob around, or maybe it was just that they got along so well together; Hughie, who had a streak of mischief the other two did not, and yet so very like them; Jims and Patsy, the positive and negative sides of a self-sufficient whole; and poor quenched Frank, the only one who seemed plagued by fear and insecurity. All of them save Jims and Patsy, were grizzled now, indeed Bob and Frank were white-haired, but they didn't really look very different from the way she remembered them as a little girl.

"I don't know whether I ought to give you a beer," Bob said doubtfully, standing with a cold bottle of Swan in his hand.

The remark would have annoyed her intensely even half a day ago, but at the moment she was too happy to take offense.

"Look, love, I know it's never occurred to you to offer me one through the course of our sessions with Rain, but honestly I'm a big girl now, and I can handle a beer. I promise it isn't a sin." She smiled.

"Where's Rainer?" Jims asked, taking a full glass from Bob and handing it to her.

"I had a fight with him."

"With *Rainer*?"

"Well, yes. But it was all my fault. I'm going to see him later and tell him I'm sorry."

None of the Unks smoked. Though she had never asked for a beer before, on earlier occasions she had sat smoking defiantly while they talked with Rain; now it took more courage than she could command to produce her cigarettes, so she contented herself with the minor victory of the beer, dying to gulp it down thirstily but mindful of their dubious regard. Ladylike sips, Justine, even if you are dryer than a secondhand sermon.

"Rain's a bonzer bloke," said Hughie, eyes twinkling.

Startled, Justine suddenly realized why she had grown so much in importance in their thoughts: she had caught herself a man they'd like to have in the family. "Yes, he is rather," she said shortly, and changed the subject. "It was a lovely day, wasn't it?"

All the heads bobbed in unison, even Frank's, but they didn't seem to want to discuss it. She could see how tired they were, yet she didn't regret her impulse to visit them. It took a little while for near-atrophied senses and feelings to learn what their proper functions were, and the Unks were a good practice target. That was the trouble with being an island; one forgot there was anything going on beyond its shores.

"What's Desdemona?" Frank asked from the shadows where he hid.

Justine launched into a vivid description, charmed by their horror when they learned she would be strangled once a night, and only remembered how tired they must be half an hour later when Patsy yawned.

"I must go," she said, putting down her empty glass. She had not been offered a second beer; one was apparently the limit for ladies. "Thanks for listening to me blather."

Much to Bob's surprise and confusion, she kissed him good night; Jack edged away but was easily caught, while Hughie accepted the farewell with alacrity. Jims turned bright red, endured it dumbly. For Patsy, a hug as well as a kiss, because he was a little bit of an island himself. And for Frank no kiss at all, he averted his head; yet when she put her arms around him she could sense a faint echo of some intensity quite missing in the others. Poor Frank. Why was he like that?

Outside their door, she leaned for a moment against the wall. Rain loved her. But when she tried to phone his room the operator informed her he had checked out, returned to Bonn.

No matter. It might be better to wait until London to see him, anyway. A contrite apology via the mail, and an invitation to dinner next time he was in England. There were many things she didn't know about Rain, but of one characteristic she had no doubt at all; he would come, because he hadn't a grudging bone in his body. Since foreign affairs had become his forte, England was one of his most regular ports of call.

"You wait and see, my lad," she said, staring into her mirror and seeing his face instead of her own. "I'm going to make England your most important foreign affair, or my name isn't Justine O'neill."

It had not occurred to her that perhaps as far as Rain was concerned, her name was indeed the crux of the matter. Her patterns of behavior were set, and marriage was no part of them. That Rain might want to make her over into Justine Hartheim never even crossed her mind. She was too busy remembering the quality of his kiss, and dreaming of more.

There remained only the task of telling Dane she couldn't go to Greece with him, but about this she was untroubled. Dane would understand, he always did. Only somehow she didn't think she'd tell him all the reasons why she wasn't able to go. Much as she loved her brother, she didn't feel like listening to what would be one of his sternest homilies ever. He wanted her to marry Rain, so if she told him what her plans for

Rain were, he'd cart her off to Greece with him if it meant forcible abduction. What Dane's ears didn't hear, his heart couldn't grieve about.

"Dear Rain," the note said. "Sorry I ran like a hairy goat the other night, can't think what got into me. The hectic day and everything, I suppose. Please forgive me for behaving like an utter prawn. I'm ashamed of myself for making so much fuss about a trifle. And I daresay the day had got to you, too, words of love and all, I mean. So I tell you what-you forgive me, and I'll forgive you. Let's be friends, please. I can't bear to be at outs with you. Next time you're in London, come to dinner at my place and we'll formally draft out a peace treaty."

As usual it was signed plain "Justine." No words even of affection; she never used them. Frowning, he studied the artlessly casual phrases as if he could see through them to what was really in her mind as she wrote. It was certainly an overture of friendship, but what else? Sighing, he was forced to admit probably very little. He had frightened her badly; that she wanted to retain his friendship spoke of how much he meant to her, but he very much doubted whether she understood exactly what she felt for him. After all, now she knew he loved her; if she had sorted herself out sufficiently to realize she loved him too, she would have come straight out with it in her letter. Yet why had she returned to London instead of going to Greece with Dane? He knew he shouldn't hope it was because of him, but despite his misgivings, hope began to color his thoughts so cheerfully he buzzed his secretary. It was 10 a.m. Greenwich Mean Time, the best hour to find her at home.

"Get me Miss O'neill's London flat," he instructed, and waited the intervening seconds with a frown pulling at the inner corners of his brows.

"Rain!" Justine said, apparently delighted. "Did you get my letter?"

"This minute."

After a delicate pause she said. "And will you come to dinner soon?"

"I'm going to be in England this coming Friday and Saturday. Is the notice too short?"

"Not if Saturday evening is all right with you. I'm in rehearsal for Desdemona, so Friday's out."

"Desdemona?"

"That's right, you don't know! Clyde wrote to me in Rome and offered me the part. Marc Simpson as Othello, Clyde directing personally. Isn't it wonderful? I came back to London on the first plane."

He shielded his eyes with his hand, thankful his secretary was safely in her outer office, not sitting where she could see his face. "Justine, Herzchen, that's marvelous news!" he managed to say enthusiastically. "I was wondering what brought you back to London."

"Oh, Dane understood," she said lightly, "and in a way I think he was quite glad to be alone. He had concocted a story about needing me to bitch at him to go home, but I think it was all more for his second reason, that he doesn't want me to feel excluded from his life now he's a priest."

"Probably," he agreed politely.

"Saturday evening, then," she-said. "Around six, then we can have a leisurely peace treaty session with the aid of a bottle or two, and I'll feed you after we've reached a satisfactory compromise. All right?"

"Yes, of course. Goodbye, Herzchen." Contact was cut off abruptly by the sound of her receiver going down; he sat for a moment with his still in his hand, then shrugged and replaced it on its cradle. Damn Justine! She was beginning to come between him and his work. She continued to come between him and his work during the succeeding days, though it was doubtful if anyone suspected. And on Saturday evening a little after six he presented himself at her apartment, empty-handed as usual because she was a difficult person to bring gifts. She was indifferent to flowers, never ate candy and would have thrown a more expensive offering carelessly in some corner, then forgotten it. The only gifts Justine seemed to prize were those Dane had given her.

"Champagne before dinner?" he asked, looking at her in surprise.

"Well, I think the occasion calls for it, don't you? It was our first-ever breaking of relations, and this is our first-ever reconciliation," she answered plausibly, indicating a comfortable chair for him and settling herself on the tawny kangaroo-fur rug, lips parted as if she had already rehearsed replies to anything he might say next. But conversation was beyond him, at least until he was better able to assess her mood, so he watched her in silence. Until he had kissed her it had been easy to keep himself partially aloof, but now, seeing her again for the first time since, he admitted that it was going to be a great deal harder in the future.

Probably even when she was a very old woman she would still retain something not quite fully mature about face and bearing; as though essential womanliness would always pass her by. That cool, self-centered, logical brain seemed to dominate her completely, yet for him she owned a fascination so potent he doubted if he would ever be able to replace her with any other woman. Never once had he questioned whether she was worth the long struggle. Possibly from a philosophical standpoint she wasn't. Did it matter? She was a goal, an aspiration.

"You're looking very nice tonight; Herzchen," he said at last, tipping his champagne glass to her in a gesture half toast, half acknowledgment of an adversary.

A coal fire simmered unshielded in the small Victorian grate, but Justine didn't seem to mind the heat, huddled close to it with her eyes fixed on him. Then she put her glass on the hearth with a ringing snap and sat forward, her arms linked about her knees, bare feet hidden by folds of densely black gown.

"I can't stand beating around the bush," she said. "Did you mean it, Rain?"

Suddenly relaxing deeply, he lay back in his chair. "Mean what?"

"What you said in Rome ... That you loved me."

"Is that what this is all about, Herzchen?"

She looked away, shrugged, looked back at him and nodded. "Well, of course."

"But why bring it up again? You told me what you thought, and I had gathered tonight's invitation wasn't extended to bring up the past, only plan a future."

"Oh, Rain! You're acting as if I'm making a fuss! Even if I was, surely you can see why."

"No, I can't." He put his glass down and bent forward to watch her more closely. "You gave me to understand most emphatically that you wanted no part of my love, and I had hoped you'd at least have the decency to refrain from discussing it."

It had not occurred to her that this meeting, no matter what its outcome, would be so uncomfortable; after all, he had put himself in the position of a suppliant, and ought to be waiting humbly for her to reverse her decision. Instead he seemed to have turned the tables neatly. Here she was feeling like a naughty schoolgirl called upon to answer for some idiotic prank.

"Look, sport, you're the one who changed the status quo, not me! I didn't ask you to come tonight so I could beg forgiveness for having wounded the great Hartheim ego!"

"On the defensive, Justine?"

She wriggled impatiently. "Yes, damm it! How do you manage to do that to me, Rain? Oh, I wish just once you'd let me enjoy having the upper hand!"

"If I did, you'd throw me out like a smelly old rag," he said, smiling.

"I can do that yet, mate!"

"Nonsense! If you haven't done it by now you never will. You'll go on seeing me because I keep you on the hop-you never know what to expect from me."

"Is that why you said you loved me?" she asked painfully. "Was it only a ploy to keep me on the hop?"

"What do you think?"

"I think you're a prize bastard!" she said through her teeth, and marched across the rug on her knees until she was close enough to give him the full benefit of her anger. "Say you love me again, you big Kraut prawn, and watch me spit in your eye!"

He was angry, too. "No, I'm not going to say it again! That isn't why you asked me to come, is it? My feelings don't concern you one bit, Justine. You asked me to come so you could experiment with your own feelings, and it didn't enter your mind to consider whether that was being fair to me."

Before she could move away he leaned forward, gripped her arms near the shoulders and clamped her body between his legs, holding her firmly. Her rage vanished at once; she flattened her palms on his thighs and lifted her face. But he didn't kiss her. He let go of her arms and twisted to switch off the lamp behind him, then relaxed his hold on her and laid his head back against the chair, so that she wasn't sure if he had dimmed the room down to glowing coals as the first move in his love-making, or simply to conceal his expression. Uncertain, afraid of outright rejection, she waited to be told what to do. She should have realized earlier that one didn't tamper with people like Rain. They were as invincible as death. Why couldn't she put her head on his lap and say: Rain, love me, I need you so much and I'm so sorry? Oh, surely if she could get him to make love to her some emotional key would turn and it would all come tumbling out, released ...

Still withdrawn, remote, he let her take off his jacket and tie, but by the time she began to unbutton his shirt she knew it wasn't going to work. The kind of instinctive erotic skills which could make the most mundane operation exciting were not in her repertoire. This was so important, and she was making an absolute mess of it. Her fingers faltered, her mouth puckered. She burst in to tears.

"Oh, no! *Herzchen*, *liebchen*, don't cry!" He pulled her onto his lap and turned her head into his shoulder, his arms around her. "I'm sorry, Herzchen, I didn't mean to make you cry."

"Now you know," she said between sobs. "I'm a miserable failure; I told you it wouldn't work! Rain, I wanted so badly to keep you, but I knew it wouldn't work if I let you see how awful I am!"

"No, of course it wouldn't work. How could it? I wasn't helping you, Herzchen." He tugged at her hair to bring her face up to his, kissed her eyelids, her wet cheeks, the corners of her mouth. "It's my fault, Herzchen, not yours. I was paying you back; I wanted to see how far you could go without encouragement. But I think I have mistaken your motives, *nicht wahr*?" His voice had grown thicker, more German. "And I say, if this is what you want you shall have it, but it shall be together."

"Please, Rain, let's call it off! I haven't got what it takes. I'll only disappoint you!"

"Oh, you've got it, Herzchen, I've seen it on the stage. How can you doubt yourself when you're with me?"

Which was so right her tears dried.

"Kiss me the way you did in Rome," she whispered. Only it wasn't like the kiss in Rome at all. That had been something raw, startled, explosive; this was very languorous and deep, an opportunity to taste and smell and feel, settle by layers into voluptuous ease. Her fingers returned to the buttons, his went to the zipper of her dress, then he covered her hand with his and thrust it inside his shirt, across skin matted with fine soft hair. The sudden hardening of his mouth against her throat brought a helpless response so acute she felt faint, thought she was falling and found she had, flat on the silky rug with Rain looming above her. His shirt had come off, perhaps more, she couldn't see, only the fire glancing off his shoulders spread over her, and the beautiful stern mouth. Determined to destroy its discipline for all time, she locked her fingers in his hair and made him kiss her again, harder, harder!

And the feel of him! Like coming home, recognizing every part of him with her lips and hands and body, yet fabulous and strange. While the world sank down to the minute width of the firelight lapping against darkness, she opened herself to what he wanted, and learned something he had kept entirely concealed for as long as she had known him; that he must have made love to her in imagination a thousand times. Her own experience and newborn intuition told her so. She was completely disarmed. With any other man the intimacy and astonishing sensuality would have appalled her, but he forced her to see that these were things only she had the right to command. And command them she did. Until finally she cried for him to finish it, her arms about him so strongly she could feel the contours of his very bones.

The minutes wore away, wrapped in a sated peace. They had fallen into an identical rhythm of breathing, slow and easy, his head against her shoulder, her leg thrown across him. Gradually her rigid clasp on his back relaxed, became a dreamy, circular caress. He sighed, turned over and reversed the way they were lying, quite unconsciously inviting her to slide still deeper into the pleasure of being with him. She put her palm on his flank to feel the texture of his skin, slid her hand across warm muscle and cupped it around the soft, heavy mass in his groin. To feel the curiously alive, independent movements within it was a sensation quite new to her; her past lovers had never interested her sufficiently to want to prolong her sexual curiosity to this languid and undemanding aftermath. Yet suddenly it wasn't languid and undemanding at all, but so enormously exciting she wanted him all over again.

Still she was taken unaware, knew a suffocated surprise when he slipped his arms across her back, took her head in his hands and held her close enough to see there was nothing controlled about his mouth, shaped now solely because of her, and for her. Tenderness and humility were literally born in her in that moment. It must have shown in her face, for he was gazing at her with eyes grown so bright she couldn't bear them, and bent over to take his upper lip between her own. Thoughts and senses merged at last, but her cry was smothered soundless, an unuttered wail of gladness which shook her so deeply she lost awareness of everything beyond impulse, the mindless guidance of each urgent minute. The world achieved its ultimate contraction, turned in upon itself, and totally disappeared.

Rainer must have kept the fire going, for when gentle London daylight soaked through the folds of the curtains the room was still warm. This time when he moved Justine became conscious of it, and clutched his arm fearfully.

"Don't go!"

"I'm not, Herzchen." He twitched another pillow from the sofa, pushed it behind his head and shifted her closer in to his side, sighing softly. "All right?"

"Yes."

"Are you cold?"

"No, but if you are we could go to bed."

"After making love to you for hours on a fur rug? What a comedown! Even if your sheets are black silk."

"They're ordinary old white ones, cotton. This bit of Drogheda is all right, isn't it?"

"Bit of Drogheda?"

"The rug! It's made of Drogheda kangaroos," she explained.

"Not nearly exotic or erotic enough. I'll order you a tiger skin from India."

"Reminds me of a poem I heard once:

Would you like to sin
With Elinor Glyn
On a tiger skin?
Or would you prefer
To err with her
On some other fur?"

"Well, Herzchen, I must say it's high time you bounced back! Between the demands of Eros and Morpheus, you haven't been flippant in half a day." He smiled.

"I don't feel the need at the moment," she said with an answering smile, settling his hand comfortably between her legs. "The tiger skin doggerel just popped out because it was too good to resist, but I haven't got a single skeleton left to hide from you, so there's not much point in flippancy, is there?" She sniffed, suddenly aware of a faint odor of stale fish drifting on the air. "Heavens, you didn't get any dinner and now it's time for breakfast! I can't expect you to live on love!"

"Not if you expect such strenuous demonstrations of it, anyway."

"Go on, you enjoyed every moment of it."

"Indeed I did." He sighed, stretched, yawned. "I wonder if you have any idea how happy I am." "Oh, I think so," she said quietly:

He raised himself on one elbow to look at her. "Tell me, was Desdemona the only reason you came back to London?"

Grabbing his ear, she tweaked it painfully. "Now it's my turn to pay you back for all those headmasterish questions! What do you think?"

He prized her fingers away easily, grinning. "If you don't answer me, Herzchen, I'll strangle you far more permanently than Marc does."

"I came back to London to do Desdemona, but because of you. I haven't been able to call my life my own since you kissed me in Rome, and well you know it. You're a very intelligent man, Rainer Moerling Hartheim."

"Intelligent enough to have known I wanted you for my wife almost the first moment I saw you," he said.

She sat up quickly. "Wife?"

"Wife. If I'd wanted you for my mistress I'd have taken you years ago, and I could have. I know how your mindworks; it would have been relatively easy. The only reason I didn't was because I wanted you for my wife and I knew you weren't ready to accept the idea of a husband."

"I don't know that I am now," she said, digesting it.

He got to his feet, pulling her up to stand against him. "Well, you can put in a little practice by getting me some breakfast. If this was my house I'd do the honors, but in your kitchen you're the cook."

"I don't mind getting your breakfast this morning, but theoretically to commit myself until the day I die?" She shook her head. "I don't think that's my cup of tea, Rain."

It was the same Roman emperor's face, and imperially unperturbed by threats of insurrection. "Justine, this is not something to play with, nor am I someone to play with. There's plenty of time. You have every reason to know I can be patient. But get it out of your head entirely that this can be settled in any way but marriage. I have no wish to be known as anyone less important to you than a husband."

"I'm not giving up acting!" she said aggressively.

"Verfluchte Kiste, did I ask you to? Grow up, Justine! Anyone would think I was condemning you to a life sentence over a sink and stove! We're not exactly on the breadline, you know. You can have as many servants as you want, nannies for the children, whatever else is necessary."

"Erk!" said Justine, who hadn't thought of children.

He threw back his head and laughed. "Oh, Herzchen, this is what's known as the morning after with a vengeance! I'm a fool to bring up realities. so soon, I know, but all you have to do at this stage is think about them. Though I give you fair warning-while you're making your decision, remember that if I can't have you for my wife, I don't want you at all."

She threw her arms around him, clinging fiercely. "Oh, Rain, don't make it so hard!" she cried.

Alone, Dane drove his Lagonda up the Italian boot, past Perugia, Firenze, Bologna, Ferrara, Padova, better bypass Venezia, spend the night in Trieste. It was one of his favorite cities, so he stayed on the Adriatic coast a further two days before heading up the mountain road to Ljubljana, another night in Zagreb. Down the great Sava River valley amid fields blue with chicory flowers to Beograd, thence to Nis, another night. Macedonia and Skopje, still in crumbling ruins from the earthquake two years before; and Tito-Veles the vacation city, quaintly Turkish with its mosques and minarets. All the way down Yugoslavia he had eaten frugally, too ashamed to sit with a great plate of meat in front of him when the people of the country contented themselves with bread.

The Greek border at Evzone, beyond it Thessalonika. The Italian papers had been full of the revolution brewing in Greece; standing in his hotel bedroom window watching the bobbing thousands of flaming torches moving restlessly in the darkness of a Thessalonika night, he was glad Justine had not come.

"Pap-an-dre-out! Pap-andre-out! Pap-an-dre-out!" the crowds roared, chanting, milling among the torches until after midnight.

But revolution was a phenomenon of cities, of dense concentrations of people and poverty; the scarred countryside of Thessaly must still look as it had looked to Caesar's legions, marching across the stubble-burned fields to Pompey at Pharsala. Shepherds slept in the shade of skin tents, storks stood one-legged in nests atop little old white buildings, and everywhere was a terrifying aridity. It reminded him, with its high clear sky, its brown treeless wastes, of Australia. And he breathed of it deeply, began to smile at the thought of going home. Mum would understand, when he talked to her.

Above Larisa he came onto the sea, stopped the car and got out. Homer's wine-dark sea, a delicate clear aquamarine near the beaches, purple-stained like grapes as it stretched to the curving horizon. On a greensward far below him stood a tiny round pillared temple, very white in the sun, and on the rise of the hill behind him a frowning Crusader fortress endured. Greece, you are very beautiful, more beautiful than Italy, for all that I love Italy. But here is the cradle, forever.

Panting to be in Athens, he pushed on, gunned the red sports car up the switchbacks of the Domokos Pass and descended its other side into Boeotia, a stunning panorama of olive groves, rusty hillsides, mountains. Yet in spite of his haste he stopped to look at the oddly Hollywoodish monument to Leonidas and his Spartans at Thermopylae.

The stone said: "Stranger, go tell the Spartans that here we lie, in obedience to their command." Its truck a chord in him, almost seemed to be words he might have heard in a different context; he shivered and went on quickly.

In melted sun he paused for a while above Kamena Voura, swam in the clear water looking across the narrow strait to Euboea; there must the thousand ships have sailed from Aulis, on their way to Troy. It was a strong current, swirling seaward; they must not have had to ply their oars very hard. The ecstatic cooings and strokings of the ancient black-garbed crone in the bath-house embarrassed him; he couldn't get away from her fast enough. People never referred to his beauty to his face anymore, so most of the time he was able to forget it. Delaying only to buy a couple of huge, custard-filled cakes in the shop, he went on down the Attic coast and finally came to Athens as the sun was setting, gilding the great rock and its precious crown of pillars.

But Athens was tense and vicious, and the open admiration of the women mortified him; Roman women were more sophisticated, subtle. There was a feeling in the crowds, pockets of rioting, grim determination on the part of the people to have Papandreou. No, Athens wasn't herself; better to be elsewhere. He put the Lagonda in a garage and took the ferry to Crete.

And there at last, amid the olive groves, the wild thyme and the mountains, he found his peace. After a long bus ride with trussed chickens screeching and the all-pervasive reek of garlic in his nostrils, he found a tiny white-painted inn with an arched colonnade and three umbrellaed tables outside on the flagstones, gay Greek bags hanging festooned like lanterns. Pepper trees and Australian gum trees, planted from the new South Land in soil too arid for European trees. The gut roar of cicadas. Dust, swirling in red clouds.

At night he slept in a tiny cell-like room with shutters wide open, in the hush of dawn he celebrated a solitary Mass, during the day he walked. No one bothered him; he bothered no one. But as he passed the dark eyes of the peasants would follow him in slow amazement, and every face would crease deeper in a smile. It was hot, and so quiet, and very sleepy. Perfect peace. Day followed day, like beads slipping through a leathery Cretan hand.

Voicelessly he prayed, a feeling, an extension of what lay all through him, thoughts like beads, days like beads. Lord, I am truly Thine. For Thy many blessings I thank Thee. For the great Cardinal, his help, his deep friendship, his unfailing love. For Rome and the chance to be at Thy heart, to have lain prostrate before Thee in Thine own basilica, to have felt the rock of Thy Church within me. Thou hast blessed me above my worth; what can I do for Thee, to show my appreciation? I have not suffered enough. My life has been one long, absolute joy since I began in Thy service. I must suffer, and Thou Who suffered will know that. It is only through suffering that I may rise above myself, understand Thee better. For that is what this life is: the passage toward understanding Thy mystery. Plunge Thy spear into my breast, bury it there so deeply I am never able to with draw it! Make me suffer ... For Thee I forsake all others, even my mother and my sister and the Cardinal. Thou alone art my pain, my joy. Abase me and I shall sing Thy beloved Name. Destroy me, and I shall rejoice. I love Thee. Only Thee ...

He had come to the little beach where he liked to swim, a yellow crescent between beetling cliffs, and stood fora moment looking across the Mediterranean to what must be Libya, far below the dark horizon. Then helped lightly down the steps to the sand, kicked off his sneakers, picked them up, and trod through the softly yielding contours to the spot where he usually dropped shoes, shirt, outer shorts. Two young Englishmen talking in drawling Oxford accents lay like broiling lobsters not far away, and beyond them two women drowsily speaking in German. Dane glanced at the women and self-consciously hitched his swimsuit, aware they had stopped conversing and had sat up to pat their hair, smile at him.

"How goes it?" he asked the Englishmen, though in his mind he called them what all Australians call the English, Pommies. They seemed to be fixtures, since they were on the beach every day.

"Splendidly, old boy. Watch the current—it's too strong for us. Storm out there somewhere."

"Thanks." Dane grinned, ran down to the innocently curling wavelets and dived cleanly into shallow water like the expert Surfer he was.

Amazing, how deceptive calm water could be. The current was vicious, he could feel it tugging at his legs to draw him under, but he was too strong a swimmer to be worried by it. Head down, he slid smoothly through the water, reveling in the coolness, the freedom. When he paused and scanned the beach he saw the two German women pulling on their caps, running down laughing to the waves.

Cupping his hands around his mouth, he called to them in German to stay in shallow water because of the current. Laughing, they waved acknowledgment. He put his head down then, swam again, and thought he heard a cry. But he swam a little farther, then stopped to tread water in a spot where the undertow wasn't so bad. There were cries; as he turned he saw the women struggling, their twisted faces screaming, one with her hands up, sinking. On the beach the two Englishmen had risen to their feet and were reluctantly approaching the water.

He flipped over onto his belly and flashed through the water, closer and closer. Panicked arms reached for him ,clung to him, dragged him under; he managed to grip one woman around the waist long enough to stun her with a swift clip on the chin, then grabbed the other by the strap of her swimsuit, shoved his knee hard into her spine and winded her. Coughing, for he had swallowed water when he went under, he turned on his back and began towing his helpless burdens in.

The two Pommies were standing shoulder-deep, too frightened to venture any farther, for which Dane didn't blame them in the least. His toes just touched the sand; he sighed in relief. Exhausted, he exerted a last superhuman effort and thrust the women to safety. Fast regaining their senses, they began screaming again, thrashing about wildly. Gasping, Dane managed a grin. He had done his bit; the Poms could take over now. While he rested, chest heaving, the current had sucked him out again, his feet no longer brushed the bottom even when he stretched them downward. It had been a close call. If he hadn't been present they would certainly have drowned; the Poms hadn't the strength or skill to save them. But, said a voice, they only wanted to swim so they could be near you; until they saw you they hadn't any intention of going in. It was your fault they were in danger, your fault.

And as he floated easily a terrible pain blossomed in his chest, surely as a spear would feel, one long and red-hot shaft of screaming agony. He cried out, threw his arms up above his head, stiffening, muscles convulsed; but the pain grew worse, forced his arms down again, thrust his fists into his armpits, brought up his knees. My heart! I'm having a heart attack, I'm dying! My heart! I don't want to die! Not yet, not before I've begun my work, not before I've had a chance to prove myself! Dear Lord, help me! I don't want to die, I don't want to die!

The spasmed body stilled, relaxed; Dane turned onto his back, let his arms float wide and limp in spite of the pain. Wet-lashed, he stared—up at the soaring vault of the sky. This is it; this is Thy spear, that I in my pride begged for not an hour ago. Give me the chance to suffer, I said, make me suffer. Now when it comes I resist, not capable of perfect love. Dearest Lord, Thy pain! I must accept it, I must not fight it, I must not fight Thy will. Thy hand is mighty and this is Thy pain, as Thou must have felt it on the Cross. My God, my God, I am Thine! If this is Thy will, so be it. Like a child I put myself into Thy infinite hand. Thou art too good to me. What have I done to deserve so much from Thee, and from the people who love me better than they love anyone else? Why hast Thou given me so much, when I am not worthy? The pain, the pain! Thou art so good to me. Let it not belong, I asked, and it has not been long. My suffering will be short, quickly over. Soon I shall see Thy face, but now, still in this life, I thank Thee. The pain! My dearest Lord, Thou art too good to me. I love Thee!

A huge tremor passed through the still, waiting body. His lips moved, murmured a Name, tried to smile. Then the pupils dilated, drove all the blue from his eyes forever. Safe on the beach at last, the two Englishmen dumped their weeping charges on the sand and stood looking for him. But the placid deep blue sea was empty, vast; the wavelets ran up rushing and retreated. Dane was gone.

Someone thought of the United States Air Force station nearby, and ran for help. Not thirty minutes after Dane had disappeared a helicopter took off, beat the air frantically and swooped in ever-increasing circles outward from the beach, searching. No one expected to see anything. Drowned men sank to the bottom and didn't come up for days. An hour passed; then fifteen miles out to sea they sighted Dane floating peacefully on the bosom of the deep, arms outstretched, face turned up to the sky. For a moment they thought he was alive and cheered, but as the craft came low enough to throw the water into hissing foam, it was plain he was dead. The coordinates were given over the helicopter's radio, a launch sped out, and three hours later returned.

Word had spread. The Cretans had loved to see him pass, loved to exchange a few shy words. Loved him, though they didn't know him. They flocked down to the sea, women all in black like dowdy birds, men in old-fashioned baggy trousers, white shirts open at the collar and sleeves rolled up. And stood in silent groups, waiting.

When the launch came in a burly master sergeant sprang out onto the sand, turned back to receive a blanket-draped form into his arms. He marched a few fleet up the beach beyond the water line, and with the help of another man laid his burden down. The blanket fell apart; there was a high, rustling whisper from the Cretans. They came crowding around, pressing crucifixes to weather-beaten lips, the women softly keening, a wordles so hhhhhhhh! that had almost a melody in it, mournful, patient, earthbound, female.

It was about five in the afternoon; the barred sun was sliding westward behind the frowning cliff, but was still high enough to light up the little dark cluster on the beach, the long, still form on the sand with its golden skin, its closed eyes whose lashes were spiky from drying salt, the faint smile on the blued lips. A stretcher was brought forward, then all together Cretans and American servicemen bore Dane away.

Athens was in turmoil, rioting crowds overturning all order, but the USAF colonel got through to his superior son a special frequency band, Dane's blue Australian passport in his hand. It said, as such documents do, nothing about him. His profession was simply marked "Student," and in the back under next of kin Justine's name was listed, with her London address. Unconcerned by the legal meaning of the term, he had put her name because London was far closer to Rome than Drogheda. In his little room at the inn, the square black case which housed his priestly implements had not been opened; it waited with his suitcase for directions as to where it should be sent.

When the phone rang at nine in the morning Justine rolled over, opened a bleary eye and lay cursing it, vowing she would have the bloody thing disconnected. Because the rest of the world thought it only right and proper to commence whatever they did at nine in the morning, why did they assume the same of her?

But it rang, and rang, and rang. Maybe it was Rain; that thought tipped the balance toward consciousness, and Justine got up, slopped reeling out to the living room. The German parliament was in urgent session; she hadn't seen Rain in a week and hadn't been optimistic about her chances of seeing him for at least another week. But perhaps the crisis had resolved, and he was calling to tell her he was on his way over.

"Hello?"

"Miss Justine O'neill?"

"Yes, speaking."

"This is Australia House, in the Aldwych, you know?" The voice had an English inflection, gave a name she was too tired to hear because she was still assimilating the fact that the voice was not Rain's.

"Okay, Australia House." Yawning, she stood on one foot and scratched its top with the sole of the other.

"Do you have a brother, a Mr. Dane O'neill?"

Justine's eyes opened. "Yes, I do."

"Is he at present in Greece, Miss O'neill?"

Both feet settled into the rug, stood braced. "Yes, that's right," It did not occur to her to correct the voice, explain it was Father, not Mister.

"Miss O'neill, I very much regret to say that it is my unfortunate duty to give you some bad news."

"Bad news? Bad news? What is it? What's the matter? What's happened?"

"I regret to have to inform you that your brother, Mr. Dane O'neill, was drowned yesterday in Crete, I understand in heroic circumstances, performing a sea rescue. However, you realize there is a revolution in Greece, and what information we have is sketchy and possibly not accurate."

The phone stood on a table near the wall and Justine leaned against the solid support the wall offered. Her knees buckled, she began to slide very slowly downward, wound up in a curled heap on the floor. Not laughing and not crying, she made noises somewhere in between, audible gasps. Dane drowned. Gasp. Dane dead. Gasp. Crete, Dane, drowned. Gasp. Dead, dead.

"Miss O'neill? Are you there, Miss O'neill?" asked the voice insistently.

Dead. Drowned. My brother!

"Miss O'neill, answer me!"

"Yes, yes, yes, yes, yes! Oh, God, I'm here!"

"I understand you are his next of kin, therefore we must have your instructions as to what to do with the body. Miss O'neill, are you there?"

"Yes, yes!"

"What do you want done with the body, Miss O'neill?"

Body! He was a body, and they couldn't even say his body, they had to say the body. Dane, my Dane. He is a body. "Next of kin?" she heard her voice asking, thin and faint, torn by those great gasps. "I'm not Dane's next of kin. My mother is, I suppose."

There was a pause. "This is very difficult, Miss O'neill. If you're not the next of kin, we've wasted valuable time." The polite sympathy gave way to impatience. "You don't seem to understand there's a revolution going on in Greece and the accident happened in Crete, even more remote and hard to contact. Really! Communication with Athens is virtually impossible and we have been instructed to forward the next of kin's personal wishes and instructions regarding the body immediately. Is your mother there? May I speak to her, please?"

"My mother's not here. She's in Australia."

"Australia? Lord, this gets worse and worse! Now we'll have to send a cable to Australia; more delays. If you are not the next of kin, Miss O'neill, why did your brother's passport say you were?"

"I don't know," she said, and found she had laughed.

"Give me your mother's address in Australia; we'll cable her at once. We have to know what to do with the body! By the time cables get back and forth, this will mean a twelve-hour delay, I hope you realize that. It's going to be difficult enough without this mix-up."

"Phone her, then. Don't waste time with cables."

"Our budget does not extend to international phone calls, Miss O'neill," said that stiff voice. "Now, will you please give me your mother's name and address?"

"Mrs. Meggie O'neill," Justine recited, "Drogheda, Gillanbone, New South Wales, Australia." She spelled out the unfamiliar names for him.

"Once again, Miss O'neill, my deepest regrets."

The receiver clicked, began the interminable burr of the dial tone. Justine sat on the floor and let it slip into her lap. There was a mistake, it would all sort itself out. Dane drowned, when he swam like a champion? No, it wasn't true. But it is, Justine, you know it is, you didn't go with him to protect him and he drowned. You were his protector from the time he was a baby and you should have been there. If you couldn't save him, you should have been there to drown with him. And the only reason you didn't go with him was because you wanted to be in London so you could get Rain to make love to you.

Thinking was so hard. Everything was so hard. Nothing seemed to work, not even her legs. She couldn't get up, she would never get up again. There was no room in her mind for anyone but Dane, and her thoughts went in ever-diminishing circles around Dane. Until she thought of her mother, the Drogheda people. Oh, God. The news would come there, come to her, come to them. Mum didn't even have the lovely last sight of his face in Rome. They'll send the cable to the Gilly police, I suppose, and old Sergeant Ern will climb into his car and drive out all the miles to Drogheda, to tell my mother that her only son is dead. Not the right man for the job, and an almost-stranger. Mrs. O'neill, my deepest, most heartfelt regrets, your son is dead. Perfunctory, courteous, empty words ... No! I can't let them do that to her, not to her, she is my mother, too! Not that way, not the way I had to hear it.

She pulled the other part of the phone off the table onto her lap, put the receiver to her ear and dialed the operator.

"Switch? Trunks, please, international. Hello? I want to place an urgent call to Australia, Gillanbone one-two-one-two. And please, please hurry."

Meggie answered the phone herself. It was late, Fee had gone to bed. These days she never felt like seeking her own bed early, she preferred to sit listening to the crickets and frogs, doze over a book, remember.

"Hello?"

"London calling, Mrs. O'neill," said Hazel in Gilly.

"Hello, Justine," Meggie said, not perturbed. Jussy called, infrequently, to see how everything was.

"Mum? Is that you, Mum?"

"Yes, it's Mum here," said Meggie gently, sensing Justine's distress.

"Oh, Mum! Oh, Mum!" There was what sounded like a gasp, or a sob. "Mum, Dane's dead. Dane's dead!"

A pit opened at her feet. Down and down and down it went, and had no bottom. Meggie slid into it, felt its lips close over her head, and understood that she would never come out again as long as she lived. What more could the gods do? She hadn't known when she asked it. How could she have asked it, how could she not have known? Don't tempt the gods, they love it. In not going to see him in this most beautiful moment of his life, share it with him, she had finally thought to make the payment. Dane would be free of it, and free of her. In not seeing the face which was dearer to her than all other faces, she would repay. The pit closed in, suffocating. Meggie stood there, and realized it was too late.

"Justine, my dearest, be calm," said Meggie strongly, not a falter in her voice. "Calm yourself and tell me. Are you sure?"

"Australia House called me—they thought I was his next of kin. Some dreadful man who only wanted to know what I wanted done with the body. The body," he kept calling Dane. As if he wasn't entitled to it anymore, as if it was anyone's." Meggie heard her sob. "God! I suppose the poor man hated what he was doing. Oh, Mum, Dane's dead!"

"How, Justine? Where? In Rome? Why hasn't Ralph called me?"

"No, not in Rome. The Cardinal probably doesn't know anything about it. In Crete. The man said he was drowned, a sea rescue. He was on holiday, Mum, he asked me to go with him and I didn't, I wanted to play Desdemona, I wanted to be with Rain. If I'd only been with him! If I had, it mightn't have happened. Oh, God, what can I do?"

"Stop it, Justine," said Meggie sternly. "No thinking like that, do you hear me? Dane would hate it, you know he would. Things happen, why we don't know. The important thing now is that you're all right, I haven't lost both of you. You're all I've got left now. Oh, Jussy, Jussy, it's so far away! The world's big, too big. Come home to Drogheda! I hate to think of you all alone."

"No, I've got to work. Work is the only answer for me. If I don't work, I'll go mad. I don't want people, I don't want comfort. Oh, Mum!" She began to sob bitterly. "How are we going to live without him?"

How indeed? Was that living? God's thou wert, unto God return. Dust to dust. Living's for those of us who failed. Greedy God, gathering in the good ones, leaving the world to the rest of us, to rot.

"It isn't for any of us to say how long we'll live," said Meggie. "Jussy, thank you so much for telling me yourself, for phoning."

"I couldn't bear to think of a stranger breaking the news, Mum. Not like that, from a stranger. What will you do? What can you do?"

With all her will Meggie tried to pour warmth and comfort across the miles to her devastated girl in London. Her son was dead, her daughter still lived. She must be made whole. If it was possible.

In all her life Justine seemed only to have loved Dane. No one else, even herself. "Dear Justine, don't cry. Try not to grieve. He wouldn't have wanted that, now would he? Come home, and forget. We'll bring Dane home to Drogheda, too.

At law he's mine again, he doesn't belong to the Church and they can't stop me. I'll phone Australia House right away, and the embassy in Athens if I can get through. He must come home! I'd hate to think of him lying somewhere far from Drogheda. Here is where he belongs, he'll have to come home. Come with him, Justine."

But Justine sat in a heap, shaking her head as if her mother could see. Come home? She could never come home again. If she had gone with Dane he wouldn't be dead. Come home, and have to look at her mother's face everyday for the rest of her life? No, it didn't bear thinking of.

"No, Mum," she said, the tears rolling down her skin, hot like molten metal. Who on earth ever said people most moved don't weep? They don't know anything about it. "I shall stay here and work. I'll come home with Dane, but then I'm going back. I can't live on Drogheda."

For three days they waited in a purposeless vacuum, Justine in London, Meggie and the family on Drogheda, stretching the official silence into tenuous hope. Oh, surely after so long it would turn out to be a mistake, surely if it was true they would have heard by now! Dane would come-in Justine's front door smiling, and say it was all a silly mistake. Greece was in revolt, all sorts of silly mistakes must have been made. Dane would come in the door and laugh the idea of his death to scorn, he'd stand there tall and strong and alive, and he'd laugh. Hope began to grow, and grew with every minute they waited. Treacherous, horrible hope. He wasn't dead, no! Not drowned, not Dane who was a good enough swimmer to brave any kind of sea and live. So they waited, not acknowledging what had happened in the hope it would prove to be a mistake. Time later to notify people, let Rome know.

On the fourth morning Justine got the message. Like an old woman she picked up the receiver once more, and asked for Australia.

"Mum?"

"Justine?"

"Oh, Mum, they've buried him already; we can't bring him home! What are we going to do? All they can say is that Crete is a big place, the name of the village isn't known, by the time the cable arrived he'd already been spirited away somewhere and disposed of. He's lying in an unmarked grave somewhere! I can't get a visa for Greece, no one wants to help, it's chaos. What are we going to do, Mum?"

"Meet me in Rome, Justine," said Meggie.

Everyone save Anne Mueller was there around the phone, still in shock. The men seemed to have aged twenty years in three days, and Fee, shrunken birdlike, white and crabbed, drifted about the house saying over and over." Why couldn't it have been me? Why did they have to take him? I'm so old, so old! I wouldn't have minded going, why did it have to be him? Why couldn't it have been me? I'm so old!" Anne had collapsed, and Mrs. Smith, Minnie and Cat walked, slept tears.

Meggie stared at them silently as she put the phone down. This was Drogheda, all that was left. A little cluster of old men and old women, sterile and broken.

"Dane's lost," she said. "No one can find him; he's been buried somewhere on Crete. It's so far away! How could he rest so far from Drogheda? I'm going to Rome, to Ralph de Bricassart. If anyone can help us, he can."

Cardinal de Bricassart's secretary entered his room.

"Your Eminence, I'm sorry to disturb you, but a lady wishes to see you. I explained that there is a congress, that you are very busy and cannot see anyone, but she says she will sit in the vestibule until you have time for her."

"Is she in trouble, Father?"

"Great trouble, Your Eminence, that much is easy to see. She said I was to tell you her name is Meggie O'neill." He gave it a lilting foreign pronunciation, so that it came out sounding like Meghee Onill.

Cardinal Ralph came to his feet, the color draining from his face to leave it as white as his hair.

"Your Eminence! Are you ill?"

"No, Father, I'm perfectly all right, thank you. Cancel my appointments until I notify you otherwise, and bring Mrs. O'neill to me at once. We are not to be disturbed unless it is the Holy Father."

The priest bowed, departed. O'neill. Of course! It was young Dane's name, he should have remembered. Save that in the Cardinal's palace everyone just said Dane. Ah, he had made a grave mistake, keeping her waiting. If Dane was His Eminence's dearly loved nephew then Mrs. O'neill was his dearly loved sister.

When Meggie came into the room Cardinal Ralph hardly knew her. It was thirteen years since he had last seen her; she was fifty-three and he was seventy-one. Both of them aged now, instead of only him. Her face hadn't changed so much as settled, and into a mold unlike the one he had given her in his imagination. Substitute a trenchant incisiveness for sweetness, a touch of iron for softness; she resembled a vigorous, aging, willful martyr rather than the resigned, contemplative saint of his dreams. Her beauty was as striking as ever, her eyes still that clear silvery grey, but both had hardened, and the once vivid hair had faded to a drab beige, like Dane's without the life. Most disconcerting of all, she wouldn't look at him for long enough to satisfy his eager and loving curiosity.

Unable to greet this Meggie naturally, he stiffly indicated a chair. "Please sit down."

"Thank you," she said, equally stilted.

It was only when she was seated and he could gaze down upon her whole person that he noticed how visibly swollen her feet and ankles were.

"Meggie! Have you flown all the way through from Australia without breaking your journey? What's the matter?"

"Yes, I did fly straight through," she said. "For the past twenty-nine hours I've been sitting in planes between Gilly and Rome, with nothing to do except stare out the window at the clouds, and think." Her voice was harsh, cold.

"What's the matter?" he repeated impatiently, anxious and fearful.

She lifted her gaze from her feet and looked at him steadily.

There was something *awful* in her eyes; something so dark and chilling that the skin on the back of his neck crawled and automatically he put his hand up to stroke it.

"Dane is dead," said Meggie.

His hand slipped, flopped like a rag doll's into his scarlet lap as he sank into a chair. "Dead?" he asked slowly. "Dane dead?"

"Yes. He was drowned six days ago in Crete, rescuing some women from the sea."

He leaned forward, put his hands over his face. "Dead?" she heard him say indistinctly. "Dane dead? My beautiful boy! He can't be dead! Dane-he was the perfect priest-all that I couldn't be. What I lacked he had." His voice broke. "He always had it-that was what we all recognized-all of us who aren't perfect priests. Dead? Oh, dear Lord!"

"Don't bother about your dear Lord, Ralph," said the stranger sitting opposite him. "You have more important things to do. I came to ask for your help-not to witness your grief. I've had all those hours in the air to go over the way I'd tell you this, all those hours just staring out the window at the clouds knowing Dane is dead. After that, your grief has no power to move me."

Yet when he lifted his face from his hands her dead cold heart bounded, twisted, leaped. It was Dane's face, with a suffering written upon it that Dane would never live to feel. Oh, thank God! Thank God he's dead, can never now go through what this man has, what I have. Better he's dead than to suffer something like this.

"How can I help, Meggie?" he asked quietly, suppressing his own emotions to don the soul-deep guise of her spiritual counselor.

"Greece is in chaos. They've buried Dane somewhere on Crete, and

I can't find out where, when, why. Except I suppose that my instructions directing that he be flown home were endlessly delayed by the civil war, and Crete is hot like Australia. When no one claimed him, I suppose they thought he had no one, and buried him." She leaned forward in her chair tensely. "I want my boy back, Ralph, I want him found and brough home to sleep where he belongs, on Drogheda. I promised Jims I'd keep him on Drogheda and I will, if I have to crawl on my hands and knees through every graveyard on Crete. No fancy Roman priest's tomb for him, Ralph, not as long as I'm alive to put up a legal battle. He's to come home."

"No one is going to deny you that, Meggie," he said gently. "It's consecrated Catholic ground, which is all the Church asks. I too have requested that I be buried on Drogheda."

"I can't get through all the red tape," she went on, as if he hadn't spoken. "I can't speak Greek, and I have no power or influence. So I came to you, to use yours. Get me back my son, Ralph!"

"Don't worry, Meggie, we'll get him back, though it may not be very quickly. The-Left are in charge now, and they're very anti-Catholic. However, I'm not without friends in Greece, so it will be done. Let me start the wheels in motion immediately, and don't worry. He is a priest of the Holy Catholic Church, we'll get him back."

His hand had gone to the bell cord, but Meggie's coldly fierce gaze stilled it.

"You don't understand, Ralph. I don't want wheels set in motion. I want my son back-not next week or next month, but now! You speak Greek, you can get visas for yourself and me, you'll get results. I want you to come to Greece with me now, and help me get my son back."

There was much in his eyes: tenderness, compassion, shock, grief. But they had become the priest's eyes too, sane, logical, reasonable. "Meggie, I love your son as if he were my own, but I can't leave Rome at the moment.

I'm not a free agent-you above all others should know that. No matter how much I may feel for you, how much I may feel on my own account, I can't leave Rome in the midst of a vital congress. I am the Holy Father's aide." She reared back, stunned and outraged, then shook her head, half-smiling as if at the antics of some inanimate object beyond her power to influence; then she trembled, licked her lips, seemed to come to a decision and sat up straight and stiff. "Do you really love my son as if he were your own, Ralph?" she asked. "What would you do for a son of yours? Could you sit back then and say to his mother, No, I'm very sorry, I can't possibly take the time off? Could you say that to the mother of your son?"

Dane's eyes, yet not Dane's eyes. Looking at her; bewildered, full of pain, helpless.

"I have no son," he said, "but among the many, many things I learned from yours was that no matter how hard it is, my first and only allegiance is to Almighty God."

"Dane was your son too," said Meggie.

He stared at her blankly. "What?"

"I said, Dane was your son too. When I left Matlock Island I was pregnant. Dane was yours, not Luke O'neill's."

"It isn't true!"

"I never intended you to know, even now," she said. "Would I lie to you?" "To get Dane back? Yes," he said faintly.

She got up, came to stand over him in the red brocade chair, took his thin, parchment-like hand in hers, bent and kissed the ring, the breath of her voice misting its ruby to milky dullness. "By all that you hold holy, Ralph, Is wear that Dane was your son. He was not and could not have been Luke's. By his death I swear it."

There was a wail, the sound of a soul passing between the portals of Hell. Ralph de Bricassart fell forward out of the chair and wept, huddled on the crimson carpet in a scarlet pool like new blood, his face hidden in his folded arms, his hands clutching at his hair.

"Yes, cry!" said Meggie. "Cry, now that you know! It's right that one of his parents be able to shed tears for him. Cry, Ralph! For twenty-six years I had your son and you didn't even know it, you couldn't even see it. Couldn't see that he was you all over again! When my mother took him from me at birth she knew, but you never did. Your hands, your. feet, your face, your eyes, your body. Only the color of his hair was his own; all the rest was you. Do you understand now? When I sent him here to you, I said it in my letter. What I stole, I give back. Remember? Only we both stole, Ralph. We stole what you had vowed to God, and we've both had to pay."

She sat in her chair, implacable and unpitying, and watched the scarlet form in its agony on the floor. "I loved you, Ralph, but you were never mine. What I had of you, I was driven to steal. Dane was my part, all I could get from you. I vowed you'd never know, I vowed you'd never have the chance to take him away from me. And then he gave himself to you, of his own free will. The image of the perfect priest, he called you. What a laugh I had over that one! But not for anything would I have given you a weapon like knowing he was yours. Except for this. Except for this! For nothing less would I have told you. Though I don't suppose it matters now. He doesn't belong to either of us anymore. He belongs to God."

Cardinal de Bricassart chartered a private plane in Athens; he, Meggie and Justine brought Dane home to Drogheda, the living sitting silently, the dead lying silently on a bier, requiring nothing of this earth anymore.

I have to say this Mass, this Requiem for my son. Bone of my bone, my son. Yes, Meggie, I believe you. Once I had my breath back I would even have believed you without that terrible oath you swore. Vittorio knew the minute he set eyes on the boy, and in my heart I, too, must have known. Your laugh behind the roses from the boy-but my eyes looking up at me, as they used to be in my innocence. Fee knew. Anne Mueller knew. But not we men. We weren't fit to be told. For so you women think, and hug your mysteries, getting your backs on us for the slight God did you in not creating you in His Image. Vittorio knew, but it was the woman in him stilled his tongue. A masterly revenge.

Say it, Ralph de Bricassart, open your mouth, move your hands in the blessing, begin to chant the Latin for the soul of the departed. Who was your son. Whom you loved more than you loved his mother. Yes, more! For he was yourself all over again, in a more perfect mold.

"In Nomine Patris, et Filii, et Spiritus Sancti ..."

The chapel was packed; they were all there who could be there. The Kings, the O'Rourkes, the Davieses, the Pughs, the MacQueens, the Gordons, the Car-michaels, the Hopetons. And the Clearys, the Drogheda people.

Hope blighted, light gone. At the front in a great lead-lined casket, Father Dane O'neill, covered in roses. Why were the roses always out when he came back to Drogheda? It was October, high spring. Of course they were out. The time was right.

"Sanctus ... Sanctus ... Sanctus ..."

Be warned that the Holy of Holies is upon you. My Dane, my beautiful son. It is better so. I wouldn't have wanted you to come to this, what I already am. Why I say this for you, I don't know. You don't need it, you never needed it. What I grope for, you knew by instinct. It isn't you who is unhappy, it's those of us here, left behind. Pity us, and when our times come, help us.

"Missa est ... Requiescat in pace ... ."

Out across the lawn, down past the ghost gums, the roses, the pepper trees, to the cemetery. Sleep on, Dane, because only the good die young. Why do we mourn? You're lucky, to have escaped this weary life so soon. Perhaps that's what Hell is, a long term in earth-bound bondage. Perhaps we suffer our hells in living ... .

The day passed, the mourners departed, the Drogheda people crept about the house and avoided each other; Cardinal Ralph looked early at Meggie, and could not bear to look again. Justine left with Jean and Boy King to catch the afternoon plane for Sydney, the night plane for London. He never remembered hearing her husky bewitching voice, or seeing those odd pale eyes. From the time when she had met him and Meggie in Athens to the time when she went with Jean and Boy King she had been like a ghost, her camouflage pulled closely around her. Why hadn't she called Rainer Hartheim, asked him to be with her? Surely she knew how much he loved her, how much he would want to be with her now? But the thought never stayed long enough in Cardinal Ralph's tired mind to call Rainer himself, though he had wondered about it off and on since before leaving Rome. They were strange, the Drogheda people. They didn't like company in grief; they preferred to be alone with their pain.

Only Fee and Meggie sat with Cardinal Ralph in the drawing room after a dinner left uneaten. No one saida word; the ormolu clock on the marble mantel ticked thunderously, and Mary Carson's painted eyes stared a mute challenge across the room to Fee's grandmother. Fee and Meggie sat together on a cream sofa, shoulders lightly touching; Cardinal Ralph never remembered their being so close in the old days. But they said nothing, did not look at each other or at him.

He tried to see what it was he had done wrong. Too much wrong, that was the trouble. Pride, ambition, a certain unscrupulousness. And love for Meggie flowering among them. But the crowning glory of that love he had never known. What difference would it have made to know his son was his son? Was it possible to love the boy more than he had? Would he have pursued a different path if he had known about his son? Yes! cried his heart. No, sneered his brain.

He turned on himself bitterly. Fool! You ought to have known Meggie was incapable of going back to Luke. You ought to have known at once whose child Dane was. She was so proud of him! All she could get from you, that was what she said to you in Rome. Well, Meggie .... In him you got the best of it. Dear God, Ralph, how could you not have known he was yours? You ought to have realized it when he came to you a man grown, if not before. She was waiting for you to see it, dying for you to see it; if only you had, she would have gone on her knees to you. But you were blind. You didn't want to see. Ralph Raoul, Cardinal de Bricassart, that was what you wanted; more than her, more than your son. More than your son!

The room had become filled with tiny cries, rustles, whispers; the clock was ticking in time with his heart. And then it wasn't in time anymore. He had got out of step with it. Meggie and Fee were swimming to their feet, drifting with frightened faces in a watery insubstantial mist, saying things to him he couldn't seem to hear.

"Aaaaaaah!" he cried, understanding.

He was hardly conscious of the pain, intent only on Meggie's arms around him, the way his head sank against her. But he managed to turn until he could see her eyes, and looked at her. He tried to say, Forgive me, and saw she had forgiven him long ago. She knew she had got the best of it. Then he wanted to say something so perfect she would be eternally consoled, and realized that wasn't necessary, either. Whatever she was, she could bear anything. Anything! So he closed his eyes and let himself feel, that last time, forgetfulness in Meggie.

(选自 Colleen McCullough. *The Thorn Birds*. New York: Avon Books, 1977. pp. 594 - 651.)

Questions

1. How is the relationship between Dane and Justine?
2. Whom does Justine fall in love with?
3. Why is Fiona punished by her family?
4. Is Justine a pure girl? Why or why not?
5. Are Fee and Paddy good parents? Could or should they have been better?

Unit 12

Ray Douglas Bradbury: *Fahrenheit 451*

Ray Douglas Bradbury was born on August 22, 1920 in Waukegan Illinois. He was an American author and screenwriter. He worked in a variety of genres, including fantasy, science fiction, horror, and mystery fiction.

Bradbury was surrounded by an extended family during his early childhood. An aunt read him short stories when he was a child. Bradbury attended Los Angeles High School and was active in the drama club. He often roller-skated through Hollywood in hopes of meeting celebrities. Among the creative and talented people Bradbury met were special-effects pioneer Ray Harryhausen and radio star George Burns. Bradbury's first pay as a writer, at age 14, was for a joke he sold to George Burns to use on the Burns and Allen radio show. Bradbury began writing his own stories at age 11, during the Great Depression. In his youth, he spent much time in the Carnegie library in Waukegan, reading such authors as H. G. Wells, Jules Verne, and Edgar Allan Poe. At 12, Bradbury began writing traditional horror stories and said he tried to imitate Poe until he was about 18. In addition to comics, he loved Edgar Rice Burroughs, creator of *The Warlord of Mars* which impressed him so much that at the age of 12, he wrote his own sequel. The young Bradbury was also a cartoonist and loved to illustrate.

At age 17, Bradbury read stories published in *Astounding Science Fiction*, and read everything by Robert A. Heinlein, Arthur C. Clarke, and the early writings of Theodore Sturgeon and A. E. van Vogt. Bradbury cited H. G. Wells and Jules Verne as his primary science-fiction influences. Bradbury identified with Verne, saying, "he believes the human being is in a strange situation in a very strange world, and he believes that we can triumph by behaving morally." Bradbury admitted that he stopped reading science-fiction books in his 20s and embraced a broad field of literature that included Alexander Pope and poet John Donne.

Bradbury had just graduated from high school when he met Robert Heinlein, then 31 years old. Bradbury recalled, "he was well known, and he wrote humanistic science fiction, which influenced me to dare to be human instead of mechanical."

Bradbury's first published story was "Hollerbochen's Dilemma", which appeared in the January 1938 number of Forrest J. Ackerman's fanzine *Imagination*! In July 1939, Ackerman gave 19-year-old Bradbury the money to head to New York for the First World Science Fiction Convention in New York City, and funded Bradbury's fanzine, titled *Futuria Fantasia*. Bradbury wrote most of its four issues, each limited to under 100 copies. Between 1940 and 1947, he was a contributor to Rob Wagner's film magazine, *Script*.

Ray Bradbury is one of those rare individuals whose writing has changed the way people think. His more than five hundred published works—short stories, novels, plays, screenplays, television scripts, and verse—exemplify the American imagination at its most creative. His major works include *The Martian Chronicles* (1950), *Fahrenheit* 451 (1953), *Dandelion Wine* (1957), *Something Wicked This Way Comes* (1962), *The Halloween Tree* (1972), *Death Is a Lonely Business* (1985), *A Graveyard for Lunatics* (1990), *Green Shadows, White Whale* (1992), *From the Dust Returned* (2001), *Let's All Kill Constance* (2002), *Farewell Summer* (2006). Ray Bradbury's style of writing always included hidden meanings that presented a central theme of the dangers of unchecked technology. Many factors in Ray Bradbury's life had contributed to his style of writing and the themes that he wanted to present to society.

The New York Times called Bradbury "the writer most responsible for bringing modern science fiction into the literary mainstream." On June 6, 2012, in an official public statement from the White House Press Office, President Barack Obama said: "For many Americans, the news of Ray Bradbury's death immediately brought to mind images from his work, imprinted in our minds, often from a young age. His gift for storytelling reshaped our culture and expanded our world. But Ray also understood that our imaginations could be used as a tool for better understanding, a vehicle for change, and an expression of our most cherished values. There is no doubt that Ray will continue to inspire many more generations with his writing, and our thoughts and prayers are with his family and friends."

Theme

Fahrenheit 451 presents a future American society where books are outlawed and "firemen" burn any that are found. The boo's tagline explains the title: "Fahrenheit 451—the temperature at which book paper catches fire, and burns." The lead character is a fireman named Montag who becomes disillusioned with the role of censoring works and destroying knowledge, eventually quitting his job and joining a resistance group who memorize and share the world's greatest literary and cultural works. Two major themes are resistance to conformity and control of individuals via technology and mass media. Bradbury explores how the government is able to use mass media to influence society and suppress individualism through book burning. The characters Beatty and Faber point out the American population is to blame. Due to their constant desire for a simplistic, positive image, books must be suppressed. Beatty blames the minority groups, who would take offense to published works that displayed them in an unfavorable light. Faber went further to state that the American population simply stopped reading on their own. He notes that the book burnings themselves became a form of entertainment to the general public.

Term

Science fiction: It's a popular modern branch of prose fiction that explores the probable consequences of some improbable or impossible transformation of the basic conditions of human existence. This transformation need not be brought about by a technological invention, but may involve some mutation of known biological or physical reality, e. g. time travel, extraterrestrial invasion, ecological catastrophe. Science fiction is a form of literary fantasy or romance that often draws upon earlier kinds of utopian and apocalyptic writing. The term itself was first given general currency by Hugo Gernsback, editor of the American magazine *Amazing Stories* from 1926 onwards, and it is usually abbreviated to SF; before this, such works were called *scientific romances* by H. G. Wells. Several early precedents have been claimed for the genre—notably Mary Shelley's *Frankenstein*—but true modern séance fiction begins with Jules Verne's *Voyage au Centre de la Terre* and H. G. Wells' *The Time Machine*. Once uniformly dismissed as pulp trash, SF gained greater respect during the 1950s, as writers like Isaac Asimov, Ray Bradbury, etc. expanded its range. SF has also had an important influence on postmodernist fiction by writers not devoted to this genre alone: Thomas Pynchon, Kurt Vonnegut, and Doris Lessing are significant examples.

Excerpt

Part One The Hearth and the Salamander

IT WAS A PLEASURE TO BURN

It was a special pleasure to see things eaten, to see things blackened and changed. With the brass nozzle in his fists, with this great python spitting its venomous kerosene upon the world, the blood pounded in his head, and his hands were the hands of some amazing conductor playing all the symphonies of blazing and burning to bring down the tatters and charcoal ruins of history. With his symbolic helmet numbered 451 on his stolid head, and his eyes all orange flame with the thought of what came next, he flicked the igniter and the house jumped up in a gorging fire that burned the evening sky red and yellow and black. He strode in a swarm of fireflies. He wanted above all, like the old joke, to shove a marshmallow on a stick in the furnace, while the flapping pigeon-winged books died on the porch and lawn of the house. While the books went up in sparkling whirls and blew away on a wind turned dark with burning.

Montag grinned the fierce grin of all men singed and driven back by flame.

He knew that when he returned to the firehouse, he might wink at himself, a minstrel man, burnt-corked, in the mirror. Later, going to sleep, he would feel the fiery smile still gripped by his face muscles, in the dark. It never went away, that smile, it never ever went away, as long as he remembered.

He hung up his black-beetle-coloured helmet and shined it, he hung his flameproof jacket neatly; he showered luxuriously, and then, whistling, hands in pockets, walked across the upper floor of the fire station and fell down the hole. At the last moment, when disaster seemed positive, he pulled his hands from his pockets and broke his fall by grasping the golden pole. He slid to a squeaking halt, the heels one inch from the concrete floor downstairs.

He walked out of the fire station and along the midnight street toward the subway where the silent, air-propelled train slid soundlessly down its lubricated flue in the earth and let him out with a great puff of warm air an to the cream-tiled escalator rising to the suburb.

Whistling, he let the escalator waft him into the still night air. He walked toward the comer, thinking little at all about nothing in particular. Before he reached the corner, however, he slowed as if a wind had sprung up from nowhere, as if someone had called his name.

The last few nights he had had the most uncertain feelings about the sidewalk just around the corner here, moving in the starlight toward his house. He had felt that a moment before his making the turn, someone had been there. The air seemed charged with a special calm as if someone had waited there, quietly, and only a moment before he came, simply turned to a shadow and let him through. Perhaps his nose detected a faint perfume, perhaps the skin on the backs of his hands, on his face, felt the temperature rise at this one spot where a person's standing might raise the immediate atmosphere ten degrees for an instant. There was no understanding it. Each time he made the turn, he saw only the white, unused, buckling sidewalk, with perhaps, on one night, something vanishing swiftly across a lawn before he could focus his eyes or speak.

But now, tonight, he slowed almost to a stop. His inner mind, reaching out to turn the corner for him, had heard the faintest whisper. Breathing? Or was the atmosphere compressed merely by someone standing very quietly there, waiting?

He turned the corner.

The autumn leaves blew over the moonlit pavement in such a way as to make the girl who was moving there seem fixed to a sliding walk, letting the motion of the wind and the leaves carry her forward. Her head was half bent to watch her shoes stir the circling leaves. Her face was slender and milk-white, and in it was a kind of gentle hunger that touched over everything with tireless curiosity. It was a look, almost, of pale surprise; the dark eyes were so fixed to the world that no move escaped them. Her dress was white and it whispered. He almost thought he heard the motion of her hands as she walked, and the infinitely small sound now, the white stir of her face turning when she discovered she was a moment away from a man who stood in the middle of the pavement waiting.

The trees overhead made a great sound of letting down their dry rain. The girl stopped and looked as if she might pull back in surprise, but instead stood regarding Montag with eyes so dark and shining and alive, that he felt he had said something quite wonderful. But he knew his mouth had only moved to say hello, and then when she seemed hypnotized by the salamander on his arm and the phoenix-disc on his chest, he spoke again.

"Of course," he said, "you're a new neighbour, aren't you?"

"And you must be—" she raised her eyes from his professional symbols, "—the fireman." Her voice trailed off.

"How oddly you say that."

"I'd—I'd have known it with my eyes shut," she said, slowly.

"What—the smell of kerosene? My wife always complains," he laughed. "You never wash it off completely."

"No, you don't," she said, in awe.

He felt she was walking in a circle about him, turning him end for end, shaking him quietly, and emptying his pockets, without once moving herself.

"Kerosene," he said, because the silence had lengthened, "is nothing but perfume to me."

"Does it seem like that, really?"

"Of course. Why not?"

She gave herself time to think of it. "I don't know." She turned to face the sidewalk going toward their homes. "Do you mind if I walk back with you? I'm Clarisse McClellan."

"Clarisse. Guy Montag. Come along. What are you doing out so late wandering around? How old are you?"

They walked in the warm—cool blowing night on the silvered pavement and there was the faintest breath of fresh apricots and strawberries in the air, and he looked around and realized this was quite impossible, so late in the year.

There was only the girl walking with him now, her face bright as snow in the moonlight, and he knew she was working his questions around, seeking the best answers she could possibly give.

"Well," she said, "I'm seventeen and I'm crazy. My uncle says the two always go together. When people ask your age, he said, always say seventeen and insane. Isn't this a nice time of night to walk? I like to smell things and look at things, and sometimes stay up all night, walking, and watch the sun rise."

They walked on again in silence and finally she said, thoughtfully, "You know, I'm not afraid of you at all."

He was surprised. "Why should you be?"

"So many people are. Afraid of firemen, I mean. But you're just a man, after all ..."

He saw himself in her eyes, suspended in two shining drops of bright water, himself dark and tiny, in fine detail, the lines about his mouth, everything there, as if her eyes were two miraculous bits of violet amber that might capture and hold him intact. Her face, turned to him now, was fragile milk crystal with a soft and constant light in it. It was not the hysterical light of electricity but—what? But the strangely comfortable and rare and gently flattering light of the candle. One time, when he was a child, in a power—failure, his mother had found and lit a last candle and there had been a brief hour of rediscovery, of such illumination that space lost its vast dimensions and drew comfortably around them, and they, mother and son, alone, transformed, hoping that the power might not come on again too soon ...

And then Clarisse McClellan said:

"Do you mind if I ask? How long have you worked at being a fireman?"

"Since I was twenty, ten years ago."

"Do you ever read any of the books you bum?"

He laughed. "That's against the law!"

"Oh. Of course."

"It's fine work. Monday bum Millay, Wednesday Whitman, Friday Faulkner, burn' em to ashes, then bum the ashes. That's our official slogan."

They walked still further and the girl said, "Is it true that long ago firemen put fires out instead of going to start them?"

"No. Houses. have always been fireproof, take my word for it."

"Strange. I heard once that a long time ago houses used to burn by accident and they needed firemen to stop the flames."

He laughed.

She glanced quickly over. "Why are you laughing?"

"I don't know." He started to laugh again and stopped "Why?"

"You laugh when I haven't been funny and you answer right off. You never stop to think what I've asked you."

He stopped walking, "You are an odd one," he said, looking at her. "Haven't you any respect?"

"I don't mean to be insulting. It's just, I love to watch people too much, I guess."

"Well, doesn't this mean anything to you?" He tapped the numerals 451 stitched on his char— coloured sleeve.

"Yes," she whispered. She increased her pace. "Have you ever watched the jet cars racing on the boulevards down that way?"

"You're changing the subject!"

"I sometimes think drivers don't know what grass is, or flowers, because they never see them slowly," she said. "If you showed a driver a green blur, Oh yes! he'd say, that's grass! A pink blur? That's a rose—garden! White blurs are houses. Brown blurs are cows. My uncle drove slowly on a highway once. He drove forty miles an hour and they jailed him for two days. Isn't that funny, and sad, too?"

"You think too many things," said Montag, uneasily.

"I rarely watch the 'parlour walls' or go to races or Fun Parks. So I've lots of time for crazy thoughts, I guess. Have you seen the two—hundred—foot—long billboards in the country beyond town? Did you know that once billboards were only twenty feet long? But cars started rushing by so quickly they had to stretch the advertising out so it would last."

"I didn't know that!" Montag laughed abruptly.

"Bet I know something else you don't. There's dew on the grass in the morning."

He suddenly couldn't remember if he had known this or not, and it made him quite irritable.

"And if you look"—she nodded at the sky— "there's a man in the moon."

He hadn't looked for a long time.

They walked the rest of the way in silence, hers thoughtful, his a kind of clenching and uncomfortable silence in which he shot her accusing glances. When they reached her house all its lights were blazing.

"What's going on?" Montag had rarely seen that many house lights.

"Oh, just my mother and father and uncle sitting around, talking. It's like being a pedestrian, only rarer. My uncle was arrested another time—did I tell you? —for being a pedestrian. Oh, we're most peculiar."

"But what do you talk about?"

She laughed at this. "Good night!" She started up her walk. Then she seemed to remember something and came back to look at him with wonder and curiosity. "Are you happy?" she said.

"Am I *what*?" he cried.

But she was gone—running in the moonlight. Her front door shut gently.

"Happy! Of all the nonsense."

He stopped laughing.

He put his hand into the glove—hole of his front door and let it know his touch. The front door slid open.

Of course I'm happy. What does she think? I'm *not*? he asked the quiet rooms. He stood looking up at the ventilator grille in the hall and suddenly remembered that something lay hidden behind the grille, something that seemed to peer down at him now. He moved his eyes quickly away.

What a strange meeting on a strange night. He remembered nothing like it save one afternoon a year ago when he had met an old man in the park and *they* had talked ... .

Montag shook his head. He looked at a blank wall. The girl's face was there, really quite beautiful in memory: astonishing, in fact. She had a very thin face like the dial of a small clock seen faintly in a dark room in the middle of a night when you waken to see the time and see the clock telling you the hour and the minute and the second, with a white silence and a glowing, all certainty and knowing what it has to tell of the night passing swiftly on toward further darknesses but moving also toward a new sun.

"*What?*" asked Montag of that other self, the subconscious idiot that ran babbling at times, quite independent of will, habit, and conscience.

He glanced back at the wall. How like a mirror, too, her face. Impossible; for how many people did you know that refracted your own light to you? People were more often—he searched for a simile, found one in his work—torches, blazing away until they whiffed out. How rarely did other people's faces take of you and throw back to you your own expression, your own innermost trembling thought?

What incredible power of identification the girl had; she was like the eager watcher of a marionette show, anticipating each flicker of an eyelid, each gesture of his hand, each flick of a finger, the moment before it began. How long had they walked together? Three minutes? Five?

Yet how large that time seemed now. How immense a figure she was on the stage before him; what a shadow she threw on the wall with her slender body! He felt that if his eye itched, she might blink. And if the muscles of his jaws stretched imperceptibly, she would yawn long before he would.

Why, he thought, now that I think of it, she almost seemed to be waiting for me there, in the street, so damned late at night ...

He opened the bedroom door.

It was like coming into the cold marbled room of a mausoleum after the moon had set. Complete darkness, not a hint of the silver world outside, the windows tightly shut, the chamber a tomb— world where no sound from the great city could penetrate. The room was not empty.

He listened.

The little mosquito—delicate dancing hum in the air, the electrical murmur of a hidden wasp snug in its special pink warm nest. The music was almost loud enough so he could follow the tune. He felt his smile slide away, melt, fold over, and down on itself like a tallow skin, like the stuff of a fantastic candle burning too long and now collapsing and now blown out. Darkness. He was not happy. He was not happy. He said the words to himself. He recognized this as the true state of affairs. He wore his happiness like a mask and the girl had run off across the lawn with the mask and there was no way of going to knock on her door and ask for it back.

Without turning on the light he imagined how this room would look. His wife stretched on the bed, uncovered and cold, like a body displayed on the lid of a tomb, her eyes fixed to the ceiling by invisible threads of steel, immovable. And in her ears the little Seashells, the thimble radios tamped tight, and an electronic ocean of sound, of music and talk and music and talk coming in, coming in on the shore of her unsleeping mind. The room was indeed empty. Every night the waves came in and bore her off on their great tides of sound, floating her, wide—eyed, toward morning. There had been no night in the last two years that Mildred had not swum that sea, had not gladly gone down in it for the third time.

The room was cold but nonetheless he felt he could not breathe. He did not wish to open the curtains and open the French windows, for he did not want the moon to come into the room. So, with the feeling of a man who will die in the next hour for lack of air, he felt his way toward his open, separate, and therefore cold bed.

An instant before his foot hit the object on the floor he knew he would hit such an object. It was not unlike the feeling he had experienced before turning the corner and almost knocking the girl down. His foot, sending vibrations ahead, received back echoes of the small barrier across its path even as the foot swung. His foot kicked. The object gave a dull clink and slid off in darkness.

He stood very straight and listened to the person on the dark bed in the completely featureless night. The breath coming out of the nostrils was so faint it stirred only the furthest fringes of life, a small leaf, a black feather, a single fibre of hair.

He still did not want outside light. He pulled out his igniter, felt the salamander etched on its silver disc, gave it a flick ...

Two moonstones looked up at him in the light of his small hand—held fire; two pale moonstones buried in a creek of clear water over which the life of the world ran, not touching them.

"Mildred !"

Her face was like a snow—covered island upon which rain might fall; but it felt no rain; over which clouds might pass their moving shadows, but she felt no shadow. There was only the singing of the thimble—wasps in her tamped—shut ears, and her eyes all glass, and breath going in and out, softly, faintly, in and out of her nostrils, and her not caring whether it came or went, went or came.

The object he had sent tumbling with his foot now glinted under the edge of his own bed. The small crystal bottle of sleeping—tablets which earlier today had been filled with thirty capsules and which now lay uncapped and empty in the light of the tiny flare.

As he stood there the sky over the house screamed. There was a tremendous ripping sound as if two giant hands had torn ten thousand miles of black linen down the seam. Montag was cut in half. He felt his chest chopped down and split apart. The jet—bombs going over, going over, going over, one two, one two, one two, six of them, nine of them, twelve of them, one and one and one and another and another and another, did all the screaming for him. He opened his own mouth and let their shriek come down and out between his bared teeth. The house shook. The flare went out in his hand. The moonstones vanished. He felt his hand plunge toward the telephone.

The jets were gone. He felt his lips move, brushing the mouthpiece of the phone. "Emergency hospital." A terrible whisper.

He felt that the stars had been pulverized by the sound of the black jets and that in the morning the earth would be thought as he stood shivering in the dark, and let his lips go on moving and moving.

They had this machine. They had two machines, really. One of them slid down into your stomach like a black cobra down an echoing well looking for all the old water and the old time gathered there. It drank up the green matter that flowed to the top in a slow boil. Did it drink of the darkness? Did it suck out all the poisons accumulated with the years? It fed in silence with an occasional sound of inner suffocation and blind searching. It had an Eye. The impersonal operator of the machine could, by wearing a special optical helmet, gaze into the soul of the person whom he was pumping out. What did the Eye see? He did not say. He saw but did not see what the Eye saw. The entire operation was not unlike the digging of a trench in one's yard. The woman on the bed was no more than a hard stratum of marble they had reached. Go on, anyway, shove the bore down, slush up the emptiness, if such a thing could be brought out in the throb of the suction snake. The operator stood smoking a cigarette. The other machine was working too.

The other machine was operated by an equally impersonal fellow in non—stainable reddish—brown overalls. This machine pumped all of the blood from the body and replaced it with fresh blood and serum.

"Got to clean 'em out both ways," said the operator, standing over the silent woman. "No use getting the stomach if you don't clean the blood. Leave that stuff in the blood and the blood hits the brain like a mallet, bang, a couple of thousand times and the brain just gives up, just quits."

"Stop it!" said Montag.

"I was just sayin'," said the operator.

"Are you done?" said Montag.

They shut the machines up tight. "We're done." His anger did not even touch them. They stood with the cigarette smoke curling around their noses and into their eyes without making them blink or squint. "That's fifty bucks."

"First, why don't you tell me if she'll be all right?"

"Sure, she'll be O.K. We got all the mean stuff right in our suitcase here, it can't get at her now. As I said, you take out the old and put in the new and you're O.K."

"Neither of you is an M.D. Why didn't they send an M.D. from Emergency?"

"Hell!" The operator's cigarette moved on his lips. "We get these cases nine or ten a night. Got so many, starting a few years ago, we had the special machines built. With the optical lens, of course, that was new; the rest is ancient. You don't need an M.D. case like this; all you need is two handy men, clean up the problem in half an hour. Look"—he started for the door—"We gotta go. Just had another call on the old ear—thimble. Ten blocks from here. Someone else just jumped off the cap of a pillbox. Call if you need us again. Keep her quiet. We got a contra—sedative in her. She'll wake up hungry. So long."

And the men with the cigarettes in their straight—lined mouths, the men with the eyes of puff—adders, took up their load of machine and tube, their case of liquid melancholy and the slow dark sludge of nameless stuff, and strolled out the door.

(选自 Ray Douglas Bradbury. *Fahrenheit 451*. New York: Ballantine Books, Inc., 1953. pp.3-14.)

Questions

1. What is the symbolic meaning of the title?
2. Why did author set the protagonist's occupation as a firefighter?
3. Why is Clarisse missing?
4. How do you understand the character Captain Beatty?
5. What does Beatty's death imply?